THE BOY IN THE MIRROR

John D. Fennell

Happy Easter Noah.
Granda - Grandma
x

Books by John D. Fennell

THE MYSTICAL MIRROR Trilogy:

Book 1: The Boy in the Mirror
Book 2: The Book of Mysteries
Book 3: Guardians of the Mirror

THE ROMAN TIME MACHINE Series:

Book 1: Vesuvius
Book 2: The Prophecy

For Alex and Oli
My two little stars

Chapter One

The Great Storm

Porthgarrick, Cornwall
Some years ago

It all began on a beautiful summer's day, when a flash of lightning appeared against a clear blue sky. Jagged and uncommonly bright, it hung in the air a second or two longer than was normal, like a dazzling crack in the heavens. The peal of thunder that followed moments later was deafening. On and on it roared, like a jet plane coming into land, rattling windowpanes, setting off car alarms.

Sam's fifty-year-old heart skipped a beat. The realisation of what was happening forced the air from his lungs, made his blood run cold.

When silence finally returned, he hurried out of the busy supermarket, bags of groceries in each hand, and looked up at the sky, dreading what he would see. Dark, threatening clouds were swirling overhead, growing at speed, devouring the blue sky in a manner that was shockingly unnatural. It was as though someone had filmed a dramatic build-up of black cloud and was now playing it back at five times the speed. The last few shafts of warm sunlight vanished before his eyes, as if at the flick of a switch.

'No, no, no!' he cried out. Like all those around him, he could not take his eyes from the gathering storm overhead. 'Bill, you fool! What have you done?'

Momentarily paralysed by the shock of what he was seeing, he could scarcely think let alone move. He had seen this all

1

before, instantly knew what was happening, recognised the telltale signs but simply did not want to believe his eyes. What on earth was Bill playing at? How could he be so foolish?

Against the black sky, the next streak of lightning was even more blinding, the next crash of thunder, yet more ear-splitting. Barely a second later, another explosion of light and noise, then another: a salvo of three thunderbolts in quick succession, so ferocious that buildings shook and a small child screamed and burst into tears. Sam dropped the bags at his feet, spilling groceries all around him, and ran across the car park towards his car as the first spots of rain struck his face. In his haste to unlock the car, he fumbled with his bunch of keys and dropped them. Raindrops, large and heavy, poked the shirt on his back like admonishing fingers, as he reached down to retrieve the keys.

His mind was racing uncontrollably. What was he going to do? How was he going to find Bill? There was only one place to start.

Once inside the car, he tore out of the car park with a screech of tyres, leaving a trail of beeping horns and shaking fists in his wake, as people vented their anger at his reckless driving. But he neither saw their red faces, nor heard their raised voices: he was focused as never before. He raced from the outskirts towards the centre of the town. All around him, streetlights were blinking on in the gathering gloom, headlights becoming more dazzling with every passing moment.

And then the rain came. What had been a spattering of drops on the windscreen became a deluge in the blink of an eye, as sudden and as violent as the storm that continued to rage above him. The pummelling of raindrops on his roof was deafening, and even on full speed, his windscreen wipers struggled to cope. As he raced into town, the road ahead became nothing more than a mass of indistinct shapes, of smears of red and white lights. But he simply could not afford to slow down, for he knew there was too much at stake.

By the time he arrived at *Morladron House,* it was as dark as night, the house nothing more than a silhouette. Isolated and eerily foreboding in any weather, it stood on a cliff top overlooking the small town. For a fleeting instant, the old, stone house flashed into life when a jagged bolt of lightning struck a nearby field, before it was once again swallowed up by the darkness.

Through the torrent of rain before him, he could just make out the faint glow of light from a ground-floor window.

The car skidded to a halt on the gravel driveway. Sam flung open the door and, without worrying to close it behind him, raced towards the house. In the few seconds it took to arrive at the porch, his T-shirt became soaked. With trembling hands, he unlocked the large wooden door and stumbled into the dark hallway in his haste to enter, water dripping from his body.

'Hello, Sam,' said a familiar, cold voice.

Sam slammed the front door behind him, partially dulling the roar of the rain outside. He flicked on the light in the hallway. And there, sitting at the bottom of the grand staircase a few paces in front of him, was a thickset man in his fifties, with greying hair. The spitting image of himself. The man who should not have been there.

'For goodness' sake, Bill!' he snapped. 'What are you doing here? Have you seen what's happening outside?'

'I've been waiting here for ages,' replied the man with an

unnerving calmness and an icy stare. 'If you'd turned up earlier, we could have avoided this. Besides,' he added with a faint smile playing at the corner of his mouth, 'you'd locked the door, so I couldn't get out.'

Sam threw his arms wide with exasperation. 'I've been out. And you never told me you were coming today.'

'I don't need your permission every time I come here,' growled Bill. 'Anyway, that doesn't matter. We're wasting time.'

The loudest clap of thunder Sam had ever heard in his life shook the ancient house, rattled the windows. For a moment, he was convinced the house had been struck. Maybe it had.

'Bill, you have to go back.'

'I don't think so,' snorted Bill.

Just then, Sam heard a baby crying in the next room. A young woman carrying the baby in her arms appeared in the doorway to the lounge. Her face was creased with anxiety.

'What's going on?' she said in a tremulous voice.

'Oh, my good grief, Bill,' gasped Sam. He thought he was going to be sick. 'What are *they* doing here?'

Bill stood up and moved towards Sam. 'You're a clever chap, Sam. I'm sure you can work it out.'

Sam swallowed hard. His heart was pounding in his chest. He moved to the hallway window and pointed outside just as another flash of lightning lit up the driveway. 'Have you seen it out there? You can't stay here. You've got to go back before someone is killed. You've got to go back – now!'

'No, Sam. You're the one who's going back,' replied Bill, and with that, he produced a small handgun from his trouser pocket.

Sam gasped. 'Is this a joke?' he demanded, just when he

thought there could be no more surprises.

Bill laughed a mirthless laugh. 'I don't think you need me to answer that, now do you?' he replied waving the gun.

'Have you gone completely insane?'

With obvious growing impatience, Bill moved a pace closer to Sam and pointed the gun into his face. 'That's enough talking for now. Let's get going.' Sam was about to speak when Bill forestalled him. 'We're going to fetch your family.'

'I don't think so,' said a defiant but trembling Sam.

'You don't really have a choice. If I shoot you and your family, well, that also solves my problem. I'm giving you the option to avoid any bloodshed.'

'You can't be serious. Go back, Bill. We'll discuss this another time, when the weather's calmed down. We'll sort something out.'

'What, and have you bury the mirror? I don't think so, Sam.' He then pressed the barrel of the gun into Sam's forehead. 'Now, move.'

What choice did Sam have? If he stood his ground, Bill could just shoot him and then go after his family. A horrible, sickening feeling of regret washed through him. What had he done? It was too late: the genie was out of the bottle. He had been a fool to think he could remain master of the situation for so long. He could have, should have, foreseen that something like this would happen eventually. He could do no more than sigh with resignation.

Without averting his gaze from his captive, Bill instructed the woman behind him to hurry out to Sam's car, which was waiting in front of the house. When she opened the front door, the rain was still pelting down, the sky still as black as coal. Sam turned slowly around and watched her dash through the rain with her swaddled baby still in her arms, and clamber into the back of his car.

With a prod of the gun between his shoulder blades, Sam was ushered out through the door. Just as the two men stood in the porch, a tree in the front garden was struck by lightning and burst into flames, casting an eerie light across the driveway, until the rain extinguished the fire in a matter of moments.

'This is madness, Bill,' insisted Sam.

Undeterred, Bill shoved him in the back again, and out into the hammering rain. They descended the steps onto the gravel, the rain soaking their clothing to the skin in an instant.

Once more, Sam turned to his doppelgänger in a last desperate attempt to make him see sense. 'Bill, this is–'

An explosion of light erupted in front of Sam, blinding him, searing the water from his body. He was flung to the ground and almost blacked out. He thought he heard a woman screaming. For several seconds, he lay prostrate and dazed on the wet gravel, the rain pummelling his back. His ears were ringing, his sight temporarily gone. He dragged himself to his knees, rubbed his sore eyes. Slowly, his sight returned.

Bill had gone.

Where the man had been standing but a moment earlier, the gravel was black and steaming in the rain. Nothing of Bill was left, no trace save for the shiny medallion the size of a large hand, lying face down with its thick chain curled around it. Sam reached over and picked it up. There was still time to make everything right, even if it was now too late to save Bill.

The car engine roared into life behind him. He spun round just in time to see the headlights explode into life. The young woman was behind the wheel, her face pale with fright and shock. He cursed himself for having left the car keys in the ignition in his haste to enter the house earlier. As the car began moving, Sam flung his arms onto the bonnet and fixed the woman firmly in his gaze.

'Stop!' he pleaded. 'Wait. I'll take you back.'

She glared back at him as if to indicate that she had no intention of returning. Her face then screwed into a grimace, and without warning, the car accelerated in a tight arc, flinging Sam backwards onto the gravel. He watched helplessly as the car skidded erratically away down the driveway and out of sight.

For a terrible moment, Sam was unsure what to do. Wiping the rain from his face, he sprang to his feet, stuffed the medallion into his pocket and darted back inside the house. With his heart pounding, he fumbled around in a cupboard in the hallway until he located another set of car keys, and then ran back outside across the driveway to the double garage, which stood opposite the house. Another violent burst of three successive lightning bolts lit up the town down in the valley. The metal garage door rattled with the force of the thunder that followed.

Sam started up his second car and tore off down the road in pursuit of the woman. Leaning forward across the steering wheel, his eyes straining through the unrelenting rain on his windscreen, he scanned the road ahead for the fleeing car. Lightning struck a nearby field, and in the split second of illumination, he caught a glimpse of the other car heading down the hill into the blurred lights of the town below. In desperation, he accelerated still further, scraping bushes, mounting grass verges in the dark as he went, his own safety an irrelevance.

At last, he reached the town and the almost comforting amber glow of streetlights. He slowed down to survey the scene. But the car had vanished. He shot his head left and right, but there was no sign of it. Two or three other vehicles were moving tentatively about the roads, causing ripples in the thin layer of surface water that covered everything. Several brave, or perhaps foolish, souls were running through the deluge, soaking wet despite their coats. There was even a couple dragging their screaming children behind them as if fleeing some disaster. But the woman and child he really wanted to see had gone.

Another terrifying thunderbolt caused him to jerk his head to the left.

And then he saw it, tall and spiralling into the black sky, swirling like a massive plume of smoke, destroying everything in its path. And then he knew why people were braving the elements to be outside: a huge tornado was tearing a path through the town like an angry giant.

'Oh, no!' he gasped in horror. 'What have we done?'

His heart missed a beat. In an instant, he forgot about Bill, about the woman and her child. His thoughts immediately turned to his own family. He floored the accelerator and raced across the bridge in the centre of the town. The river below was flowing in a torrent, the like of which he had never seen before. Every couple of seconds, he glanced through his side window at the monster carving its way through his town, swaying like a massive spinning top, changing its direction apparently in a random fashion, unconcerned by the devastation it was causing. Behind it, two smaller whirlwinds had formed, writhing like snakes ready to pounce on their prey.

Panic swept through his body. His breathing became shallow. If anything happened to his own family, he would never be able to forgive himself.

He turned into a residential road of terraced houses on both sides. He scraped the side of a parked car, lost his wing mirror. Above him, to his left just behind the row of houses, roared the main tornado, as if following him, watching him, waiting for an opportune moment to strike. And then, as he raced down the road, it changed direction, burst into the line of houses with a deafening crash. Bricks and tiles, and pieces of wood, pieces of fractured furniture, spiralled into the air. A brick landed suddenly on the roof of his car, creating a dent. The twister then moved along the terraced houses, demolishing everything in its path, as if they were made of nothing more than matchsticks. People ran out of their houses, darting in all directions, splashing in the puddles, screaming as debris flew all around them. At least, he thought, it was still early afternoon, and therefore many of the houses would be empty. But he knew number eight was not.

By now, Sam was only a few houses in front of the tornado. He skidded to a halt in the middle of the road in front of number eight and sprinted through the unrelenting rain towards the house. He thumped on the door with both fists, thumped again and again, his desperation almost causing him to cry like a terrified child. As he waited for several agonising seconds, he watched as the line of approaching destruction edged closer and closer. Windows were blown out, trees torn to shreds in an instant, bricks funnelled into the air.

The door flew open. 'What's going on?' screamed his daughter. He could barely hear her voice over the devastation to his left.

He yelled at her to get her child with such a voice, such a pleading expression that brooked no argument. The moment she reappeared with her baby, he dragged them violently out of the doorway towards the car, the force of the wind almost knocking them to the ground. His daughter glanced over her shoulder just as the tornado devoured her neighbour's house. But for the noise of terrible destruction, Sam would have heard her screams of terror.

The engine was still running. As the car pulled away, his daughter's house disappeared behind a swirl of debris, fragments large and small flying in all directions, raining down on the car.

'Dad, what's going on?' demanded his daughter, her eyes wide with shock and terror.

Sam did not respond until he saw the tornado receding slowly in his rear-view mirror. 'Where's Matt?' he demanded, breathlessly.

'What? He's at work.' The baby was crying wildly. 'For heaven's sake, Dad, what's happening?'

'I don't know,' he lied. For the time being, it was safer not to tell her the truth. 'We need to go somewhere safe.'

He changed up a gear and accelerated down a side street, only one thing on his mind: get back to the house and safety. His daughter seemed too shocked and too busy trying to comfort her screaming baby to ask any more awkward questions.

A jagged crack of lightning arced across the black sky in front of them. It was hard to believe it was still only three o'clock in the afternoon on what had earlier been a hot summer's day. By now, large areas of the town had been plunged into blackness when the storm had destroyed streetlamps and taken down power lines. But with an immense amount of skill and a large slice of luck, Sam soon found himself driving away from the town and up the hill towards *Morladron House*.

His mind had just begun to consider what he was going to do on the other side when it happened. A blinding flash of white light filled the windscreen, and he lost control of the car. Whether the road just in front of the car had been struck or the car itself, he could not be sure, but the next thing he knew, the vehicle had come to a standstill, and he was lying stunned against the deflating airbag on the steering wheel. Having spun through one hundred and eighty degrees on the wet road, the car was now facing back down the hill and was listing to one side, the passenger-side wheels stuck in a ditch by the side of the road. Although the engine had cut out, the headlights were still casting a bright but rain-smeared pool of light ahead of them.

Immediately, Sam turned to his right, and saw his daughter slumped forward, the swaddled baby safely cradled in her arms. Once more, the baby began crying, instantly awaking its mother.

Sam touched her shoulder. 'Are you okay?'

She looked up and out of the windscreen. 'I think so.'

Sam turned the key in the ignition, but nothing happened. A flash of lightning lit up the hillside in front of them, and in the brief moment of illumination, they caught sight of a tall, dark, swirling column, creeping its way erratically across a field towards the road, towards them.

'Dad!' screamed his daughter.

'I know. I saw it.'

Sam repeatedly turned the key with a renewed urgency, but

it steadfastly refused to ignite the engine. The tornado burst through the hedgerow to their right with a maelstrom of leaves and twigs and glided into the pool of light in front of the car. It was smaller than the vast twister that had just destroyed his daughter's house but no less dangerous.

'We have to get out of the car,' yelled Sam, but seeing his daughter's door was wedged against the hedgerow, he grabbed the baby from her arms and ordered her to follow him out of the driver's door.

The moment he stumbled out of the car into the pouring rain, he heard the roar of the tornado, felt its force trying to drag him towards it, trying to devour him and the child. He reached his free arm into the car and pulled his daughter out onto the road, just as the gyrating funnel began clawing at the bonnet. He dragged his daughter to her feet and implored her to run up the hill after him.

Barely had he turned to run, when he heard her fall over behind him and scream his name. He turned around, but she had gone, vanished behind the towering, sinister whirlwind that writhed only a couple of metres from him. He had a split second to make a decision. He chose to run.

Sheltering his screaming grandchild from the rain as best he could, he sprinted up the hill, pumping his legs as fast as he knew how, until his lungs felt like they would burst, and his heart would explode. Not daring to look back, he could sense the thing pursuing him at a leisurely pace, as if it were savouring the chase.

At last, he reached the gates to his house, still open after his earlier hasty exit. He splashed across the gravel and bounded up the steps to the front door. As he fumbled to open the door, he heard the gravel on the driveway being sucked up behind him, like the sound of a large wave crashing onto a shingly beach.

Finally, he was inside and leaping up the stairs two at a time and racing into the study at the end of the landing. He could hear the tornado drawing ever closer, howling its menace in the black sky. It was drawing up gravel and mud and branches, and hurling them at the stone walls, clawing against the old house, trying to reach him and the baby. He heard a window smash downstairs.

A flash of lightning lit up the room, and there in the corner, he saw what he so desperately sought. He rushed across the floor, tore away a blanket to reveal a tall but narrow mirror, angled slightly upwards on its wooden stand. Whilst still holding the screaming infant in one arm, he reached out and pressed a palm against the cold glass of the mirror.

And then he and the baby vanished in a second.

Almost straightaway, the whirlwind seemed to lose some of its terrible force. Its assault on the side of the house subsided, until the whole massive cone began to shrink in size, before spiralling into a tall and thin wisp of harmless smoke.

Thunder pealed overhead for one last time as the rain began to ease its intensity. From nowhere, a break appeared in the clouds, and a dazzling beam of brilliant sunlight burst through onto the house below, like a spotlight on a stage.

Within a few short minutes, the rain had stopped altogether, and shafts of sunlight arrowed down onto the town. And then, all was serene and quiet once more.

Chapter Two

Morladron House

Porthgarrick, Cornwall
Present day

'Rachel Trump,' said an indignant Mrs Tyler, the French teacher. 'As you seem to want to talk through my entire lesson, perhaps you'd like to stand up and explain to the class how reflexive verbs work.'

Rachel immediately stopped talking and looked up at the teacher with a smirk. 'Er … je suis … Oh, I don't know, Miss,' she replied, grinning at the girl sitting next to her.

'No, no. Come on now,' insisted the teacher. 'Stand up and tell us. I'm sure you must have been discussing reflexive verbs with your friends just now.'

With her friends around her whispering sarcastic encouragement, she slowly dragged herself to her feet. The whole class turned to watch her rise. But Tom Paget watched her more intently than most. He studied her sweet, delicate features, and the wavy, dark brown hair, which cascaded over her shoulders. Even after three years of verbal abuse and disdainful looks, Rachel Molly Trump was still the loveliest thing he had ever set eyes upon.

A face appeared in front of his, blocking his pleasant view and jolting him abruptly from his daydream. It was a round face with a shock of blond hair and was by some way *not* the loveliest thing he had ever set eyes upon.

'You're staring again,' muttered his friend, Jake McBean,

with a disapproving frown.

'No, I wasn't,' replied Tom, far too quickly to be convincing.

'Oh, you so were,' whispered Jake in his soft Scottish accent.

'Yeah, well, what if I was? She's a great-looking girl.'

'But she hates you!' insisted Jake.

'Settle down, please,' said Mrs Tyler. 'Now come on, Rachel. You're not going to sit down till you've said in French: I get up – at eight o'clock – in the morning.'

Rachel sighed petulantly and crossed her arms. 'Sorry, but I don't know,' she said. Then, seeing the determined look on her teacher's face, sighed again. '*Je … lever …* something. Oh, how should I know?'

The half of the class who knew the answer, laughed. The half who did not, remained nervously silent, praying Mrs Tyler would not ask them.

Jake turned again to Tom. 'Really, Tom. What do you see in her? I mean, she's not exactly the brightest tool in the shed.'

'The brightest tool in the shed?' chuckled Tom.

'Oh, you know what I mean. She's not exactly going to win an intellectual debate now, is she?'

'Maybe not. But look at her – she's gorgeous.'

'Do the words shallow and skin-deep mean anything to you?' grinned Jake.

'You're just jealous,' replied Tom, more loudly than he had intended.

'Thomas Paget and Jake McBean,' said Mrs Tyler, turning sharply towards the two boys. 'Is there something you wish to share with the class?'

'Er, no,' replied Tom. 'I was just discussing the answer.'

15

'Which is?' pressed Mrs Tyler.

'Well, er ... *Je me lève à huit heures du matin*?' he said hopefully.

'Yes, well done, Tom,' said a mildly surprised Mrs Tyler.

Most of the class groaned its grudging praise, whilst Rachel shot him the filthiest of looks.

And then the bell rang to signify the end of the school day, much to Tom's relief. To remind her pupils of the homework she wanted them to do, Mrs Tyler had to raise her voice above the noise of scraping chairs, closing books and excitable conversations.

As Rachel and her knot of glamorous friends started walking towards the door, she muttered: 'What's the point of learning this rubbish? It's, like, a complete waste of my time.'

'Well, you chose to do it,' said one of her friends.

'No, I didn't,' spat Rachel. 'My parents made me.'

'Never mind,' continued the girl with a snigger. 'I'm sure Paget will help you with your homework, won't you, Paget?'

Tom was clearing up his books when he heard his name mentioned and looked up. 'Er, yeah,' he said with a hopeful smile. 'I could help you out, if you like?'

Rachel gave him a look of utter contempt. 'Oh, please! Get out of my way, loser,' she said, and brushed past him, such that he had to take a step backwards to maintain his balance. As she turned her back on Tom and stormed out of the room, her small coterie of friends stared at him briefly with smirks on their faces, before following Rachel into the corridor.

'I told you, mate,' said Jake, leaning close to his friend. 'You're wasting your time with that evil witch.'

As the two friends sauntered home after school, Tom fished

out a tennis ball from his school bag, and they began the game of catch they played almost every day. After tossing the ball to his friend, Jake threw the ball high into the air.

'You're just showing off now,' said Jake, in his usual deadpan manner, as Tom nonchalantly caught the tennis ball in his left hand.

Then it was Tom's turn to launch the ball high over a telephone line across the road.

With arms and legs pumping in ungainly fashion, Jake set off down the road, eyes squinting upwards into the bright blue sky. Yet despite his stocky frame, he managed to follow the flight of the ball and held the catch. 'Is that the best you can do?' he said, and promptly hurled the ball skyward with all his considerable might.

For a brief moment, Tom was dazzled by the blazing sun, but as soon as he caught sight of the ball against the summer sky, he sprinted along the pavement, looking far more of an athlete than his friend, and pouched the catch, once again using only his left hand.

'What a catch!' he exclaimed. 'And still he only needs one hand.'

'You still won't get in the cricket team, mate,' said Jake.

'Of course I will,' replied Tom confidently. 'For my fielding alone.'

'You're just trying to impress that Trump girl. I know your game.'

Tom picked up his rucksack, and the two boys resumed their walk home.

'Honestly, Tom,' continued Jake, 'I really don't understand what you see in that girl. She treats you like a piece of poo, and still you keep coming back for more.'

'She's just a normal fourteen-year old, Jake, like the rest of us. Full of confusing emotions and hormones. One day she'll change, she'll mature and realise just what a really nice chap I am …'

'Aye, when hell freezes over.'

'And when she does,' continued Tom, undaunted, 'I'll be there waiting for her.'

'Maybe, but at the moment, I'm afraid … she hates you!'

'Well, I wouldn't say hates exactly,' protested Tom.

Jake laughed. 'You're right. I wouldn't say hate – she loathes you.'

'I don't expect you to understand true love.'

'You're mad, Tom. Stark raving bonkers, mate.'

'One day, my friend. One day,' said Tom wistfully, and tossed himself a catch. 'You'll see.'

'Aye, one day I'll win a cross-country run.' Whereupon both boys burst out laughing at the thought of the portly Jake winning a running race.

Though Tom was able to laugh about it, his three-year obsession with Rachel Trump was feeling increasingly like nothing more than an exercise in pain and futility. Maybe it was about time he tried to forget her and move on.

Presently, they reached the road bridge that spanned the river in the centre of Porthgarrick. To their right, the river snaked its way through the wooded hills in the distance and down into the town, and a couple of hundred metres to their left it flowed out into the sparkling blue sea, cutting the town in half. Overlooking the wharves on either side of the river, where small boats were moored, were large stone buildings, originally built as warehouses but now, for the most part, shops, restaurants and bars. Both sides of the valley rose high above the river and were covered with houses of all shapes and sizes, some brightly coloured, whilst others looked rather drab and weathered by the sea air. As the eye travelled upwards, larger more prosperous houses came into view, detached properties with impressive views across the valley and out to sea.

As they crossed the bridge, Tom looked up at the buildings on the far side, and as ever one particular house stood out from the rest. Standing aloof over the rest of the town, the two-storey mansion house, faced with silver-grey stone, stood like a small castle perched on the highest point of the far side of the valley. It overlooked the sea to the left and every other building in the town in front and to the right. Despite local legend speaking of a mighty castle having once existed on the spot centuries earlier, no evidence to support such a myth had ever been uncovered. Now that it was derelict and boarded up, it looked more than ever like a haunted house from a low-budget horror film. Indeed, in the playgrounds and pubs of Porthgarrick, tales were constantly being recounted of ghostly sightings and unexplained happenings in and around the old house. Even though Tom knew the tales to be irrational, he nonetheless felt an inexplicable attraction to the house every time he saw it. Particularly as it had, at one time, belonged to his family.

When they had crossed the river and begun to walk up the hill towards their respective homes, Tom turned to Jake and said: 'Let's go and take a look at the house.'

Jake paused for a moment, before agreeing.

It was good of Jake not to object, thought Tom, particularly as Tom made him trek up the road that led past the house at least once every week after school. But then they both knew that Tom had no desire to go home any earlier than was necessary. Besides, such a hot and sunny day demanded they stay outside as long as possible.

After a short, energetic walk, which had made Jake puff and pant all the way, they arrived at the wrought iron gates in front of the house. A thick chain and a large padlock had been attached to the rusting gates, together with a sign that warned trespassers to keep out. Yet every time he saw the sign and the lock, Tom had to fight the compulsion to clamber over and take a look inside.

Jake pulled back a clump of ivy and read a sign carved into a large boulder next to the gates: '*Morladron House*. What's wrong with Seaview Cottage or something normal like that?'

'Ah, well,' began Tom with infectious enthusiasm. 'It's named after *Morlard the Mighty*, a giant who came down from the skies and built a towering castle made entirely of glass and–'

'Nice story. But Mrs Meadow says the name means pirates in Cornish, and probably comes from when the house was owned by pirates or smugglers.'

'You have to go and spoil a perfectly good legend, don't you?' sighed Tom in mock disappointment.

He looked at the house again with its boarded windows and sinister appearance, and the urge to enter grew and grew. It was as though a voice in his head were telling him there were answers in there, answers to questions that had haunted him ever since he had learnt to speak.

'Let's go in,' he said suddenly.

'Now why would we want to do that?' sighed Jake.

'Why, what's wrong?'

For a moment, Jake looked stunned that his friend finally

seemed to be serious about breaking in. 'Well, firstly, it's probably very unstable and could collapse at any time. And secondly, someone might see you.'

'This place used to belong to my family,' insisted Tom. 'But I don't know anything about it.'

Despite constant questioning from Tom over the years, his father stubbornly refused to tell him anything about the connection to their family. Indeed, he had only found out that it had been in his mother's family for generations after a casual conversation with a neighbour, who had clearly wanted to impress him with the ridiculous story of a ghost he had once seen stalking the grounds of the house. And then of course, his father's refusal to discuss the house had fuelled Tom's curiosity even further.

'You just said it yourself,' continued Jake, 'the house *used* to belong to your family. It doesn't anymore. Now come on. Don't be daft.' He then moved impatiently away from the gates, clearly intent on resuming their journey home.

'I'm going in,' said Tom, with a glint in his eye.

'No, you're not. Don't be a fool.'

After a cursory look around him to check the coast was clear, and before Jake could say another word, Tom clambered up the gates, and jumped down onto the ground on the other side.

'Tom, come back, you idiot,' yelled Jake, seizing the gate in his large hands and looking nervously around him.

Tom simply grinned at his friend. 'Just stay there and keep watch. I'll be five minutes, that's all.'

And then he was gone, running over the driveway, which was more weeds than gravel, towards the house. The urge to explore inside was overwhelming, was pulling him towards the house almost against his will, like a mermaid luring a ship onto rocks. There was no obvious way in: all the ground-floor windows were boarded up, graffiti scrawled across them, and the large wooden front door looked as solid and impenetrable as the day it had been fitted. Yet he had to find a way in, just had to.

He ran round to the back of the house.

Jake was nervous, uncomfortable. Tom was always dragging him up here and making him wait whilst his friend stared longingly at the house and talked nonsense about his family, and about legends and ghosts. But Tom had never tried to break in before. What would happen if Tom were caught? The last thing his friend needed was another beating from his father.

'Oh, look. It's Mr Bean,' squawked an unpleasant voice behind him.

He spun round, instantly recognising the voice, feeling a shiver run down his spine. Rachel Trump and three of her friends were standing in the road staring at him with malevolent looks, their faces now plastered with make-up.

'That was Paget who just went in, wasn't it?' said Rachel before Jake could speak.

'Er, no. There's, er, no one in there,' he stammered. 'I was just looking at the–'

'Nice try, Mr Bean,' said Rachel, as she reached into her pocket, and pulled out her bright pink mobile phone. 'Let's see what the police have to say.'

'No, please!' pleaded Jake, and took a step towards the girl.

'Stay there, fat boy,' sneered Rachel, and reached out a hand in front of Jake's chest, whilst the other hand began tapping into her phone.

'Come on, Rachel,' continued Jake in increasing desperation. 'Tom's never done anything to you. He's just having a quick look. This house used to belong to his family.'

'I don't care if it belonged to the Queen. He's trespassing.'

Jake took a sudden lunge for the phone, but Rachel, as if expecting such a move, swung her arm over her head, taking the phone out of reach. Her three friends formed a semi-circle around Jake, casting him condescending and baleful looks.

'Now, now, Mr Bean,' taunted Rachel, and held the phone to her ear. 'We all know you're not going to try anything, don't we?'

She was right. As stocky as he was, Jake had never hit a boy in anger, let alone a girl; it simply wasn't in his nature. Tom used to tease him, saying you knew when Jake was really angry when he frowned at you. So he glanced back at the house, briefly contemplated climbing over the gates to warn his friend, but quickly realised he would never make it. Feeling desperately powerless, he resorted to the only option left to him: he began calling out Tom's name, whilst the girls stood and jeered, and Rachel spoke into her phone.

Almost as if an invisible hand were guiding him, Tom immediately found a way into the enclosed rear garden through a small gap in the giant hedge. Like an explorer in the jungle, he beat a path through the overgrown bushes and grass, until he arrived at a stone terrace at the rear of the mansion. Above him, loomed the grey house, silent and sinister. Just as at the front, all the windows and doors had been boarded up, and large tentacles of ivy had spread up the walls like the feelers of a giant beast trying to prise a way into the house.

Tom's eyes scanned every block of stone, every wooden board, searching for a way to break in. There was no way he was going to turn back now. The same strange sixth sense that had egged him on this far was pushing him forward, feeding his confidence.

Towards one end of the house, a large bush had been allowed to grow unchecked and was now concealing one of the ground-floor windows. Tom pulled back some branches to take a closer look. Various creepers and weeds were smothering the wooden board. He tugged them off and saw that a section of the window frame to which the board was nailed was rotten. Spurred on by his growing excitement, he pulled at the corner of the board with all his might until it yielded with a crack, and there before him was a small black hole, just big enough for him to climb through.

His pulse was racing, adrenalin coursing through his veins. The exhilaration he felt was growing by the second, without his really knowing why. The voice of reason inside his head, which told him there were countless dangers ahead, was reduced to a whimper, buried deep at the back of his mind, supplanted by the voice that was spurring him on inexorably.

And then he was inside the dark and cool interior of the house, oblivious to the small tears in his trousers and the grazes to his arms, sustained when he had scrambled through the hole. Unable to bear the wait until his eyes had grown accustomed to the dark, he brushed himself off and moved forwards. There was a crunch of unknown debris under his feet and a stale smell in his nostrils. He felt like an archaeologist, the first person to enter an Egyptian tomb in three thousand years. The anticipation of what treasures he would find within was almost too much to bear.

He felt his way through a doorway and then into a corridor, and suddenly found himself in a spacious hallway with a grand wooden staircase to his left. In front of him, dozens of tiny strings of bright sunlight were suspended from the boarded windows down to the floor, shafts of light carrying swirls of dust.

He thought he heard his name being called, and shivered. What if the ghost stories were true? He stopped and then heard it again. It sounded like Jake was shouting out to him. But he was meant to go upstairs, he just knew it. Whatever Jake wanted to tell him would have to wait. So up he climbed.

As his pupils dilated, and the scene around him began to take shape, he saw a landing with many closed doors leading off it. A pigeon cooed above him and then abruptly flew away, the flapping of its wings reverberating loudly around him and toying with his nerves.

He tried all the doors, peeked into all the rooms. Some were nearly empty; others contained the barest amount of furniture. All were dark and ghostly.

Finally, he came to a closed door at the end of the landing and immediately noticed that a light appeared to be on in the room: a bright light was shining from under the door. With his heart pounding faster and faster, he opened the door, and a sudden blast of light blinded him. He shielded his eyes and edged sideways into the room. When he peered through his fingers, he saw that a beam of sunlight had burst through a hole in the roof and was shining on a tall rectangular mirror at the back of the room where the light was then being diverted towards the doorway like a searchlight.

Jake was still calling out his name and sounding more and

more fraught with every cry. But the mirror intrigued him. He dragged it away from the blinding beam of light to take a closer look. It was a little taller and wider than he was and was tilted slightly backwards on a sturdy wooden stand. An ornate wooden frame, as wide as a hand, ran along all four edges, and was covered in elaborate carvings of animals, plants, fiendish faces and all manner of indecipherable letters and hieroglyphics. He ran a finger around the carving of a ghoulish head, the size of a large apple, felt the large teeth in its gaping mouth and the bulging eyes in its evil-looking face.

He then ran a hand across the surface of the mirror itself, gathering dust and dirt as he went, until he could see his own wide-eyed face staring back at him with all the wonderment he felt inside. He wiped clean a strip down to his feet, and looked up and down at the reflection of his entire thin figure, from the black shoes and trousers, and white shirt of his school uniform, to the light brown hair on his head. Instinctively, he straightened his tie and promptly felt a strange tingling sensation in the ends of his fingers. He turned his hand over and stared at the blackened fingertips. There was nothing there, yet he could feel something, like a fading charge of static.

Once more, he was drawn towards the mirror like iron to a magnet. His hand reached out and the palm pressed onto the glass. For a brief moment, the tingling returned and spread throughout his entire body, a pleasant, energising sensation of warmth and elation. He could have remained like that with his palm stuck to the mirror for ages.

Jake cried out again. A moment later, the wail of a distant police siren drifted into the house. At first, Tom tried to ignore it, but then it grew louder, and suddenly, he realised the source of Jake's anguish. His only thought was to hide the mirror. He simply could not let it fall into the hands of another. The magic he felt sure it somehow possessed was his and his alone. So he heaved it across the room, straining against the cumbersome weight of the thing. It kept sticking in the uneven floorboards, almost as though it were digging its heals into the floor, reluctant to be moved from the spot it had no doubt occupied for years.

The siren was louder still. Then it faded to a groan and stopped. At last, Tom had moved the mirror into a corner of the room behind a large dresser and turned it around to face the wall. He hurried out of the room, closed the door behind him and started to run down the stairs, just as he heard voices and the jangle of keys outside.

He was barely halfway down when the front door flew open in front of him. A rectangle of blinding light poured into the house, stopping him in his tracks. Three black silhouettes stood on the threshold, faceless and menacing. Tom knew it was pointless to run. He shielded his eyes with an arm and walked solemnly down the last few steps to accept his fate.

Whilst a scruffy old man locked the front door behind them, two policemen escorted Tom into their waiting car. As they drove away, Tom saw on one side his friend Jake, his face screwed with trepidation, and on the other side the pretty face of Rachel Trump laughing loudly with three of her friends. When she caught Tom's gaze, her eyes narrowed, and a mixture of smugness and malice spread across her face.

'Mr Paget?' inquired one of the policemen, when the front door opened.

'Yeah,' replied a scruffy, middle-aged man with a sullen

look. His hair was unkempt, his chin unshaven, and though he was tall, he hunched his shoulders. His stomach was straining to break out of a dirty and creased shirt. All in all, he looked much older than his forty-two years.

'Is this your son?' the policeman continued, pointing at Tom who stood motionless, with his head bowed in shame.

His eyes narrowed and he peered at the boy. 'Of course it's my son,' he replied gruffly. 'Why? What's he done?'

'We caught him breaking into that old house on the hill, *Morladron House.*'

Tom's father glared at his son. 'You idiot,' he spat, then turned to the two policemen and added: 'I'm sorry about this, officers. I'll deal with this. It won't happen again, I assure you.'

Tom was directed into the house, while his father and the policemen chatted for a further minute or two on the doorstep. But he was not interested in what they had to say, only about what was to come. When he heard the front door slam shut and saw his father enter the lounge, he braced himself.

'So, come on then,' began his dad. 'What on earth were you doing up there?'

Tom stood tall, determined not to cower, even though his legs were like jelly. 'I'm sorry, Dad,' he began, his voice already faltering. 'I just wanted to …' He could not find the right words. Then again, what was the point? No matter the explanation he offered, it would be rejected and thrown back in his face with interest.

'Just wanted to what?' shouted his father suddenly. 'Just wanted to embarrass me, make me look a fool, is that it?'

'I wasn't doing any harm,' replied Tom, through bared teeth.

'What have I told you about going up to that house, eh?

You steer clear of it, do you hear me? It's nothing but trouble.'

But that response only fuelled Tom's burning curiosity. 'What do you mean, Dad, it's nothing but trouble? You tell me I should never go there, but you never tell me why?'

'Don't answer me back, boy.' His father's face was turning red, his fists clenching. 'It has nothing to do with you. If you go there again–'

'It has something to do with mum, doesn't it?' The question had come out even before the thought had formed in his mind, erupting from his subconscious, almost against his will.

His father's face hardened even further, anger bursting from every pore. 'How dare you?' he bellowed.

'I'm fourteen, Dad. I'm not a kid anymore. I have a right to know.' Tom knew he had touched a raw nerve, a topic he had never dared broach since his early childhood. His father's reaction, maybe the adrenalin too, gave him the strength to probe deeper into the past, to find the answers he had wanted for so long. The image of his father finally opening up to him, of his collapsing to the floor in tears and hugging his son, flashed through his mind.

But his father was not so easily broken. 'What are you talking about? You don't have a right to anything …'

'What happened to mum?' Tom refused to buckle under his father's piercing gaze. And was that a flicker of emotion he saw in the man's eyes? 'Tell me,' he asked softly. 'What happened to her?'

'Your mother is dead, that's all you need to know. And if she could see you now–'

'Talk to me, Dad,' pleaded Tom, feeling he was getting somewhere.

'Shut up, you pathetic little boy,' said his father, and cursed through clenched teeth with such feeling and hatred that the notion he would ever put an arm around Tom and have a consoling chat instantly seemed foolish and misguided.

And that particular dream was shattered completely when Tom saw his father clench a fist and draw it back. Tom saw it all in slow motion, saw the fist flying towards him. He would have had the time to react, to evade the blow or to simply block it but did neither. He refused to believe that his dad was about to strike him again until it was too late. He fell to the floor as much from shock as from the force of the blow. Dazed, and hurting, inside as well as out, he stared back up at his father who glowered down at him.

'Get up, you pathetic child. You make me sick.'

And with that, Tom's father spun around and stormed out of the house.

Chapter Three

Michael Paget

As Jake left the classroom, he gave Tom a wan smile and a pat on the shoulder. The rest of the pupils filed out whispering to one another and glancing back at Tom who was left sitting alone at his desk. Rachel Trump and her friends were the last to leave, having sat at the back of the classroom causing trouble as usual. Tom's eyes followed Rachel out of the door as she turned briefly towards him and blew him a mock kiss. When the door shut noisily behind her, he returned his gaze back to the top of his desk.

The teacher, Mrs Meadow, moved forward, turned a chair around and sat facing Tom across the desk. He looked up at her, desperate to maintain his blank expression. Anything else would be a sign of weakness and would court unwanted comments of sympathy. She was short and plump, and was, he guessed, from the greying streaks in her otherwise dark hair, in her forties. And she had a tendency to wear large, flowery dresses, as if declaring to the world that she cared not one jot what others thought of her appearance. She scrutinised Tom through a narrow pair of glasses. But despite a fearsome reputation for being strict, her face could suddenly break into one of the kindest smiles Tom had ever seen. In short, he had always liked the deputy head.

'So, Tom,' said Mrs Meadow, removing her glasses, which were then left hanging on a pink cord around her neck. 'You know why I asked you stay behind, don't you?'

'I think I can guess,' mumbled Tom.

Mrs Meadow smiled encouragingly, and immediately, Tom felt his defences crumbling. 'What happened, Tom?' she asked, and stared pointedly at his black eye.

The throbbing around his left eye socket seemed to intensify with the attention cast upon it. 'I fell over,' he lied, and straightaway felt a pang of guilt.

'Come on, Tom. We both know that's not what happened.'

Every time she spoke his name, he felt reassured. Maybe it was because his dad hardly ever called him Tom. 'It's complicated,' he said finally.

Mrs Meadow sighed, somehow completely without impatience and full of sympathy. 'Shall I tell you what I think happened?' She did not wait for his response before continuing. 'You were caught and arrested up at that old house, taken home where your father got angry … and then he hit you.'

Tom did not answer but retained his impassive expression, even though inside he wanted more and more to talk. On their way to school that morning, he had told Jake everything, just as he had told his best friend the last time his father had struck him. In that sense, Jake was his release valve, the one person he could talk to without fear of judgement or leg-pulling. But Mrs Meadow was an adult; if he told her, there would be consequences: care homes, foster parents and who knew what else. It was best to let things sort themselves out, as they eventually would, or so he always convinced himself.

'You don't have to put up with this,' continued Mrs Meadow.

Funny, that was exactly what Jake was always saying. Yet it was never a helpful solution, just a trite and empty comment that people said.

'Tom, I can help you do something about this. But if you don't talk to me, I can't do anything.'

'I told you – I fell,' insisted Tom. As much as he liked her, he still did not feel ready to talk.

Mrs Meadow sighed again. 'Oh, Tom. At least tell me what you were doing up at that house. It's so unlike you to get into trouble.'

However, now here was a topic he did feel comfortable discussing with her. She had to be about the same age his mother would have been, had she still been alive. Perhaps Mrs Meadow knew something about her or about *Morladron House*.

'I wasn't stealing or anything,' he began, with a sudden melting of his cold expression. 'It used to belong to my family. And I just – I want to know what happened, why my dad won't talk about it. I don't suppose you know anything about the house, do you?'

Mrs Meadow smiled again. 'I'm afraid not. All I know is that it used to belong to your grandfather before your father inherited it. There were rumours that your father got into financial difficulties and had to sell it, but no one wanted to buy it. So in the end he had to get rid of it for next to nothing. But that's only rumour. I don't really know much else. No one seems to.'

That was why he liked her: anyone else, any other teacher, would have harped on about his trespassing on private property. Yet Mrs Meadow was always more interested in finding out about her pupils, what made them behave the way they did, than simply chastising them. Somehow, she was exactly how he had always imagined his mother would have been.

'And my mother?' he asked hopefully.

'Tom,' she said, shaking her head. 'I honestly don't know. But after we heard that your mother had died, your father became ill, started drinking and lost his job. But that is still no excuse for the way he treats you.'

'But he's still my dad.'

'Yes, Tom, he is. But that doesn't give him the right to hit you.' But seeing Tom's frown, she promptly stood up. 'When you're ready to talk, come and see me, please. I really believe I can help you, Tom, if you'll let me.'

Tom simply nodded and returned to his blank expression.

Mrs Meadow was the closest thing he had to a mother.

The next day dawned warm and sunny once again. Tom rose early and left the house well before he was due to meet Jake on their way to school. It was such a lovely morning, and he had so much to ponder that he decided to amble down to the sea before school but not to the main beach, as there would be too many morning joggers and dog walkers to distract him. He wanted to be alone. So instead, with his small rucksack strapped to his back, he scrambled down a rocky path that led from the cliffs near *Morladron House* down to the sea. Once down in the rocky cove, he clambered over large boulders and splashed through small rock pools, until he spotted the opening to a small cave that he and Jake had discovered a few years earlier. He finally came to rest on a smooth boulder in front of the cave, sat himself down and gazed out across the sea, the strong smell of salt and seaweed filling his nostrils. A pair of seagulls cawed overhead.

His left eye socket was still swollen and uncomfortable, but his pleasure at watching the waves breaking gently over the rocks just in front of him, and the sun sparkling on the blue ocean beyond, was undimmed. It was an idyllic spot. And as no one else seemed willing or able to take the hazardous journey down the cliff, it was ideally suited to someone who wanted nothing more than quiet contemplation.

Tom had half expected to skulk into the dank cave and lick his wounds, reflecting on what Mrs Meadow had said to him the previous day, but instead he found only one thing was going through his mind over and over again: the strange mirror in *Morladron House*. It was hard to forget the bizarre feeling of euphoria he had experienced upon touching the glass. He had intended to pass his moment of solitude mulling over other things in his complicated life, but time and again, his mind kept returning to the mirror, until he finally gave in to the voice in his head that cried out as loudly as the seagulls above. After glancing at his watch and satisfying himself that there was still plenty of time, he resolved to break into *Morladron House* once more.

With renewed vigour, he clambered up the rocks until he reached the top. This time he was much more careful to scan his surroundings, and when he was at last satisfied that he was not being watched, he scrambled over the gate into the grounds of the house.

With the same excitement, the same growing anticipation, he entered the house via the same route as before. To his relief, no one had thought to question him about how he had gained access to the house, so the loose board he had found two days ago had not yet been reattached.

At last, there he was, standing in front of the dusty mirror once more, almost not daring to touch the glass this time, yet knowing he imminently would. That same strange, compelling impulse was there, something like a voice in his head telling him over and over again to reach out and touch the glass.

At that time of the morning the sun was on the opposite side of the house to when he had first come across the room two days previously, so the room was darker than before, full of eerie shadows. For a few long seconds, he stared at his own reflection, fighting the urge to touch the mirror. Inevitably, his attention was drawn to the dark bruising around his left eye. He reached out and touched the reflection of the black eye, as if he could somehow soothe the discomfort it was causing him.

A faint shower of sparks seemed to erupt from his left hand as it touched the glass. The same tingling sensation crept through his fingers and up his forearm. He seemed to lose consciousness for a split second as if he had nodded off.

And the next thing he knew, he was standing in a strange place, staring at such an alien environment it felt like a bizarre dream. Although there was no sense of weightlessness, he seemed to be floating in space, with thousands of tiny stars twinkling all around him. A myriad of smoke-like ribbons of light drifted about slowly, aimlessly, noiselessly, multi-coloured and translucent, like the fragments from a thousand shattered rainbows. It was a strangely warm, comforting place, with no feeling of menace whatsoever.

After a few seconds, his eyes began to focus on a figure directly in front of him, no more than a dozen paces away. As he looked closer, he saw his frozen mirror-image staring blankly back at him, right arm stretched out before him, reflecting Tom's own outstretched left arm. At first, it appeared that he was gazing into a mirror, looking at the framed image of himself, identical in almost every way. Except the boy was wearing a smart blazer and had spiky, gelled hair. Tom was about to lower his arm, still expecting to see his reflection do the same, when instead it lowered its arm first and then spoke.

'Who are you?' it said in Tom's own voice, and then took a step forward.

'Hi,' was all Tom could say. Surely he was simply looking at his own reflection. How daft would that be, talking to himself in a mirror? Perhaps Jake was right: he *was* going mad.

'What just happened?' continued his startled reflection, and began looking sharply left and right, and up and down. When the boy spun around to look behind him, Tom realised that what had looked like the frame of a large mirror was in fact a tall oblong of shimmering light directly behind the boy.

Almost without realising, as if instinctively mirroring the boy's movements, Tom found himself turning around, and was suddenly confronted with his very own rectangle of light directly behind him. It was as tall and thin as the mirror he had just touched only a minute or two earlier, and, although the light was blurred and shimmering, as if looking at an image through water, he quickly realised he was peering back into the gloomy room in *Morladron House* where he had been only moments earlier. When Tom touched the window of light before him, it was as cold and unyielding as a pane of glass. Somehow, he had travelled through to the other side of the mirror, but now there appeared to be no way back.

As if that shocking realisation had struck both boys at the same time, they spun round simultaneously to face one another once more. Cautiously, the two boys walked towards one another, but whilst the boy in the dark school blazer was casting glances all around him, mesmerized by the wisps of coloured mist that floated around them like silk scarves floating on a gentle breeze, Tom could not help staring at the other boy. The likeness was uncanny, unnerving.

When the boy looked downwards, Tom followed his gaze. They were both standing on a pathway, no more than a couple of metres wide that ran between their two mirrors. Shimmering with all the colours of a rainbow, it swayed lazily, almost imperceptibly from side to side. Tom squatted down and found it to be as smooth and as hard as glass. It was cold to the touch but made no noise when he tapped it. In fact, there was no sound to be heard anywhere, except the noise of Tom's pulse racing in his ears at an ever-increasing rate.

The other boy came cautiously forward, glancing nervously at what appeared to be a sheer drop into nothingness on either side of the path.

'Where on earth are we?' asked Tom.

'How should I know?' replied the boy, his mind and his eyes elsewhere. 'One minute I was touching that stupid mirror, and the next I'm here with you in this place.'

A light flashed on in Tom's mind. 'Did you say you touched a mirror?'

'Yes,' said the boy, and pointed behind him to the oblong of light. 'The mirror was in the spare room in my house. I just wandered in, and felt I had to touch it for some reason. Next thing I know – wham! – I'm in here, wherever here is.'

Tom noticed that the light behind the boy was much brighter than his own but had the same blurred, watery quality to it. 'I just touched a mirror in that old house back there,' he said, pointing over his shoulder. 'We must have touched the mirrors at the same time. It must have … I dunno … triggered something.'

'Oh, yeah, right,' snorted the boy.

'How else do you explain what just happened?'

The boy screwed his face into a frown, weighing up Tom's theory. 'Who are you, anyway?' he asked, almost as though he could not think of anything else to say.

'My name's Tom Paget.'

The boy's face froze, and for the first time Tom felt he had the boy's full attention, his eyes staring unblinkingly into Tom's. 'I'm Michael Paget. Michael Thomas Paget.'

Tom gasped. 'I'm … Thomas Michael Paget.'

Michael blinked at last. 'W – What?' he said.

Tom could have asked a hundred different questions, but only one thing mattered for the moment. 'Listen, I've no idea what's happening. But if we got here by touching a mirror at the same time, maybe we can get back by touching the backs of the mirrors at the same time.'

Michael's face brightened into a smile. 'Yes, good thinking. It's worth a try.'

They retreated towards their respective portals, until Michael abruptly spun round. 'Wait,' he said. 'If this works, wait exactly one minute and touch the mirror again. If we come back through, we might have discovered something really cool.'

'Okay, yes. Good idea,' replied Tom, excitedly checking that he was wearing his watch, which he was.

After a brief countdown, they pressed their palms to the cold, smooth surfaces. The same sensation of static crept up Tom's arm, the same split second of unconsciousness hit him. And then he was standing back in the dark room, this time with his back to the mirror, and his left arm outstretched in front of him. Immediately, he spun round and saw nothing but his own startled expression staring back at him from the dusty mirror. The strange void had gone, vanished, and instantly it felt like he had just awoken from a particularly bizarre dream.

But then he remembered what they had just agreed and hurriedly checked his watch. After several agonising seconds, he placed his left palm on the mirror again. Nothing happened. He waited. Still nothing. Maybe it really had been just a dream. Yet he longed to go back, felt strangely empty and sad at the thought he could never go back.

Three seconds later, he was standing back in the void facing his doppelgänger once more, and a tremendous feeling of relief and euphoria swept over him.

This time, the two boys hurried towards one another. One of the many iridescent swirls that were floating about drifted between them like an exotic bird flying in slow motion, before moving off aimlessly towards the stars. Tom's excitement and wonder were reflected in Michael's face.

'This is incredible,' said Michael, wide-eyed. 'If we can travel backwards and forwards to our own houses, why don't we try swapping over? I'll go through your mirror and you go through mine.'

Tom gleefully agreed. They ran over to one another's portals, agreed to return in exactly one minute and then touched the shimmering windows of light simultaneously.

A moment later and Tom was standing in a bright, sun-lit room, so crammed full of boxes and furniture that only a narrow path of carpet was visible leading to the closed door at the far side of the room. He turned around and saw a mirror identical to his own, except that it looked cleaner, and the wide wooden frame was a shade lighter. He leant over a cardboard box on a table to peer out of the large window to his left and gasped in awe at what he saw. He was looking across a picturesque valley, at dozens of houses arranged in rows up the far side, each one vaguely familiar. Somehow it seemed to be Porthgarrick, yet at the same time it was different. And then his eyes roamed to the right, and immediately caught sight of the familiar shape and presence of *Morladron House*, perched on top of the far valley wall overlooking the sea to the right – when it should have been on the left. He was looking at a mirror image of his home town.

However, there was no time to dwell on what he had seen. After glancing at his watch, he hurriedly returned to the mirror, touched its surface and was promptly transported back into the void with Michael.

'You live in Porthgarrick,' said Tom, rushing towards Michael.

'Yeah,' he replied. 'And you live in a dirty old house.'

'That's not my house,' laughed Tom. 'The mirror's in *Morladron House*.'

Michael looked blankly at him. 'Where?'

'You know, that old house at the top of the hill.'

'Oh, I see. You mean these mirrors allow us to travel from one side of the valley to the other.' Michael looked disappointed. 'I thought we were travelling from one part of the country to another.'

Tom thought the boy must be joking, but as he studied the familiar face, he saw no sign of humour, only puzzlement. He could feel his own exasperation rising. If he could see what was happening, why could Michael not?

'Michael, don't you see? That, over there,' he said, pointing at the portal that led back to his own world, 'is my Porthgarrick, and this here is your Porthgarrick. We're not travelling across the valley – we're travelling between your world and mine. We both live in Porthgarrick. But in different worlds.'

For a moment, Michael's face was blank, but then his mouth slowly curved into a smile. 'Wow,' he said simply.

'How could this be possible?' asked Tom, the wild enthusiasm returning.

'I don't know. But it's great, isn't it? So, what's your world like?'

'What's *your* world like?' countered Tom, and both boys laughed.

'Why don't we find out?' asked Michael. 'We look alike. So we could just swap places for a while.'

Tom loved the idea. 'Let's come back this evening and–'

'Why wait? Let's swap now,' proposed Michael. 'Come on, it would be great.'

Tom had to think for a moment. His heart was racing. This was all happening so quickly. The idea of exploring an entirely new world was thrilling beyond words, surely every child's dream. What would it be like? What would he find? The small voice in his head that told him to be cautious was quickly silenced by a tide of uncontrollable excitement.

'If we synchronise watches,' continued Michael, his face a picture of bubbling anticipation, 'and agree to come back at, let's say, four o'clock this afternoon …'

'That's a long time. Are you sure about this?'

'Of course,' replied Michael confidently. 'Look, I trust myself, so I trust you. We're the same person really, aren't we? Just in different worlds.'

It was hard not to feed off Michael's enthusiasm and confidence.

'So, I take it you do go to school?' asked Michael. Tom nodded. 'Then where's your blazer? You can't go to school like that.'

'Of course I go to school, but it's summer. We don't have to wear them when it's hot.'

Michael began peeling off his blazer. 'Well, in my world you'll get shot for not wearing a blazer at any time of the year. And your tie?'

Tom took the blazer from Michael and then sheepishly fished out his crumpled tie from a trouser pocket. After removing his rucksack, he put on both items.

'Make sure you're tidy, otherwise you'll get *me* into trouble,' grinned Michael. 'You scruffy little urchin.'

'I'll bear that in mind,' smiled Tom.

'Oh, that's a nice-looking shiner you've got there, Tom, my friend.'

'Yeah,' replied Tom uneasily, the joy draining from his face. As ever, the socket seemed to throb more when it was being studied by someone else. 'After school, go straight to *Morladron House*. It would be better if you didn't go to my house,' he added sombrely.

'Well, I don't know where you live, anyway.'

'It's probably best for both of us if we keep it that way.'

'Okay,' replied Michael slowly. 'I won't ask.'

Once they had exchanged brief details about their respective schools, and Tom had explained how to get out of his *Morladron House,* the excitement returned, and the two boys prepared to go their separate ways.

'Wait,' said Tom. 'You haven't told me anything about your family. Who else is in the house?' The thought had suddenly occurred to him: Michael clearly lived in a different house, went to a much stricter school. If there were differences in their otherwise similar worlds, did it mean his mother was still alive? Yet he dared not ask the question outright.

'Oh, don't worry. My dad's about to go to work, and I hardly speak to my stepmum. In fact, I hardly say anything to either of them, to be honest. So just keep quiet, and they won't notice a thing.'

Tom had noticed Michael's face drop perceptibly at the mention of his stepmother. He instantly recognised the sad look in his face, had seen it so many times in the mirror himself. It seemed they had both lost their mothers. Perhaps their worlds were not so dissimilar, after all.

After a quick countdown, the two boys touched the portals simultaneously and vanished from the void into one another's worlds.

Chapter Four

Through the Mirror

Following Michael's directions, Tom quietly left the cluttered room containing the mirror, went into the boy's bedroom and picked up his school bag. It had been agreed that they might as well have one another's rucksacks, as the books and timetables in them were only relevant in their respective schools. When he flicked through one of the books, he was horrified to see that all the words were in an odd-looking foreign language, until he realised that it was English after all, but that all the words were back to front: the mirror image of his own language. Though he was still able to read it slowly, he was going to look a complete fool in class. Maybe this was not going to be such a good idea after all.

'Hurry up, Michael,' cried a woman's voice from downstairs. 'Remember, I'm not driving you to school today – you'll have to walk.'

When he moved onto the landing, Tom heard voices downstairs and the chink of spoons on breakfast bowls. His throat went dry, his palms began to sweat and his mind was flooded with doubts. What would he do if they could tell he was not Michael? It was all beginning to feel like a very bad idea.

With trepidation, he plodded down the stairs, and when he reached the bottom, a slim, attractive woman, who was walking away from him down the hallway towards the kitchen, glanced back over her shoulder and smiled warmly at him.

'Quick. Come and have some breakfast before you go,' said the woman cheerily.

And with that, she padded off back into the kitchen, carrying a baby in her arms and leaving Tom no option but to follow her. As he entered the kitchen, she sat down opposite him at a small table and gave him another smile.

The house was so very different to his own. All the rooms he had seen were bigger, cleaner, more welcoming than his own. The house, the smiles, the calm were so alien to what he was used to that they made him feel uncomfortable.

'Morning, Michael,' said a familiar voice to his right.

He turned, looked at the man who had just come to join them at the table, and froze. It was his father. The voice, the eyes, even the way he held his coffee mug in two hands with his elbows on the table, were unmistakable. Yet this was not *his* father. His hair was neatly trimmed and combed, and his face thinner and more youthful. A smartly pressed shirt hung on his slim, athletic-looking body. And he was smiling.

'You all right, son?' asked Michael's father with a puzzled air. 'You look like you've seen a ghost.'

Tom realised he was staring, mouth open. 'Er, yeah,' he said quickly, looking away. 'I'm fine … Dad.'

The man then stood up abruptly, and Tom flinched involuntarily. Again Michael's father looked perplexed.

'You sure you're okay, son?' he asked. 'You're a bit jumpy this morning.'

'No, really. I'm fine. Just a bit tired that's all,' replied Tom, and hastily sat down at the breakfast table.

Out of the corner of his eye, he thought he saw the two adults exchange a confused glance. Maybe it was nothing, or maybe his behaviour was so strange to them that they knew already that he was not Michael. He immediately chastised himself for being so irrational. It was ridiculous to think they could know anything. After all, he looked identical to their son.

'Ouch!' said Michael's stepmother suddenly. 'How did you get that black eye?'

Tom had forgotten about that. 'I fell over upstairs,' he replied quickly.

'You ought to get that seen to,' she persisted.

'I'm fine, really,' said Tom, and grabbed a packet of breakfast cereal, hoping to divert attention away from his eye. Michael had said he did not speak much to his parents, so Tom reasoned that that was the best way to react.

Whilst Tom poured himself a small bowl of cornflakes, Michael's father went over to a dishwasher and placed his empty mug inside. When he returned to the table, Tom had begun devouring his breakfast with gusto, keen to finish and get out of the room as quickly as possible. Above him, Michael's father was about to leave the kitchen when he stopped abruptly.

'You're eating with your left hand,' he said, perplexed.

Tom froze mid-mouthful and his blood ran cold. Maybe this was the moment they would find out.

'Michael, I've told you before,' continued the man, 'it's okay to be right-handed. Don't worry what they say at school. If they start trying to change you again, they'll have me to answer to. You make sure you tell me if that happens. Please don't feel you have to conform.'

Hurriedly, Tom swapped the spoon into his right hand. 'Er, sorry. Yeah, you're right.'

Using his wrong hand, he then proceeded to eat the remainder of his breakfast awkwardly and in twice the time it would normally have taken him. Much to his relief, Michael's father soon left the room to prepare for work, and the stepmother was too involved with her baby to engage him in any further conversation. He could not get out of the house soon enough, as much to escape from Michael's family, as to begin exploring this new world.

Finally, he was back outside again, with the bright morning sunshine warming his face. He turned around and looked back at Michael's large detached house with a tinge of envy. It was a beautifully renovated, old stone house with large picture windows, which afforded impressive views across the valley below. If the town was anything like his own Porthgarrick, the location of the house alone, high up the side of the valley, indicated there was money in Michael's family. Clearly, Michael's father had a better job than his own dad.

He quickly told himself not to be so materialistic and headed down the valley towards the centre of town. As he neared the bottom of the valley, the traffic was increasing in volume but not in noise. Sleek-looking cars hummed past in almost total silence, driving on the right-hand side of the road. He stood and watched them in awe, realising they were all electric: quiet and pollution free. Road signs and posters were nearly all electronic and animated, indicating a use of technology that was far more widespread than in his own world.

He wandered onto the bridge in the centre of Porthgarrick and peered across at the town. Most of the old buildings were the same as those he was used to, only on the opposite banks of the river. However, the longer he studied the scene, the more one particular difference began to stand out above all else: everything was so much cleaner than in his own town. There was no litter, no graffiti that he could see. All the houses and shops were well maintained, many with multi-coloured flower boxes in the windows. Only the smell of salt and seafood, and the crying of seagulls circling overhead were the same. It was not that his own town was at all bad, in fact he loved his home town, but simply that this place seemed like paradise.

He was about to continue across the bridge towards school, when it suddenly occurred to him that he was going in the wrong direction. The whole place was the complete mirror image of his own town. Therefore, the school was back the other way, on the same side of the valley as Michael's house. Realising he was in danger of being late, he hurried back whence he had come. He ran along the streets, all of which were familiar yet confusing. He kept disappearing down the wrong turning and then having to turn around abruptly and come back when he realised he was going the wrong way.

Eventually, he came to the conclusion that he had to calm down and think his way out of this problem logically. He pictured the route to school in his mind, and then simply started reversing the directions, so that a right turn became a left turn and vice versa. It worked, and he soon caught sight of the familiar-looking school on the edge of town.

As he neared the school, a large billboard high on the gable end of a house caught his eye, with its bright and animated image. A clean-shaven Ed Sheeran in a black suit and tie was standing on a rostrum waving at a cheering crowd in front of him. The large slogan in back-to-front lettering underneath was tricky to decipher but read: *Success Requires Sacrifice.*

Intrigued, he stared at the moving image for a short while. It was clearly Ed Sheeran, but he looked more like a politician than a singer.

A couple of agitated boys ran past him, sweating in their black school blazers, dragging him back to the present. School was about to start. At least by turning up at the last minute he had avoided meeting anyone who might have known him; he would be able to sit quietly in class whilst he got to know the pupils around him, and worked out who were Michael's friends and who were not. At last, excitement began to fill him once more when he knew that the real fun was about to begin.

Somehow, Tom managed to negotiate the morning without anyone suspecting he was not Michael. But then, he thought, why would they? After all, the idea that he had an exact look-alike in a parallel world would have been preposterous to him only a few hours ago, so the very notion would scarcely have occurred to anyone else, even if his behaviour was different to what they were used to.

It had certainly proved to be an unusual experience. He had tried to keep note-taking to a minimum, but when left with no choice in order to avoid attracting undue attention, he had endeavoured to conceal his writing behind his free hand in case anyone were to see him writing the wrong way round, let alone with the wrong hand. And certain lessons had proved to be harder to negotiate than others. History, for one, had been particularly fascinating because, although he had been vaguely familiar with many of the events, the protagonists had been completely unknown to him.

However, English had proved especially awkward, for when he had had to read aloud in class, his reading was laboured and disjointed. Starting at the back of a book and reading from right to left and back to front was distinctly tricky, which had caused much mirth in the classroom. Eventually, the teacher had lost her patience and reprimanded him for intentionally playing the fool, as she saw it, just to elicit laughs from his friends. It was all too easy to imagine Michael having the same problems in Tom's world.

Much to his surprise (or maybe he should not have been surprised, he began to wonder), Michael was friends with many of the same people that Tom was in his world, though their personalities were always very different. Most of Michael's friends, it seemed, were troublemakers who always sat at the back of the classroom disrupting the lessons, something Tom was not used to at all. But as long as his poor reading had continued to annoy the teachers and to make Michael's friends laugh, none of them had suspected for a moment that Tom was not Michael.

Tom quickly noticed that everyone, not just he and Michael, had their first and middle names reversed. And so it turned out that Michael's best friend was one Sean Jake McBean, whom he thought it best to seek out once breaktime arrived, having only sat with him once that morning when he had had little chance to talk to him.

The playground was a mass of black blazers under a hot, glaring sun. Tom had quickly established that Michael's school operated a very strict uniform policy, according to which all the girls had to wear black trousers, and everyone had to wear their blazers at all times, even outside when it was hot. Any transgressions and pupils were summarily dispatched to the headmaster's office.

After a quick scan, Tom spotted Sean with a couple of

friends at the edge of the playground, his mop of blond hair standing out against the black of his clothing. As he approached the group, he could see Sean's smiling face over the top of a dark-haired girl who had her back to Tom, and who was in animated conversation with the three boys in front of her.

Sean grinned broadly when he saw Tom approaching. 'Hey, Michael,' he said. 'Fancy a wee bit of fun?'

The agitated girl barely glanced at Tom, before turning back to face the imposing figure of Sean leering down at her. 'Give me back that book, you idiot,' she demanded.

And Tom's heart skipped a beat. It was Rachel Trump, or whatever she was called in this world. Except that she had her dark brown hair swept back in a ponytail and wore small and stylish glasses. It was so unmistakably Rachel Trump, yet somehow so different, too.

'You give me one good reason why I should give you this book back,' said Sean, leaning forwards and looking down at the girl with a menacing smirk on his face, whilst waving the book above her head. He had the same Scottish accent as Jake, yet what sounded easy-going and musical when spoken by Jake was somehow cold and aggressive in Sean.

'Just give it back, McBean,' continued the girl, with a glare.

'Why should I, you little cow? You keep showing me up in class, sucking up to the teachers and pretending you know everything. You need to be taught a wee lesson.'

Although increasingly intimidated by Sean's stocky figure and threatening voice, Tom stepped in. 'Come on, Sean,' he said in his best conciliatory voice. 'Give her the book back.'

Sean shot him a look of utter bewilderment, which quickly changed to one of suspicion and then of annoyance. 'What's up with you?' he snarled.

'Nothing Jake ... er, I mean, Sean. Look, she's not doing any harm. Let's just leave her be.'

'I don't need your help, thank you very much,' snapped the girl.

But neither Tom nor Sean was now looking at her; their eyes were firmly fixed on one another. For a horrible moment, the broad-shouldered Sean stood staring coldly at Tom with such menace in his eyes that Tom feared he was about to punch him. But then his face broke into a knowing smile.

'I know what you're up to. But you can do better than this stuck-up cow.'

After punching Tom playfully but firmly on his upper arm, Sean gave him the girl's paperback, and then, after one last evil smirk at whom he thought was his friend Michael, walked away with his two companions.

'Sorry about that,' said Tom, turning to the girl.

'What do you care?' she replied, and promptly snatched the book from his hand. Briefly, she flashed those fierce, hazel eyes at him, a familiar look behind unfamiliar glasses.

'It's ... er ...' His mind was racing as fast as his heart was pounding. What was Rachel's middle name? He should know this. At last, it came to him. 'It's Molly, isn't it?' he said.

'Well, it hasn't changed since yesterday, as far as I know.' She then began striding away across the busy playground, weaving impatiently between several boys playing football, who promptly jeered at her for getting in the way of their game.

Tom hurried after her. 'Sorry. Yes, of course. Anyway, call me To..., er, I mean Michael. Call me Michael.'

'I don't really want to call you anything, Paget.' She neither looked at him nor stopped.

'We're not really friends, are we?'

Molly slowed her pace to look at him. 'Well, actually, Paget, I only pretend to hate your guts because I'm really madly in love with you,' she said, and gave him a brief and sarcastic smile.

For a short moment, Tom laughed nervously, but then, when he saw Molly's face was unmoved, he quickly stopped, rather embarrassed. She had the same fiery eyes that Rachel had, but there seemed to be an intelligence behind them that most definitely was not there in Rachel. It was hard to suppress the excitement, the leap of joy in his heart, at meeting this newer, more intelligent version of the girl he adored. Yet he would be no better off than he currently was with Rachel, unless he could convince Molly he was not Michael, whom she clearly disliked.

She rolled her eyes at him and strode off again.

Then it came to him. Honesty, after a fashion, was the only way forward.

'Listen,' he began in a low voice, trying to keep up with her. 'I'm not actually Michael.'

'Really,' muttered Molly, disinterested.

'No. My name is … Tom. I'm Michael's cousin. We … look identical, so every now and then we swap lives just for a laugh. I pretend to be him, and he pretends to be me.'

'Oh, please. Is that the best you can do?'

'No, really. I can prove it. I've got this black eye.'

She glanced at him. 'Shame it's not both eyes.'

'When you see me tomorrow, I won't have it. Then when I come back in a couple of days, it'll be back again.' He was already planning his next trip. Now that he had met her, there was no way on earth he would not be coming back.

'Gosh,' Molly said. 'It's amazing what make-up can do these days, isn't it?' She forced a smile once more, before resuming her face of thunder. 'I'm not stupid, you know, Paget.'

By now, Tom's mind was racing almost as fast as they were walking. 'Ah, ah! I know. Michael is right-handed, isn't he?'

'I can't say I've ever been bothered to look.'

'I'll write something down for you, and then you'll see that I'm left-handed.'

Molly stopped abruptly and looked up at Tom, a frown so unbecoming of such a pretty face. 'Look, what is it you want exactly?'

'I was just hoping we could be friends,' he replied meekly.

'Ha!' she scoffed. 'I know what you're interested in, and it's not friendship. I suppose you staged that little scene back there, did you? Just to make you look like the hero, come to rescue the poor damsel from the frightful ogre. Honestly, you'll have to come up with something better than that.'

And with that, she stormed off so briskly that Tom's path was blocked by a group of boys before he could move to follow her. He watched her disappear into the crowd and wondered what on earth Michael could have done to have made her hate him so much.

Later that afternoon, Tom walked into a classroom and saw an empty chair next to Molly. The desks in the room were arranged in pairs, and clearly Molly's best friend had yet to arrive. He seized his moment and sat down next to her, ignoring the taunts from Sean and his friends at the back of the class.

A look of utter disgust appeared on Molly's face when she saw him. 'What are you doing? Go and sit back there with your brain-dead friends.'

Just then, Molly's friend turned up and loomed over Tom, louring. 'Yeah, come on, Paget, move,' she said. 'I sit there.'

'Sorry,' said Tom, with the most apologetic face he could pull. 'It's just for today. I promise.'

Molly and her friend exchanged glances and sighs. Then, as Molly stood up to move away, the teacher entered the classroom and barked at everyone to sit down immediately with such authority that Molly had to reluctantly sink back into her chair, whilst her friend shuffled off to another seat.

After a short while, Tom turned to Molly with a grin and whispered: 'Hi.'

She responded with a look of contempt and revulsion, as if a terrible smell had entered her nostrils. But he was used to that from Rachel, and Molly's looks of disgust were nothing compared to Rachel's. He knew it would take time to gain her trust. He could wait.

During the lesson, the whole class was instructed to work in pairs. Molly, however, steadfastly refused to even acknowledge Tom's presence, burying her nose in her books instead. It was clear that she really did not like Michael at all.

'I'll write something down,' muttered Tom, glancing between the teacher and Molly. 'Anything you like, and then you'll see that I'm left-handed.'

'How about writing: get lost,' replied Molly, without looking at him.

Undeterred, Tom continued: 'I tell you what – watch this,' he said, and began writing as fast as he could two lines from Shakespeare's *Julius Caesar*, which he had had to learn the week before.

Molly, her curiosity piqued, could not help looking to see what he was doing, and, as he wrote, a flicker of amazement danced across her face, before vanishing behind her cold exterior.

'Of all the skills you could have taught yourself,' she began, 'you've learnt how to write Shakespeare backwards, with the wrong hand. That's really going to help you in the future.'

'Backwards?' said Tom, before realising what he had done and cursing under his breath. 'Ah, yes. Oops.' He paused. 'Look, I'm really not Michael. My name really is Tom. Think of a test, any test you like. What could I do to prove to you that I'm not Michael?'

'Look,' sighed Molly, finally turning to look at him. 'I really don't care who you're pretending to be. Why are you bothering with all this again? You know I don't like you.'

'Again?' murmured Tom. 'Michael likes you, doesn't he?' he said, as much to himself as to Molly.

'I don't like you,' she repeated, ignoring him. 'I've never liked you and I never will like you. And I certainly don't fancy you. You're wasting your time with your childish games. We are never going to be friends. So please – leave me alone.' And with that she returned to her books.

Tom recognised when he was beaten. Yet he nevertheless smiled to himself. He had, he hoped, sown the seeds, aroused her curiosity. The next time they met, he would continue to fuel any doubts she may have had. He may have lost the first skirmish, but he was not defeated yet.

When Tom re-entered the void, there was only one real concern on his mind: had Michael enjoyed being Tom? For if he had found the whole experience boring, any future exchange would be in jeopardy. And now that he had met Molly, the thought of only seeing her again infrequently, or worse still, never again, was too terrible to contemplate. He need not have worried.

'Wow!' said Michael, when the two boys drew close. 'That was so cool. Your world is awesome.' His face was wide-eyed like a child at Christmas. 'We have to do that again.'

For several minutes, the two boys exchanged funny stories about reading and writing backwards and getting lost in the mirror image of their respective towns. Much to Tom's relief, Michael was as keen as him to repeat the experience as soon as possible.

'How about the day after tomorrow?' suggested Michael with glee.

'Yeah, why not?'

'Excellent. What about eight in the morning?' Tom nodded. 'Good. But do you think we should tell anyone about this? I mean friends or anybody? Cos I was getting some funny looks from your friends at times.'

'Likewise,' smiled Tom. 'But no one would believe us if we told them the truth. But I did try telling someone that we were identical-looking cousins who swapped lives now and then for a laugh, just to try to explain my rather odd behaviour.'

'That's a good one. I'll have to remember that.'

'Anyway, I'd better give you this back,' said Tom, peeling off the blazer and handing it to Michael.

'Don't ever forget this – or your tie,' said Michael, as he put his blazer back on. 'You'll get me into real trouble if you do.'

'Just one more thing,' said Tom, as they were about to go their separate ways. 'What made you touch the mirror this morning? I mean, the chances of us both touching it at the same time are virtually nil.'

'I've always been touching that mirror since I was a kid. Weird really. Can't explain it.'

It was then that Tom realised it had not been the house itself that had been pulling him towards it all these years like a mermaid singing to a ship, but the mirror inside the house. Michael's mirror was in a different house altogether, and, moreover, Michael seemed totally indifferent towards *Morladron House*. Something, some strange force, it seemed, had been drawing both of them towards their respective mirrors all their lives.

Yet one nagging question remained: why them?

Chapter Five

The Blazer

As much as he was desperately keen to see Jake again and discuss what had happened the previous day, Tom's mind kept returning to Molly Trump, and what he could possibly do to convince her that he was not Michael. There were, however, still another twenty-four hours to go before he would see her again, and it felt like he was counting down every single second. He simply had to get her out of his head and focus on something else.

Jake was sitting nonchalantly on a low brick wall at the end of the road, waiting as usual for Tom to join him on their walk to school. As with all Tom's friends, Jake never liked coming to Tom's house in case his father answered the door. Something that Tom found perfectly understandable. Most of the children in the town, and a good many adults as well, were afraid of the man and his temper. Tom very soon realised he would have to make sure that Michael never met his father.

'Oh, we decided to turn up today, did we?' said Jake sarcastically. Sarcasm or not, it was still great to hear and see his friend again after his uncomfortable encounter with Sean the previous day.

'I … yes. Oh … yesterday. Did I not …?'

'No, you did not,' continued Jake with mock anger. 'And I hope you're feeling better today.'

'Yes, I, er … Anyway, listen … What do you mean?'

'Well, you weren't exactly yourself yesterday, were you?'

The irony was too much. 'You could say that,' he laughed.

But then he suddenly became worried. 'Oh, what do you mean? What did I do?'

'What do you mean, what did I do? You really aren't quite yourself at the moment, are you?'

He was starting to get concerned. All he had really thought about the previous day was himself. He had hardly stopped to consider what was happening back in his own world. 'Listen, Jake, I can explain everything–'

'I bet you can,' said Jake, as he stood up, and flung his bag over his shoulder.

So what was Tom going to say now? Up to that point he had automatically assumed he would just trot out the story of Michael, his identical cousin, who had come down to swap lives with him for the day. But suddenly, that idea sounded absurd in his head. Jake would never believe it. He knew Tom far too well, knew he did not have such a cousin, and would know that Tom would never do something like that without forewarning his best friend at least the day before. There seemed little choice but to try to tell the truth, however ridiculous that was going to sound.

As they began walking down the slope of the valley towards the river, Tom cleared his throat. 'Right, you're probably not going to believe this, but I swear every word is true. I broke into *Morladron House* again yesterday morning before school …'

'Oh, for goodness' sake, Tom!' said an exasperated Jake.

'No, it's okay. I didn't get caught this time.'

'That's not the point, mate. Haven't you learnt your lesson?'

'Listen to me, Jake. I found a mirror in the house, and when I touched it, I ended up in this … this strange place with another boy who looks just like me. It turns out he *is* me but in a different, sort of ... parallel world. So, we decided there and then to swap places for the day.' He cringed as he spoke the words, conscious that they sounded utterly ludicrous.

'Oh, right,' said Jake, and continued walking in silence for several seconds. He then grabbed Tom's arm to stop him and looked straight into his face, before saying: 'Sorry? Do you want to run that by me again?'

'No, really, Jake. It's true. His name is Michael.'

'What, your middle name? Oh, come on. Stop messing about,' he said, with a hint of irritation creeping into his voice. He then began walking downhill again, leaving Tom to catch up with him.

'Look – I know it's hard to believe. But that's what happened. I can prove it.'

'Right. I suppose that explains why you looked and acted so cool yesterday,' said Jake, ignoring the challenge.

'It does? I mean, was I? Hey, are you saying I'm not cool?'

'And I guess that explains why you've finally managed to get Rachel to notice you. You're definitely in there now, you know.'

Something in his tone told Tom his friend was not joking. And there was a growing hint of impatience there, too.

'I am? How did he ...? What happened?'

Jake sighed and stopped once more. 'I can't believe you're still trying to win that girl over, after all she's done to you. For goodness' sake, she shopped you to the police. And then you got beaten up by your dad, all thanks to her.'

'Ah, yes, but it wasn't really–'

'Tom, you need to get a grip.' Jake was suddenly deadly serious, something Tom was not used to seeing in his friend. 'I know it's not been easy with your dad, but you need to sort your life out, work out what your priorities are. If you care more about getting Rachel than being with your friends who actually like you, then I need to know that.'

'No, but, Jake, listen–'

'No, Tom, you listen.'

It was the first time Tom had ever seen the mild-mannered Jake be so forceful, and it was very disconcerting, particularly as he felt wholly to blame.

'I'll tell you what I saw yesterday, shall I?' continued Jake. 'You thought if you put a bit of fancy hair gel in your hair, spray a wee bit of nice deodorant on and start walking with a confident swagger you'd look cool, and Rachel would suddenly start falling for you. Well, congratulations, Tom. It worked; she is starting to like the new you. But that's not you, is it? If you're going to change like that, you're going to lose your mates. It's as simple as that.'

'Oh, good grief. Sorry,' said Tom nervously. 'What did he … what did I … what happened?'

'You were mean to Clare Goodman. And you know I like her, and now she won't even speak to me cos I'm your friend.'

'I'm really sorry, Jake. But I'm telling you–'

'Don't tell me about mirrors and parallel universes, Tom,' said Jake in an almost apologetic tone that suggested he felt guilty at raising his voice to his best friend. 'We're fourteen. We're not eight-year-old kids anymore, playing knights and dragons in the back garden. You need to sort yourself out. Forget about her, move on.'

Jake then abruptly turned away and walked off at a pace, a cloud hanging over his head. Tom could have easily gone after him and caught up with him but thought better of it. It seemed more prudent to leave his friend be for a while, to allow them both time to think things through.

Tom felt puzzled and increasingly guilty. What exactly had Michael done?

When he arrived at school, Tom found it was not only Jake who was treating him differently. Several pupils he knew well enough to say hello to, glared at him suspiciously when he greeted them. With increasing unease, he sought out the shy Clare Goodman, and without knowing exactly what had been done or said, he apologised unreservedly for his behaviour the previous day, and tried to put it down to the stress he was feeling after a run-in with his father, a point he stressed by pointing at his still bruised left eye. She and her friends seemed wary and only reluctantly, and not wholly convincingly, accepted his apology.

Of course, the simple answer to avoid all this unpleasantness was to stop swapping lives with Michael immediately. He could return to his friends and his inconspicuous life. Yet, always at the forefront of his mind was the thought of seeing Molly and her world again. It was no good: there was simply no way on earth he could even contemplate not returning again. And again.

The only solution was to somehow make his life work in both worlds. And to make that happen he would have to convince both Molly and Jake of what was happening.

First of all, he would try to convince Jake, his best friend, the boy he had known for years. That had to be easier than trying to convince a girl he barely knew. So when the two boys sat down together later that day in the computer suite at neighbouring terminals, Tom decided to try his luck again.

He was about to open his mouth when Rachel flitted past

and sat nearby. 'Hi, Tom,' she said coyly, and smiled.

Tom responded with a faint, nervous smile of his own. What should have filled him with delight, having waited for years for such an acknowledgement from her, actually left him feeling decidedly uneasy. Jake glanced between the two of them and sighed with mild disgust.

'Listen, Jake,' said Tom, averting his eyes from Rachel back to Jake. 'I'm really sorry for anything that happened yesterday. But I have to go back again tomorrow, so I can prove to you that what I said earlier is true.'

'Right,' said Jake, without even looking.

'Come with me to the house tomorrow morning and watch me disappear into the mirror.'

Clearly trying to contain his anger, he glanced at Tom. 'I'm not breaking into that house with you or anybody else.' He began tapping at his keyboard, as if trying to tell Tom to leave him alone.

'But I want to prove to you what happened,' persisted Tom.

'You know full well I won't, and I can't, go into that house. So, it's very convenient that the only way to prove your story is for me to break into the house, don't you think?'

Tom was silent. It was hard to find a flaw in Jake's argument.

'Tom, why don't you just stay on this planet,' continued Jake after a moment, 'and leave this schizophrenic friend of yours behind on his planet? Then we can all be happy.'

Rachel's pretty face was glancing across at Tom, getting in his eyeline, distracting him. She smiled at him again, a vacuous smile that he found no longer interested him in the slightest.

'I have to go back, Jake,' he said finally. 'There's a girl there called Molly Trump, just like Rachel, only ... nice. The exact opposite to Rachel in fact.'

'I bet there is,' mumbled Jake, once again focusing most of his attention on the computer screen in front of him.

'Look, I'll have a word with Michael when we swap. I'll ask him to be more like me when we do this.'

'Good idea,' replied Jake absently. 'You do that.'

'I'll ask him to–'

'Listen to yourself,' snapped Jake suddenly, such that Tom started. 'You're talking about yourself in the third person. You need to see a doctor or something.'

Tom realised he was getting nowhere. 'What about this?' he said, losing patience and pointing at his black eye. 'I suppose you think I made this up as well?'

'No, of course not.'

'Then tell me this: did I have a black eye yesterday? Eh? How do you explain that?'

For a moment, Jake remained silent and maintained his stern expression. Then when the realisation of what Tom had just said had sunk in, his hard exterior melted away for a few moments. 'How did you do that?' But then he frowned again. 'Bah, you must have covered up it with make-up.'

'I'll prove it to you, Jake,' said Tom, turning back to his own computer. 'I promise you, mate: I *will* prove it to you.'

At precisely eight o'clock the next morning, Tom touched the mirror once more and was transported back into the void. The awkwardness with Jake of the previous day was largely pushed to the back of his mind. He knew he would eventually prove to his friend what was happening, and besides, he was going to see Molly again.

'Hey, Tom, my man,' said a gleeful Michael. 'You ready for this?'

'Of course,' smiled Tom.

It was still unnerving staring at someone who looked identical to himself in every way, down to the black tie with its silver emblem and the white shirt of their school uniform. In many ways, it was hard not to believe that he was simply mad and was talking to his own reflection.

'Just one thing, though, Michael,' he continued. 'I'm not as outgoing as you are. If you're trying to be me just tone it down a bit. I don't want to alienate my friends, particularly Jake who's my best mate.'

'Fair enough,' replied Michael, far too swiftly to make Tom feel comfortable. 'I trust you didn't tell him how all this happened?' he grinned.

'I tried to, but he didn't believe me.'

Michael laughed out loud. 'Don't go around telling people the truth. They'll never believe you, and you're likely to get us both locked up in a loony bin.'

'You're probably right,' conceded Tom. 'But if we're going to carry on doing this, let's at least agree to try to not get one another into trouble ...'

'I didn't get you into trouble,' snorted Michael, with a dismissive wave of the hand.

'Not exactly but–'

'You worry too much.' He paused, then, obviously seeing Tom's disquiet, added: 'Okay, I'll be a good boy, I promise. It's just ... there's more freedom in your world, and it's hard not to get carried away with what I can do. Anyway, you ready?'

Tom nodded with an encouraging smile. He at least felt better for having aired his concerns.

'I've left my blazer and school bag in the bedroom,' said Michael. 'Just, whatever you do, do not forget them.'

After Tom had given Michael his school bag, the two boys crossed over and prepared to swap lives once more. Following a brief countdown and a mutual cry of 'Good luck', they vanished from the void.

The moment Tom was back in the cluttered spare room in Michael's house, his eyes were drawn towards the window and *Morladron House* in the distance across the valley. It struck him just how similar it was to the house in his own world, dominating the skyline, yet all boarded up and lifeless. So much in their two worlds seemed to be virtually identical: people, places, buildings. On the face of it, the differences were slight and subtle. So if *Morladron House* was derelict in both worlds perhaps it shared a similar history. And if his own father was unwilling or unable to provide him with the answers he had sought ever since he could remember, then maybe this world would at least give him some clues as to the fate of his mother. The idea began to fill him with excitement. Why had he not considered that before?

He quickly grabbed Michael's school bag, and then almost tripped down the stairs in his haste to begin posing his questions. When he reached the bottom and entered the kitchen, Michael's father and stepmother were standing close to one another whispering in a disconcerting and animated manner. The moment they caught a glimpse of Tom, they stopped, turned towards him and smiled full of what struck him as guilt. For a second or two, Tom had the strange feeling that they had been talking about him, or at least talking about Michael. But no, surely that was just paranoia.

He greeted them both with a cheeriness that was probably totally unexpected and sat down at the breakfast table opposite the happy little baby, who was merrily spreading food across its face. He leant forward and pulled a funny face, causing the baby to squeal with delight. He would have to be relaxed and chatty if they were going to answer his questions, even if it ran counter to Michael's normal relationship to his parents. He hoped they would just dismiss his behaviour as the usual teenage hormones, as most adults were wont to do.

'You're very cheerful this morning, Michael,' said the stepmother, as both parents sat down at the table.

'He's probably got himself a girlfriend, haven't you, son?' said Michael's father, with a knowing grin.

'Not quite,' smiled Tom. 'It's nearly the summer holidays, that's all.'

They all chuckled, and a warmth spread through Tom, the like of which he had never experienced at home before.

Clearly not used to engaging Michael in conversation, the two adults resumed their breakfasts in silence. Or maybe, thought Tom, they were still contemplating their earlier whispered conversation. Either way, Tom had his chance.

'Dad?' he began and swallowed nervously. 'Someone at school the other day said that that house across the valley used to belong to our family. Is that true?' He thought it best not to dive straight in with a question about Michael's mother.

'You know it did,' replied Michael's father, clearly surprised at the question.

For a moment, Tom was reminded of his own short-tempered father and cursed himself for asking such a direct question.

But, as if feeling guilty at his abruptness, Michael's father put his coffee down, smiled and said: 'Yes, it was in your mother's family for generations, as far back as any records we can find.'

'So why isn't it anymore?' asked Tom with renewed enthusiasm.

Both adults exchanged a curious look, which Tom could not quite decipher. They were clearly surprised at Michael's questioning, either because he had already been told all this before, or because he had never before shown any interest in the subject. Either way, his father seemed happy enough to talk. Maybe he was just glad that his son was talking to him at all.

'Well, your grandfather couldn't keep up with the maintenance on the house. It suffered quite a lot of damage during the Great Storm, and then the poor chap went slightly doolally when you were a baby, and he had to be put away in a home. It turned out that so much needed doing to the house that in the end we decided to just sell it. But the thing is, no one wanted to buy it. All the locals said it was cursed and haunted and all sorts of rubbish like that, so even the local estate agents weren't that interested. Daft, really. But in the end, we sold it for a pittance to a developer, who then went bust, and it's been gathering dust ever since. No idea why; it's a great spot for a house. In fact, we've even considered buying it back recently. I'm sure your grandpa would like that ...'

'Grandpa's still alive?' said Tom, shocked. 'Er ... I mean ... yes, he would, wouldn't he?'

Michael's father rubbed his chin and gave Tom a puzzled look.

'Yes, you've never visited your grandfather, have you?' said Michael's stepmother. 'I think you should. He'd like that.'

'Yeah, you're right. I should,' said Tom absently, before realising he was committing Michael to something he would probably not appreciate.

However, it was hard to think about Michael when he had so many other questions to ask.

'What was the Great Storm?' he asked.

'Don't they teach you anything in school these days?' laughed Michael's father. 'That was a few years ago now. This town was hit by a freak and terrible storm that caused a huge amount of damage. Several houses were wiped out and a few people lost their lives. Scientists couldn't explain it, but said it has happened a few times throughout this town's history. Something to do with the valley and the sea and thermals, I think they said. Basically, they don't really know why. But God forbid it should ever happen again.'

Tom was totally bemused. He had never heard of any such storm in his own Porthgarrick, and as strange, not to mention interesting, as the story was, it seemed to offer none of the answers he sought. What he really wanted was to talk about Michael's mother. But how on earth was he going to phrase the question? Even if Michael's father appeared to be nothing like his own, it still did not mean Tom knew what he was like. So, no, he could not bring himself to simply ask the man a question about his wife who was probably dead. He needed more time to plan what to say. Perhaps he should ask Michael. Yes, that was it. He would ask Michael.

He desperately wanted to ask about the mirror, too, since theirs was tucked away in a room upstairs and not in *Morladron House*, which seemed odd. But then he thought it would be best to keep quiet on that score for the time being, since drawing attention to it at that stage was probably not a good idea.

'Anyway, you'd better get going, Michael,' said Michael's stepmother. 'You'll be late for school.'

As Tom approached the school, his mind was racing at a hundred miles an hour. He was worried about his relationship with Jake and how he was going to convince him of what had been happening, and thereby patch up their friendship. He was also still trying to process the information Michael's father had just given him, and how it could possibly relate to what had happened in his own world. And increasingly, he was alternately anxious and excited about seeing Molly again, and all that that would entail.

With his head buzzing with thoughts like bees in a hive, he entered the school grounds, and only slowly began to notice that more and more pupils were turning and staring at him, some with little giggles and whispers, others wide-eyed with astonishment. Eventually, the looks became too numerous to ignore. With growing self-consciousness at the attention he was attracting, he frantically tried to think what he was doing that could possibly be out of place in this world.

It was then that he realised he was not wearing Michael's blazer. In his excitement to speak to Michael's father, he had forgotten to pick it up. And now it was too late to go home and fetch it. Still, he thought, surely it would not be a problem, even if he did appear to be the only pupil not wearing one.

'Paget!' cried a harsh but familiar voice. 'Michael Paget! Come here.'

He turned sharply to his left, and there, striding purposefully towards him, was Mrs Meadow, at least this world's version of Mrs Meadow. For, whilst the short, plump figure very much belonged to his favourite teacher, her clothing was a mix of prudish greys and dour blacks, and her jet-black hair was swept back into a bun, giving her face a harsh and unfamiliar quality. She eyed him through her glasses with menacing intent. She may have looked like Mrs Meadow, but he instantly knew she was going to be nothing like the woman he knew.

'Where is your blazer, boy?' she demanded, as a small crowd of black blazers assembled around the two of them, keeping a nervous distance.

'I … er … I'm sorry, I … forgot to bring it. I left it at home. I could go and get it if you want.'

An audible gasp went around the gathering throng. Tom was still perplexed, but growing more concerned by the second, not least because of the teacher's intimidating and angry glower.

'Are you trying to be funny, Paget?'

'No. Not at all. I … um … I really have forgotten to bring it.'

'Are you totally stupid?' An unsettling look of annoyance and surprise spread across the teacher's face. 'Are you looking to be punished?'

'Er … no. I … sorry … I …It won't happen again.'

'You're right, it won't happen again,' said the teacher, and grabbed Tom's upper arm. 'Come with me.'

'Mrs Meadow … I–'

Another gasp went up around him.

'What did you call me?' she demanded in a shrill voice, and stared at him in an even more terrifying manner.

'I … er … Mrs Meadow?' he said quietly, uncertainly. Maybe she had a different first name, but surely her surname had to be the same.

'Are you trying to provoke me, Paget? You've always been trouble, but such insolence …'

She dragged him along by the arm, as the crowd of pupils, keen to keep its distance, parted before them. Too bewildered and unnerved to speak, Tom was marched through the main doors and into a small office, where they were greeted by a short but stout, middle-aged man that Tom knew from neither his own world nor the one he was in. He wore a smart grey suit and a chirpy but unnerving smile.

'Morning, Headmaster,' said the Mrs Meadow look-alike.

'Morning, Miss Doomsday,' he beamed. 'So what have we here, then?'

'Miss Doomsday?' mumbled Tom, with a barely suppressed snigger.

'Is there something wrong, Paget?' glared Miss Doomsday.

Realising he was making matters worse, Tom quickly launched into an apology. 'No, not at all. I just wanted to say that I'm really sorry. I didn't forget my blazer on purpose. I must have just been daydreaming when I got dressed this morning. I can assure you it won't happen again.'

A growing feeling of unease was rising inside him. What would he do if he were given detention after school? He had to get back home by four o'clock that afternoon at all costs, otherwise, he might end up being trapped in Michael's world for ever. His only hope was that a small piece of Mrs Meadow's decency existed inside Miss Doomsday.

'Well, I'm pleased you are repentant, Paget,' began Miss Doomsday. 'But I'm afraid the deed is done. And you know full well, what happens if someone forgets to wear their blazer.'

Miss Doomsday strutted over to a desk and removed a

long, thin piece of wood from a drawer. Tom swallowed hard when he saw it. He had never seen one in real life, but he knew exactly what a cane looked like. Miss Doomsday strode back towards him, brandishing the cane like a sword.

'You've got to be joking,' said a shocked Tom, taking a step backwards towards the closed door behind him. 'What is this? What's going on?'

'Now come on, Paget,' said Miss Doomsday, looking at him across the top of her glasses. 'Don't pretend to be so surprised. After all, it's not the first time, now is it?'

'No, no, no!' pleaded Tom. 'I forgot my blazer, that's all.' He scanned her eyes, shot a look across to the headmaster, and back again, desperately looking for signs that this was just a prank, a wind-up intended simply to frighten him into learning his lesson. But no such signs were present. Miss Doomsday's face was set with determination and a hint of suppressed anger. The headmaster's was serene, almost indifferent.

'Oh, you think you're somehow different,' said Miss Doomsday. 'You think the normal rules don't apply to you, is that it? Well, I've got news for you, young man, you are not special. You are not different. If you wilfully break the rules you must expect to be punished. Now, hold out your hand.'

'N-no. I'm not. This isn't right. You can't do this.'

'Unless I'm very much mistaken, Paget, you're right-handed, aren't you?' persisted Miss Doomsday. 'So kindly hold out your right hand now, and perhaps we can also help to correct that filthy abnormality.'

'No way!' Even if they were about to beat his weaker hand, Tom had no intention of being punished in this way, even if it meant getting into even more trouble. He would stand his ground. This had to be wrong. Surely caning children belonged in the barbaric past.

A vice-like hand suddenly grabbed his right wrist and forced his hand upwards. At the same time, another hand seized his left arm from behind, locking him to the spot.

'Now, come on, Paget,' began the headmaster whose strength surprised and frightened Tom. 'When Miss Doomsday asks you to do something, I really think you should be doing it, don't you?' His voice was almost diffident.

Tom tried to wriggle free, but the headmaster held him firmly in place.

'Come on, Michael,' continued the headmaster in a matter-of-fact tone. 'Face it like a man. It'll soon be over. Then we can all go back to work. Nurse, come in here please,' he then called out, and a few seconds later a woman appeared through a side door and entered the office.

Tom tried to protect his hand by curling his fingers tightly into a fist. But then the nurse, clearly used to such behaviour, prised his fingers open and held his palm flat in front of Miss Doomsday. Tom was powerless, his hand exposed.

Miss Doomsday's face was inscrutable when she raised the cane and delivered the first blow to his palm. It stung like mad. The second and third ones even more. The cane was rough and uneven, with slight ridges running the length of it, such that it dug into his skin and drew blood after only four blows. Pride and no small amount of anger kept Tom from making a noise, even if he had to bite his lip to do so. After ten strikes, Miss Doomsday stopped, wiped the bloodstained cane on an anti-sceptic cloth handed to her by the nurse, and returned the cane to her desk, leaving Tom's right hand a bloody mess.

'There, you see,' said the headmaster, as he released his grip. 'That wasn't so bad.'

Tom watched in silence, numb with shock, as the nurse wiped his hand, and then wrapped a small piece of bandage around the wound. He did not know whether to cry, shout out his anger, or even to laugh at the absurdity of having just been caned for nothing more than forgetting his blazer. Tears welled in his eyes, but the moment quickly passed, and rage grew inside him instead.

'I'll report this,' he said evenly. 'You can't do this. It's not legal.'

'My dear boy,' replied the headmaster calmly. 'Of course it's legal. We wouldn't do it if it wasn't legal, now would we? Every child knows if they forget their uniform this is what happens.' He smiled cheerfully, as though he were simply discussing a piece of homework that had not been quite as good as it should have been. 'And let's be honest, it works, doesn't it? After all, you're not going to forget your blazer again, are you?'

'It's about time,' began Miss Doomsday solemnly, 'that troublemaker of a father of yours started teaching you right from wrong and stopped filling your head with his seditious ideas. He's not doing you any favours, you know.'

Tom had no idea what she was talking about. Not that it mattered; he was angry beyond words, and his hand was throbbing like mad.

She then approached him once more, this time with a black blazer in one hand, hung out in front of her on a hanger. 'Here. Wear this for today,' she said. 'And make sure you bring it back at the end of the day. I think by now you know what will happen if you forget to do so.'

Chapter Six

The Scarred Hand

Tom was beginning to feel lonely. He was a complete stranger in Michael's world, alone with no friends to turn to when things were not going well, as they had not been since he had forgotten to wear his alter ego's blazer. It had been hard seeing familiar, friendly faces with unfamiliar and unfriendly personalities, knowing they would never feel inclined to comfort him.

He had spent that morning lost in his own thoughts. One minute he had sat silently in the classroom feeling sorry for himself, the next he had been seething with anger, angry with Miss Doomsday and the headmaster, and angry at this insane world in which he found himself. It made no sense at all. This world was so much like his own, yet at the same time nothing like his world. At times, the differences were staggering. Not even seeing Molly, it seemed, could wrench him from his despondent thoughts. There had been moments when he had simply wanted to go home and never come back.

At last, he had made it through to lunchtime. He was still lost in thought when he joined the queue in the school canteen. Just as he had reached the front of the queue with his tray and had finished paying for his meal, he caught sight of Sean moving away from another till nearby.

'Hi, Sean,' said Tom in a subdued voice. Sean was not his friend, but it was at least someone to talk to. 'How's it going, mate?' he added, almost without thinking.

Sean glared at him, moved closer and without warning

tipped Tom's tray over, sending his dinner to the floor with a clatter of cutlery, crockery and wooden tray. The plate of pasta with its tomato sauce, and the chocolate pudding came to a rest upside down on the floor.

'What are you doing?' demanded Tom indignantly, his fuse still short after his earlier caning.

'Oops,' replied Sean with an ugly smile.

Tom thought better of entering into an argument and simply dropped to his haunches to salvage what he could of his dinner. As he did so, Sean crouched down beside him, no doubt to give those around them the impression he was going to help.

'Just so you know, Paget,' he hissed through clenched teeth. 'I know who you are. And you are not my *mate*.' He stressed the last word with such venom that Tom swallowed his intended response.

'What's going on here?' asked a teacher who had hurried over.

Both boys stood up slowly, still sharing an icy stare.

'Nothing,' said Tom. 'It was just an accident.'

Sean glowered once more and then turned and wandered off with his friends, leaving Tom to clear up the mess. As he bent down with a cloth, Molly moved away from the till and looked down at him.

'What's the matter, Paget?' she said, in a patronising tone. 'Even your friends turning their backs on you now, are they?'

He looked up at her and replied bitterly: 'Sean is not my friend.' He then winced when he forgot the discomfort in his right hand for a moment and tried to pick up the tray.

'Oh, dear,' continued Molly, having spotted his bandaged hand. 'Been caned yet again, have we? When will you learn?'

Tom looked sorrowfully at his injured hand 'What kind of a sick world … place … is this?' he said.

Molly rolled her eyes. 'Oh, dear. Not still trying to pretend you come from somewhere else, are you?' she asked, and promptly turned and walked away.

With nothing left but an apple and a can of drink on his tray, Tom followed her into the dining hall. Once he was alongside her, he slammed his tray onto an empty table, pulled away the bandage and thrust his injured hand in front of Molly, who was wandering about looking for her friends. She stopped dead in her tracks.

'See that?' he said in a loud whisper before she could speak.

She grimaced when she saw the dried blood and torn skin, glanced at him and then moved on. But Tom was in no mood to let her walk away. He caught up with her again and thrust his hand in front of her once more.

'Go on, Molly,' he insisted. 'Take a good look. Make sure you're satisfied it's not make-up or tomato sauce or something else.'

She seemed to study his hand for a second or two, before brushing his arm aside with her shoulder. 'Get out of my way,' she replied. 'Find someone else to pester.'

'Have a look on Monday, Molly,' said Tom calling after her. 'If you want proof, take a good look at my right hand.'

'Why are you looking so glum?' asked Michael, when the two boys met up in the void. 'Don't look so worried. I was a good boy this time. I didn't upset anyone. I trust you didn't get me into any trouble.'

'No, not really,' replied Tom softly, looking away and covering his bandaged hand with his left hand. He saw no need to tell Michael about his caning. After all, he had been the one who had taken the punishment, and hopefully, that was the end of the matter as far as the school was concerned. 'I see you managed to persuade Sean that I'm not you,' he continued, hurriedly changing the subject. 'How did you manage that?'

'I just told him we were cousins, like you said.'

'And he believed you straightaway?'

'Of course,' replied Michael. 'I also tried telling your mate Jake that we are cousins, but he just looked at me funny. I'm not sure he's all there, you know.'

Tom had to smile wryly to himself. How come Sean had been so easy to convince when Jake was so sceptical? Still, it would be great to see Jake again.

'And I told that Rachel Trump girl, too,' continued Michael. 'I think she believes me now as well. She's a cracking girl, isn't she? Nothing like her equivalent in my world. Have you met Molly yet? She's a stuck-up little cow.'

As Michael continued with his rant about Molly, and returned to his rave about Rachel, Tom tuned out of the words and found himself studying Michael: his appearance, his body language, his expressions. And he realised that his double was exactly as Jake had described him: hair sculpted meticulously with hair gel, a powerful waft of deodorant emanating from him and a confident, perhaps even arrogant, demeanour. In short – nothing like himself. How had he not seen the stark differences between them before? Had he been so blinded by the excitement of what they had been doing? And just how similar were their lives? He had to find out.

'Listen, Michael,' he said. 'Do you mind if I ask you a question about your real mother?'

'My mum? What do you want to know?'

'Did she die when you were a kid?'

'No, of course not. She's still alive. Why do you ask?'

Tom was briefly taken aback. He had not expected that, had expected Michael to say that his mum had died too. 'My mum died when I was a baby, but I don't know how or why. I was hoping if our lives were so similar, we might have similar histories. So if she's still alive, where is she now?'

'She lives in France. I don't see her much these days. When she and my dad split up years ago, he got custody of me. See, she's a little bit unstable. Bit of a nutter really, but she's still my mum.' His mouth twitched with an attempt to conceal the sadness that Tom instantly saw in his face.

It was difficult for Tom to conceal his own disappointment. He had so hoped Michael could help him uncover the truth about his mother's fate, but it now seemed he could not. Yet Tom still felt so agonisingly close. Michael's world held the clues he sought, he just knew it. After all, their two worlds were so very similar, full of the same people and places. And if, in one of the worlds, only some of those same people had lived and died in a dissimilar way, then after only a few generations that world would have been populated with thousands of completely different people, living in a completely different world. But they were not.

'Anyway,' continued Michael, 'I've got football this weekend and your world hasn't. How about we swap again on Monday?'

Tom paused for a moment. He had told Molly to look at his hand on Monday, so if he turned up with his bandaged hand, she would probably never speak to him again. Besides, an extra day would give him more time to gather his thoughts and perhaps mend his friendship with Jake.

'I can't,' he said finally. 'Better make it Tuesday.'

'You're not going soft on me, are you?' glowered Michael, as if reading his mind.

The aggressive tone, the angry look, were once again traits Tom could not see reflected in himself at all. 'Sorry, Michael,' he said firmly, 'but I've got something on on Monday. We'll have to make it Tuesday.'

'Fair enough,' sighed Michael. And the anger was gone as quickly as it had come. 'Tuesday it is.'

It was Monday morning and Molly Trump was confused. Michael Paget was not exactly the nicest or the brightest pupil in the school. Yet a few days ago he had come up to her out of the blue with an imaginative and elaborate but totally ludicrous story about his being somebody else, all it seemed, with the sole intention of getting her to like him. Of course, he had tried to get friendly with her a couple of years ago, spending weeks going out of his way to be nice to her, until she had finally left him in no doubt, or so she had thought at the time, that she had no intention of ever going out with an ignorant bully. As a result, his resentment towards her had grown and grown. He had continually poked fun at her, called her hurtful names, pushed her around and generally made her life a misery. Eventually, he had seemed to grow bored of picking on her, and for over a year now he had hardly even acknowledged her existence. Then all of sudden, there he was again, trying to get to know her, trying to be her friend. What on earth was he up to? And did he really think he had a chance with her, after everything that had happened between them in the past?

Whilst she sat at the edge of the classroom, with the teacher droning on and on at the front of the room, her note taking rapidly turned into nothing more than doodling. She became momentarily cross with herself when she noticed the scribbles on her pad. She had always been so good at concentrating in class, but now annoying little thoughts kept creeping into her head. Thoughts involving that wretched Paget boy.

A short burst of whispered giggles made her cautiously look behind her. As usual, Michael Paget and his mates were messing about at the back of the classroom, faces red with suppressed laughter. When the teacher chastised them yet again with a curt instruction, they hurriedly pretended to be writing in their books. Almost despite herself, Molly could not help but look at Michael's right hand. He was scribbling away with the fluency of a natural right-hander, with his hand curled awkwardly over the page so he could see what he was writing. And the hand had no trace of a bandage on it. She was not close enough to see if there was a scar or not, but there did not appear to be any discomfort in his writing at all. And as he scribbled, he made no attempt to even glance across at her to check if she was watching him. And to add to it all, there was not the slightest bruising around his left eye.

What was she thinking? It had to be part of this ridiculous charade he was trying to play with her.

At last, the bell rang for the end of the class. The stampede out of the door began almost immediately. Molly decided to follow Michael and caught up with him in the corridor outside.

'Paget,' she said. 'Show me your right hand.'

He turned round with a big grin on his face, which vanished in an instant when he saw who it was. 'What did you say?' he asked in an ugly voice.

'I said, show me your right hand.'

He raised his right hand slowly and then presented her with a rude gesture. 'There, how about that?' He turned his head back to his mates and they all burst into laughter.

But then Molly reached out, grabbed his right hand and turned over the palm before he had time to react. It was smooth and relatively clean. She detected a faint scarring, no doubt from a previous caning or two, but it had long since healed and was barely visible.

'What are you doing, you stupid cow?' he snapped, and tore his hand back from her grip.

'She just wants to hold your hand,' laughed one of his friends.

But by this time, Molly had turned around and was marching off in the opposite direction. The torrent of childish and suggestive comments followed her down the corridor, but faded fast as she turned a corner.

What was going on? Had someone as stupid as Michael Paget really developed the ability to use some sort of horror make-up on his hand and his eye? Yet even if he had, which seemed most unlikely, she knew he had been caned for not wearing his blazer. News of his visit to Miss Doomsday's office had spread around the school almost before the caning had finished. And since everyone knew about Miss Doomsday's cane, there was no way on earth his wound could have healed over the weekend.

And just to add to the confusion, when he was pretending to be a boy called Tom, he really was completely different. He even sounded different.

What on earth was going on?

Tuesday arrived and Tom's right hand was still bound up and uncomfortable. He took a deep breath and at exactly eight o'clock in the morning he touched the mirror in *Morladron House*. At once, he was transported back into the void, a place just as mysterious and alluring in equal measure as when he had first appeared there. A group of multi-coloured wisps of cloud drifted in front of him like a friendly ghost. When his view cleared, Tom saw Michael striding towards him across the colourful pathway between them, his face taut and fierce.

'You got me into trouble,' he snarled.

'What do you mean?' asked Tom, not daring to admit he could guess where this was going.

'Don't play the innocent with me,' said Michael, stabbing a finger aggressively at Tom at point-blank range. 'You forgot the blazer, and now I've got yet another black mark on my record.'

'Yeah, and look what I got for my troubles,' replied Tom defiantly and held up his bandaged hand. 'I was the one who got punished, not you.'

'That's not the point. We had an agreement, not to get one another into trouble.'

'Look, I'm sorry I forgot the blazer, but how was I supposed to know you live in some sick world where children are caned for something trivial like that?'

'You fool!' hissed Michael. His face was red and seething. 'How could you forget the blazer?'

'It was hot and …' Tom found he could not be bothered to argue. 'I'm sorry. What's done is done. Perhaps we should stop …' He paused once more. He could not bring himself to say what he was thinking. The idea of calling a halt to their adventure was too terrible to bear. He had to find out more about his mother. And he had to see Molly again.

The silence seemed to calm Michael. He averted his gaze and turned away to look back at the shimmering mirror a dozen paces behind him, as if the two boys were sharing the same thoughts, sharing the same dread of never returning to one another's worlds. If he, Tom, felt so strongly about Molly, it stood to reason that Michael was equally infatuated with Rachel.

Michael turned around to face Tom once more and frowned. 'You owe me for this,' he said quietly.

'Yeah, I probably do,' conceded Tom.

'My parents will be out late tonight, and it just so happens that Rachel has invited me to a party this evening as well. And I really want to be there. So I'll be back at ten this evening, okay?' Although it was a question his sour face defied Tom to say no.

'Okay,' replied Tom. 'Ten o'clock it is.'

The school library was a quiet place at lunchtime on a hot summer's day. Michael's school had that much at least in common with Tom's. A teacher was on duty at a desk near the entrance, engrossed in a book. Only a handful of students were sitting at the numerous desks, browsing the bookshelves, or meandering down the aisles. At one point, Miss Doomsday wandered in to return a book, and when she caught sight of Tom busy in front of a computer, she froze for a moment in surprise, as though she had never before seen Michael in the library, before marching out again. Tom simply smiled to himself and resumed his search.

The internet, or at least the school's access to it, was

intensely frustrating in Michael's world. Almost everything he typed into the search engine came back with *Access Denied*. It did not help that he was not quite sure what he was looking for. And then on top of that, everything he read was back to front, so initially it took him twice as long to decipher what he found. But at least the more he read, the easier it became to read backwards.

He had been trying, rather randomly, to access various newspaper websites, in the hope of unearthing an old story or two about Porthgarrick or *Morladron House*, something that might give him a lead. But it soon became apparent that access to most newspapers was severely limited.

Just when he was beginning to run out of ideas, he remembered Michael's father talking about something called the Great Storm. He had even found a plaque on a small monument in the town centre, erected, so it said, in remembrance of those killed in the storm. To his knowledge, no such event had ever occurred in his own Porthgarrick, which in itself struck him as odd. So he decided to search for it.

After a few minutes, he finally came across a report from fourteen years previously:

The Cornish town of Porthgarrick is still reeling from the freak storm that struck just after midday yesterday, and which left nine people dead. Many buildings in the picturesque fishing port were destroyed, including an entire row of terraced houses, when a deadly combination of torrential rain, lightning strikes and even a series of tornadoes hit the town.

Rescue workers described the scene as horrendous. Arthur George, spokesman for the military rescue operation, said it was a miracle that there had not been more deaths considering the extent of the devastation. He did, however, concede that they had not ruled out finding more bodies, since the situation in the town was still "very confused". One eyewitness described the town as looking like it had been bombed. The town has now been sealed off by the military, while the relief operation is carried out.

Satellite pictures taken at the time confirm eyewitness accounts, which state that the storm appeared out of nowhere and without warning in the middle of what had been a sunny day. A spokesman for the Met Office indicated that the storm was very localised and centred over the small town. He went on to say that they could offer no explanation at this time for the strange phenomenon, but that it was not the first time such a freak storm had occurred in Porthgarrick. Several, albeit much milder, storms had centred over the town in the past, such as the one in 1989 when seven houses were struck by lightning within the space of five minutes. One controversial explanation claims these occurrences of freak weather could have been caused by the wind being channelled down the steep-sided valley in which Porthgarrick lies ...

Tom sat back in his chair and scratched his head. If that theory were true, he thought, why had his Porthgarrick never been hit by such violent storms?

Fascinated by the story, he went on to read eyewitness accounts of cars flying through the air and tornadoes ripping apart houses. The fact that all this had happened in Porthgarrick, right in the town where the mirror was located, seemed to him to be just too much of a coincidence.

Tom became aware of someone pulling up a chair to his right and sitting down next to him. He looked across, and to his astonishment, Molly was sitting there, her eyes scrutinising his hand rather than his face.

'Hi,' he said, unable to hide the surprise and pleasure in his voice.

'Come on, then,' she said cautiously. 'I'll humour you for the moment. Show me your hand. I know you're dying to show it to me.'

Gleefully, Tom unwound the bandage and held out his right hand. 'See!'

She recoiled slightly at the sight of the criss-cross of pink marks on his hand, some of which were still weeping in places. She then glanced up at his beaming face and back down at the hand. Though she was desperately trying to hide it, Tom could see the amazement in her face.

'So, did you check my right hand yesterday then?' continued Tom.

Molly merely gave a slight, begrudging nod.

Now that he had her attention he was not about to let go. 'And the black eye?' he said pointing to it. 'Although it's beginning to fade a little now. It obviously wasn't as bad as it looked.' He was starting to ramble nervously, so forced himself to shut up.

Molly frowned. 'I'll admit one thing, Paget. I've no idea how you're doing this, but it's very clever.'

'You still don't believe me, do you?' he chuckled.

'Are you really surprised? I hate Michael with every bone in my body. So forgive me if I'm very wary.' Her face was completely without humour. 'Even if what you say is true, you're still friendly with Michael. And I have no interest whatsoever in getting to know any of his friends or relatives either.'

Tom wound the bandage back round his hand. 'I assure you,' he said quietly, 'the more I get to know him, the less I like him, too.'

An uneasy silence fell between them.

'What do you know about the Great Storm?' asked Tom finally, turning back to his computer screen.

'We're not suddenly friends now,' said Molly, bristling with anger. She rose to her feet, fire in her eyes. 'Why are you trying to be my friend?' But before Tom could answer she went on. 'Michael was obsessed with me for a long time until I told him he had no chance. Then suddenly, you come along trying to be my friend. Sorry, but that's just too much of a coincidence. I'll admit this is a very clever trick, Paget. But don't think for one minute we'll ever be friends.'

She pushed her chair away and marched off with a face of thunder, leaving Tom to wonder whether he would ever manage to convince her that he was not Michael.

Although it was well past nine o'clock in the evening, the longest day of the year was only a few days away, and so the sun was still in the sky, sinking in the east at a snail's pace. Most of Porthgarrick was now in shadow as the sun had dipped behind the high valley walls, but the small sandy beach at the head of the valley was still bathed in a warm, golden light. Gentle lapping waves seemed to be toying with a dog at the water's edge, whilst its owners strolled hand in hand across the sand. A small and faint pall of smoke hung in the still air from a knot of people grouped around a barbecue. It was an idyllic spot at that time of year, and Molly often went for a short evening stroll after her dinner and homework, to soak in the atmosphere and clear her head.

This time, however, one figure in particular had immediately caught her eye. He was a boy of her own age, conspicuous for still being in the white shirt and dark trousers of his school uniform, and who was standing at the water's edge, occasionally skimming pebbles across the water. It was the boy who looked like Michael Paget, but who behaved, spoke and moved like someone else. She could not help but watch him for several minutes and wonder. Michael Paget was an extrovert who always craved attention and was never seen without his small group of unpleasant friends, and most certainly was never seen on the beach on his own, nor in the library for that matter. Everything about this strange figure casting stones into the sea told her it was not Michael Paget, even if the physical likeness was striking.

As she watched, mesmerised, confused, the boy turned slowly away from the sea and ambled up the beach. Hurriedly, she moved back towards the line of shops and hotels overlooking the sea, and half hid herself behind a row of parked cars. She watched as he climbed back onto the seafront and settled himself down on a bench overlooking the beach, with his back to her.

After only a few short moments, a small group of three or four boys appeared on the seafront and surrounded the bench upon which the boy was sitting. She instantly recognised the large frame and blond hair of Sean McBean, and although she was not close enough to hear what was being said, she could quickly tell that an argument had erupted. The Paget boy sprang to his feet just as Sean moved closer to him. Voices were raised, insults exchanged, from what she could make out. Paget was shoved in the chest and took a large step backwards, before regaining his balance and lunging forwards. Two of the other boys stepped in at the last minute and separated the two snarling, red-faced boys. The friends looked as confused as Molly was. It made no sense to her at all. Only the other day she had seen Sean and Michael as inseparable as ever, as thick as thieves, causing their usual amount of trouble. Had they really fallen out so quickly? And had Michael been ostracised from their entire group of friends? Ordinarily, Molly would not have cared one jot what happened to any of that particular group, but this time something very odd was going on, something she felt unable to ignore.

Sean was eventually led away by the other boys, but not before further insults and threatening gestures were cast back and forth. Paget then looked at his watch and at once reacted with some concern, for he began to march with great purpose, very nearly running in fact, away from the beach and back into the town. Molly ducked behind a car as he strode close by. She waited a couple of seconds and then moved off in pursuit. The boy headed down the high street, glancing at his watch every minute or two as he went. Luckily for Molly, there were plenty of other people to hide behind: window-shoppers, people moving to and from the many restaurants and pubs along the street. And, away from the beach, lights were coming on as the town slowly descended into twilight.

She followed him through the town, until he turned abruptly up a side street to his left and began ascending the steep side of the valley between tightly-packed houses. By now her heart was pounding with excitement, feeling like she was about to catch a villain red-handed. After waiting a few seconds to increase the gap between her and her quarry, she headed off in pursuit.

93

By now, the darkness was creeping throughout the town, providing Molly with plenty of shadows to lurk in. But the boy was in too much of a hurry, was too concerned with the time according to his watch, to ever turn around. The higher they both climbed, the more Molly's heart began to pound. She was not as fit as he appeared to be, but there was no way on earth she was about to lose sight of him, even if she was beginning to feel a slight queasiness.

Eventually, he turned to the right and disappeared around the corner into a side street. She ran the last few steps up the steep path, not wanting to lose him now. When she peered along the side street, he was crossing the road and almost saw her when he looked both ways. Her breathing was hard, painful, but the adrenaline kept her going.

He went up to a large house and disappeared through the front door. Molly's heart sank. He had simply gone home, probably had to be home by a certain time, and now her tailing him had been in vain. She slowed to a stroll as she crossed the road to take a brief look at his home.

And then she noticed that in his haste to get into the house, he had left the front door ajar. There were no lights on in the house and no curtains were drawn. Suddenly, inexplicably, she had the overwhelming urge to follow him into the house. Ignoring the potential dangers and consequences, she pushed open the door and looked down the dark hallway. There was no one in sight. Her heart was racing out of control, but she did not want to turn back now.

A dull thud came from upstairs as she moved into the hallway.

'Hello?' she called out instinctively, warily.

There was no response. So, she moved further into the

house and up the stairs, knowing it was wrong but embracing the excitement. A pool of light burst out of a doorway onto the landing, scaring the wits out of her, freezing her to a spot near the top of the stairs. But the only movement was inside the room. When she reached the landing, she stood tight against the doorframe from where the light was emanating, and then, almost millimetre by millimetre, she peered round and into the room.

Paget was standing with his back to her, staring into a full-length mirror, or so it seemed, for the mirror was angled away from the doorway, such that she could not see a reflection. But yes, it was a mirror. As he reached out his hand to touch the mirror, she could see the reflection of his hand appear on the glass. He stood motionless for a moment, holding that strange pose.

'Come on, Michael!' he muttered to himself.

For several seconds, he stood staring slightly down into the mirror, with his palm pressed against the glass, apparently waiting for something to happen, or as if he were praying.

Before Molly realised what she was doing, she had entered the cluttered room and was tip-toeing closer to him, bewildered and keen to discover what on earth he was doing. She was directly behind him, close enough to hear his deep breathing, or was it her own? She could see the mirror clearly now with its thick wooden frame and almost gasped at the sight of it. The carvings were hideous, unlike anything she had ever seen before. Figures of people and unfamiliar creatures stared back at her with leering faces and oversized eyes and teeth.

As she peered over his shoulder, tiny sparks began to fly like fireflies around the hand that touched the surface of the mirror. She reached out and placed a hand on his shoulder to get a better look. 'What are you doing, Paget?' she said in a low voice.

He started, turned his head around without releasing his touch on the mirror and said with shock and horror on his face: 'Molly? No!'

And then, within the blink of an eye, the sparks turned into tiny worms of electricity, darting up the boy's arm and towards her. She felt consciousness fading from her mind.

And then she and the boy disappeared from the room.

Chapter Seven

The Girl in the Mirror

For a heart-stopping moment, Tom was unable to move. Had she been left behind, or had she travelled through the mirror with him? Fear prevented him from turning around to check. But then he could feel a small hand on his shoulder, and instantly, he sighed with relief. He swallowed hard and then spun round to face her. Expressionless and mouth open, her pretty face seemed to be staring right through him as though she were stuck in a trance, her left arm still raised in front of her like a one-armed zombie. She blinked, but otherwise remained completely motionless.

'Oh, my–' he began.

'Who … who's that?' asked Molly, her raised hand changing into a pointed finger and indicating a spot over his shoulder.

Tom spun round again and saw a less than pleased Michael, striding along the rainbow path towards them, his face set with angry disbelief.

'That's Michael,' replied Tom quietly and with growing anxiety.

'So,' continued Molly slowly, 'you're not Michael?'

'No,' sighed Tom. 'Like I've been trying to tell you for the last few days: my name is Tom. He's the Michael you know.'

Michael, red-faced and scowling, drew up to them. 'What is *she* doing here?' he demanded.

'It … it was an accident …' began Tom. He had no real idea how it had happened, so trying to explain it to Michael was going to be impossible.

'Where am I?' mumbled a still shocked Molly, finally lowering her arm and adjusting her glasses.

'It's a kind of gateway between two worlds,' replied Tom. 'A gateway between your world and my world.'

'Oh, I see,' she said blankly. She looked around at the stars all around them and at the wisps of iridescent colour floating past, before looking back at Tom and saying: 'What?'

'What do you think you're playing at, bringing *her* here?' said Michael, with a voice that grew louder with every word he uttered.

'I think I'm having a weird dream,' said Molly, before Tom could answer. A wisp of multi-coloured smoke drifted close by, grabbed her gaze and refused to let go until it wafted aimlessly over her shoulder and away into oblivion.

Tom ignored her. 'I didn't plan this,' he said, turning back to Michael. 'She touched my shoulder just as I was coming through. I must have somehow brought her with me. How could I know it was even possible to do that?'

'Yeah, but now she knows our little secret. I can't believe you'd do this.'

'So, he's Michael,' said Molly absently, 'and you're Tom?'

'Yes!' they both said together, without releasing their mutual glare.

'And you're cousins?' she asked uncertainly.

'No!' they replied in unison with growing irritation.

'And she's meant to be the clever one,' muttered Michael.

'What's that supposed to mean, Paget?' hissed Molly, instantly snapping out of her bewilderment. She then folded her arms indignantly.

'Er … Molly,' said Tom. 'We're both called Paget.'

'You don't say. It's obvious you're … related.'

Tom was going to correct her again, but she turned sharply away, her dark-brown ponytail swaying into view, and stared once more at the surreal scene around her.

Now they were both angry at him. Yet he still failed to see how any of this was his fault. He had not done anything wrong, had he? Somehow, he had to try to appease both of them, but judging by their faces it was going to be easier said than done.

'Look, Michael,' he began calmly. 'I'll take her straight back now …'

Michael paused for a moment, his icy gaze skipping between Molly and Tom as he thought it through. Presently, a disconcerting smile grew on his face, not at all what Tom had been expecting. 'No, you wanted her in your world. So go ahead, take her with you.' He waved at Molly dismissively. 'You're welcome to her. She's nothing but trouble in my world.' With that, he took a step towards his own mirror, as if to indicate that the discussion was over.

'No, Michael,' pleaded Tom. 'You've got to take her back with you. What if she meets the other Molly, I mean Rachel? What if she meets Rachel? We don't know what could happen.'

'Who's Rachel?' asked a puzzled Molly.

'She's you … in my world,' replied Tom, whilst still looking at Michael.

'Right,' replied Molly with a frown.

'Yeah. Kind of like your cousin but not,' added Michael, his voice full of sarcasm.

Molly glowered at him. The animosity between them was plain for Tom to see.

He turned to Molly. 'You've got to go back with Michael.'

'She's not coming back with me,' insisted Michael.

'I'm not going back with him,' added Molly, and gave them both a dirty look.

'See, she doesn't want to come.' Michael raised his hands in the air and walked away.

'Michael, please. She can't stay with me.'

'I'm still here, you know,' said Molly. 'I have a say in this as well.'

'Yes, Molly. I … sorry. Look, Michael, she can't go into my world, we don't know what could happen.'

'True, but you'll just have to tell me what does happen when you get back,' smirked Michael. Finally, he seemed to have realised Tom's discomfort, seemed to be revelling in it.

'But there's nowhere for her to sleep.'

'You should have thought of that before you brought her through.'

'I didn't bring her through,' snapped Tom. 'Not on purpose, anyway.'

'No, of course you didn't. It was an accident, wasn't it?' returned Michael, his face dripping with malice. 'I'm not stupid, Tom.'

Molly scoffed just loud enough in the background to elicit a glare from Michael.

'You wanted to prove to your new girlfriend that you weren't me, didn't you?'

'No, of course not.'

'I'm not his girlfriend,' added Molly.

'Well, whatever. You brought her through, now you've got to deal with the consequences.'

For a few brief moments, Tom studied his alter ego's face.

He saw the unpleasant mix of anger and glee in the boy's eyes and the aggressive curl to his mouth, and at once, he realised he could see absolutely nothing of himself reflected in Michael. He had thought he knew his spitting-image so well, simply because he knew himself so well. But the more he looked at him, the more he knew they had nothing in common at all. Aside from appearance, they were worlds apart in more ways than one. And at that moment, he was suddenly pleased that Molly would not be going back with this complete and unpleasant stranger.

'At least come back first thing in the morning,' said Tom calmly.

'No,' grinned Michael. 'I don't feel like it. Let's make it four o'clock tomorrow afternoon.'

'Michael, please. We don't know what could happen to Rachel.'

This final mention of Rachel's name seemed to spark a doubt in Michael's mind. He paused for a moment with a pensive frown, before adding: 'Okay, okay. Let's say ... one o'clock tomorrow lunchtime. That's my final offer.' He grinned briefly and then moved towards his shimmering mirror in preparation for returning to his own world.

And straightaway, Tom knew there was no point in arguing any further.

'There, you see,' said Tom, after he and Molly had materialised into the dark room in *Morladron House*. 'I told you I wasn't Michael.'

'Yes, but you didn't tell me anything about this,' replied Molly. She let go of him as soon as she realised it was safe to do so and hurriedly took a couple of steps away from him, as if she believed he had some contagious disease.

In the gathering gloom, Tom looked at her darkened face and laughed uneasily. 'You didn't believe me when I told you I was Michael's cousin, so you were hardly going to believe any of this, were you?'

Molly frowned, though whether through displeasure or perplexity Tom could not tell. 'I suppose not,' she conceded.

Outside of the room, the night was closing in, albeit slowly on such a clear summer's evening. The only meagre light penetrating the room came from the small patches of pale sky above them, seen through the holes in the roof, leaving the room full of eerie silhouettes.

'Where are we, anyway?' asked Molly, stepping cautiously around the room.

'Welcome to my world,' replied Tom, spreading his arms wide.

'You live here?'

'Not exactly,' smiled Tom weakly. 'Anyway, we can't stay here. It's getting late and we need to find somewhere for you to stay tonight.'

'Wait a minute, Paget … er, Tom. I've got to get home.' She glanced at her watch. 'My parents will kill me for being out this late. You have to take me back.'

Tom sighed. 'Molly, I'm not sure you still understand just what has happened here. We are now in a completely different world – a different universe, I guess – to the one where you come from. Michael and I are the only ones who can travel back and forth, and we do that by touching our mirrors at the same time.'

'Oh, right. You expect me to believe that rubbish?'

Tom was incredulous. 'Well, yes, actually. How else do you

explain what just happened back there?' he said, pointing at the mirror.

Molly was silent for a moment before she said: 'But I can't stay here.'

It was getting so dark that Tom could barely make out Molly's features anymore when she stood more than a metre away. Not that he needed to see her face to sense the growing anguish she was feeling.

'I'm sorry. There is no other way. You can't go back until one o'clock tomorrow afternoon.'

'Then where am I going to sleep tonight?'

'I have no idea. That's what we need to sort out now. Come on, we'll go to my house for now until we work something out. My dad will still be down the pub with his mates till midnight at least.'

And with that, he marched her out of the room.

After leaving Molly in his otherwise empty house, Tom hurriedly made the short walk to Jake's house and rang the doorbell. Jake's father answered the door.

'Hi, Tom,' he said. 'What's up?'

'Hello, Mr McBean,' replied Tom nervously. He still had no idea what he was doing, or what he was going to do.

Mr McBean was tall and well built like his son but athletic with it. And just like Jake, he wore a ready smile, which straightaway suggested he wouldn't hurt a fly. As he looked at him, a picture entered Tom's mind of what the man would be like in Michael's world of opposite personalities. Sean's father probably drank heavily, wore a string vest over a potbelly and swore at everyone in an incomprehensible Scottish accent. Tom had to suppress a giggle at the thought.

'Sorry to disturb you at this time of night,' continued Tom, 'but could I speak to Jake for a moment?'

'Yeah, of course,' replied Mr McBean, and disappeared into the house.

Tom heard Jake's name being called. A few moments later, his friend appeared in the doorway.

'Hi,' he muttered frostily. 'What do you want?' Their friendship had been strained for a few days now.

'Jake,' said Tom hurriedly, and tugged gently on his friend's arm to pull him away from the door and out of earshot of anyone else. 'You've got to help me. There's someone in my house I want you to meet, and I don't know what to do with her.'

Jake screwed his face into a frown. 'Tom, what on earth are you talking about?'

'Look, I'm not explaining myself very well. Just come to my house now, and I'll explain everything.'

'Tom, it's quarter past ten. Can't this wait till the morning?'

'No. We have to do something before my dad gets home. And–'

'Okay. I'll ask if I can come out for five minutes. But this had better be good.'

After quickly telling his parents where he was going, Jake left the house and followed Tom. Once inside the house, Tom closed the front door behind them, concerned that Jake might run a mile when he saw Molly. They both stepped into the lounge, where Molly, who had been pacing up and down the room impatiently, stopped and stared at them.

'Oh crikey, Tom,' said Jake and stopped dead in his tracks. 'Is that who I think it is? What is she doing here?'

Before he could respond, Molly said: 'Is that McBean? Why

the heck have you brought him here?'

'No. This is my best friend Jake. And–'

'I don't need this,' said Jake and headed for the door.

Tom leapt after him and grabbed his arm. 'Wait, Jake,' he said. 'This isn't Rachel. Stay, please. I need your help.'

He looked into Tom's frantic face and then glanced across at Molly, who was glowering through her spectacles at both of them.

'Are you going to tell me what's going on here, Paget?' demanded Molly.

'What on earth are you doing with Rachel in your living room?' added a bemused Jake.

'Both of you,' shouted Tom suddenly. 'Shut up and listen to me. Molly, this is *not* Sean. This is my friend Jake. Jake, this is *not* Rachel. This is Molly. She comes from the parallel world I've been trying to tell you about.'

Jake rolled his eyes. 'Och, here we go again.'

'That really isn't Sean, is it?' muttered Molly.

'No …'

'My goodness,' she continued, and slowly lowered herself into an armchair. 'I really am in a parallel world.'

'Finally,' sighed Tom.

'What's going on, mate?' said Jake quietly, his eyes flitting between the two of them.

'Jake, like I've been trying to tell you these past few days: I've been travelling back and forth between this world and Molly's world. Only, when I came back this evening, Molly came through with me by mistake. And now she's got nowhere to stay.'

'Oh, I see,' said Jake, scratching his mop of blond hair. 'Simple as that, eh?'

'It's the truth, Jake. I promise you.'

'So, you're telling me you brought her here from another world ...'

'Yes. Well, I didn't exactly bring her ...'

'And that somehow now she's stuck here?'

'Yes, Jake.'

'Oh, right. And you just expect me to believe that?'

'Sean ... Jake ... whatever your name is,' said Molly. 'I think he's telling the truth.'

'Aye, but you would say that, wouldn't you?' Jake then turned back to Tom. 'But she looks just like Rachel,' he said, a hint of doubt creeping into his soft voice.

'Of course she looks like Rachel,' replied Tom, straining not to let the rising exasperation he felt, creep into his voice. 'It's a parallel world. There's another me, another you, another Rachel. Everybody is the same as here ... only ... different, sort of. Everyone seems to have the opposite personality.'

'So,' began Molly, rising to her feet again and scratching her head in thought. 'Anyone who's unpleasant in my world is nice in this world and vice versa. Is that what you're saying?'

'Yes, that seems to be the case,' replied Tom, and then turned to Jake. 'There, you see. When did you last hear Rachel use a phrase like "vice versa", eh?'

Jake smiled meekly. 'You're right. It's got more than one syllable in it. It can't be Rachel. I'm convinced.'

'Great,' said Tom. 'But we're wasting time. We have to find somewhere for Molly to stay until I can take her back tomorrow.'

'Why doesn't she just stay here with you?' suggested Jake, his face still a blank, still unsure what he was hearing and seeing.

'Because if my dad finds her, I'm dead. That's not an option.'

'What about the old house?'

'Yes,' agreed Tom. 'That's all I could think of, too. So, I thought if you could help me get a few things together–'

'Er, excuse me, boys,' said Molly. 'Do you mean the house we've just come from? There's no way I'm spending a night in that dirty old house. It's probably full of rats and bats and …'

'Cats?' suggested Jake, but received nothing but a withering look from Molly.

'Molly, you have to–'

'I'm not staying in that house. And that's that. Why don't I just go to a hotel or something? You do have hotels in this … frightful world of yours, don't you?'

'Yes, but I don't have the money to put you in a hotel for the night.'

'Frightful? Did she just say the word frightful?' laughed Jake. 'She really isn't Rachel, is she?'

'No, Jake. She isn't,' replied Tom through gritted teeth.

'Great,' said Molly, and then let out a heavy sigh. 'That's just … great.'

'So,' continued Jake, 'what am I like in this world of hers? Am I like … nasty or something?'

Tom put a hand to his forehead, and squeezed his eyes shut for a moment. 'Jake!'

'Yes?'

'You're really not helping.'

'No, er … sorry.'

'Listen, Jake,' resumed Tom. 'There's only one option left.'

'Oh, what's that?'

Tom hesitated and pulled a nervous face.

Then it dawned on Jake. 'No, no, no! There's no way she can stay at mine.'

'Why not?'

'Because my parents won't allow it, that's why not. They know all about Miss Rachel Trump. In fact, everybody in this town knows about Rachel Trump. They wouldn't let her into our street, let alone our house. No, I'm sorry, Tom. She can't.'

'Right,' said Molly decisively. 'That's settled then – I'm staying here tonight.'

'But you can't,' insisted Tom, his eyes wide and terrified. He swallowed hard. 'If my dad finds out ...'

'Well, we'll just have to make sure he doesn't,' said Molly. Whereupon she turned on her heel and strode up the stairs. 'I suppose I'd better find a hiding place in your bedroom.'

Jake laughed thoughtfully.

'What's the matter with you?' asked Tom.

'Ah, it's just funny,' replied Jake. 'You've always wanted Rachel in your bedroom. Well, now you do.'

Somehow, to Tom's great relief, they got through the night without incident. Inebriated, Tom's father returned home late, and then slept like a baby through the night, until it was time for him to rise and go to work. He was used to his son getting up before he did and leaving the house early, so when he did not see Tom at breakfast, it was no great surprise. Once Tom heard the front door slam shut, he let out a huge sigh of relief.

'Why are you so afraid of your dad?' asked Molly.

'You saw my black eye,' mumbled Tom, and promptly walked away.

Molly opened her mouth as if to speak, but then appeared to think better of prying further.

'Come on, let's have some breakfast,' said Tom, as he went down the stairs.

'Tom, it's getting late,' said Molly, as she followed him into the kitchen. 'You'll be late for school.'

'You sound like my mum,' he chuckled. And then he remembered. 'I mean, Michael's mum,' he added, and a pang of regret ran through him like an ice-cold stake. He managed to bury the emotion for the time being. Now was not the time to burden Molly with his problems; he had more pressing matters to consider.

After a hastily taken breakfast, Molly stood and said: 'Come on, we'll be late.'

'Whoa, hang on a second. Where do you think you're going?' asked Tom.

'To school, of course,' replied Molly.

'You can't go outside – you might be seen by someone.'

'And if you don't go to school you'll be punished again.'

Tom rubbed his still bandaged hand. 'Yeah, well. Things are a little different in this world.'

'Well, I'm not staying in this stuffy house all morning,' insisted Molly.

'You can't go outside. This isn't your world. We don't know what could happen.'

Molly frowned and adjusted her glasses. 'You came to my world and nothing happened. If we meet someone, I'll just pretend to be this Rachel girl. Now come on: show me this world of yours.'

'Oh, right. And what if you meet the real Rachel? What if something terrible happens when the same two people meet?'

'What if? What if? You worry too much.'

'Since when did you become an expert in all this?'

demanded Tom.

'Oh, and you are, I suppose?' scoffed Molly.

'No, but–'

'Come on. It'll be fine. I might as well do something while I wait to go home.'

And with that, she turned and stomped out through the front door. Tom hurriedly followed her out, wondering whether he was indeed being just a little paranoid.

He caught up with her in the street, where she was standing, shielding her eyes from the glare of yet another warm sunny day.

'This is weird,' she said, looking down into the town below them. 'I recognise it all, but it's all back to front.'

'I know,' agreed Tom. 'It's kind of cool, isn't it?'

'And all the cars are driving on the wrong side of the road.'

'No, I think it's you that drive on the wrong side of the road.'

And they shared a brief, nervous laugh.

'Look,' began Tom earnestly. 'I really think you should be hiding. This isn't a good idea for all sorts of reasons.'

'Nonsense,' smiled Molly, who suddenly seemed to be relaxed and enjoying herself. She grabbed Tom by the arm and began walking down the road. 'Show me your school,' she said, full of excitement. 'Now, where is it?' She stopped, looked down into the town to get her bearings and then pointed to a spot across the valley. 'It must be over there. Am I right?'

'Yes, but–'

They were walking again before Tom knew what to say.

'You should really go to school, Tom. I don't want you to get into trouble on my account. I'd feel bad. This is all my fault, really. I should never have followed you into your house, I mean, into Michael's house.'

'No, it was an accident,' said Tom, and then when they turned into another road he added: 'This really isn't a good idea. If–'

He became aware of a car pulling into the curb beside him. The passenger window purred down.

'Hello, Tom,' said a familiar woman's voice. 'You're running a bit late.'

Tom bent down to look into the car. 'Oh, er … Hi, Mrs M-Meadow,' he stammered. His heart sank. How on earth was he going to get out of this one? He had known it would be a mistake to go outside with Molly.

'Come on,' continued Mrs Meadow. 'Hop in. I'll run you to school.'

'Er … no, it's fine thanks. We'll walk.'

'Tom, you'll be late if you walk from here,' countered Mrs Meadow, looking at her watch. 'Now come on, hop in. Don't worry, no one will see you, if that's what you're worried about. Oh, is that Rachel Trump with you?' Her face was suddenly a picture of surprise. 'My, you look a little … different today, Rachel. Very … sophisticated.'

Molly quickly withdrew her arm from Tom's. He could feel her discomfort without needing to look at her. He had never wanted the ground to open up and swallow him so much in all his life.

Molly cleared her throat nervously. 'Hello, Mrs Doom–'

'Mrs Meadow,' interjected Tom quickly. 'Mrs Meadow. Yes, thanks, we'll come with you.'

Realising there was no way to avoid accepting the teacher's offer of a lift, he opened the car's back door. He had travelled with Mrs Meadow before in the front seat, but this time with Molly to look after, he thought it best to sit in the back with her. Yet as soon as he had ushered Molly in, sat down himself and then closed the door, he immediately felt it had been a bad choice, for it would arouse unwanted suspicion. By the time the car started off down the road, Tom thought his pounding heart would explode in his chest.

'So, are you two an item now?' asked Mrs Meadow, glancing into the rear-view mirror and instantly seeing her two passengers shift uncomfortably in their seats.

'No,' said Tom. 'I was just helping her with some, er, homework.'

'I see. Good for you,' said Mrs Meadow in a tone that suggested she did not believe a word of what Tom had just said. She no doubt thought she knew what was going on, thought Tom. If only she knew the truth.

'You're running late today, Mrs Meadow,' said Tom quickly, desperately wanting to deflect attention from the two of them.

'Oh, dramas at home with the children,' laughed the teacher. 'Nothing to worry about. Anyway, Rachel, I didn't know you had to wear glasses.'

Molly was about to speak when Tom cut in: 'No, she doesn't need to wear glasses. They're just for show, aren't they?' And he laughed nervously.

Molly smiled timidly, removed her glasses and shrugged her shoulders. 'Yes, that's right,' she chuckled uneasily.

'Oh, I see. And how's that brother of yours doing?'

'Well–'

'Oh, he's fine,' interjected Tom.

'Let the poor girl speak for herself, Tom,' said Mrs Meadow

with a benevolent smile.

Tom glanced anxiously across at Molly who cleared her throat and said: 'Er, yes. He's doing just fine actually. He's still at university studying medicine. He intends to specialise in neurology ...'

'Don't be facetious, Rachel,' said Mrs Meadow, her round face suddenly screwing into a frown.

'Er, sorry,' replied Molly, shooting a bewildered glance between the teacher's face in the rear-view mirror and Tom's horrified look. 'I wasn't being facetious–'

'Rachel's just being silly,' said Tom. 'You know what she's like.' He gave Mrs Meadow the best knowing look he could summon and then landed a playful punch on Molly's upper arm. The briefest of glares was exchanged between them.

'Yes, I suppose I do,' replied the teacher uncertainly.

Presently, they arrived at the school just as the last few pupils were meandering into the main building. When they were out of the car and safely out of Mrs Meadow's earshot, Molly grabbed Tom's arm and demanded: 'What was that all about?'

'Molly, you can't talk like that. You can't say words like ... neurology and facetious. Rachel and her brother are the same – they're not very nice and, well ... thick, basically. And her brother is certainly not at university studying medicine.'

'How was I supposed to know that?'

'Just ... try not to say anything,' said Tom.

They hurried into the building where the corridors were rapidly emptying as pupils poured into their classrooms.

'Now what are we going to do?' asked Molly.

'I don't know,' was all Tom could reply.

Jake appeared, his voice startled and urgent. 'Tom? What

are you doing here with her? Have you gone mad? I've just seen Rachel back there coming out of the toilets.'

Tom hurriedly explained what had just happened.

'But Rachel's coming this way,' said Jake. 'Molly can't come into the classroom. You can't have both of them in the same room.'

'Look, Molly,' began Tom. 'Sorry about this, but we've got to find somewhere for you to hide.'

'Perhaps I should just go and find a broom cupboard to lurk in all day, shall I?' she replied.

'Well, it wouldn't be a bad idea,' said Tom, his patience and ideas running out.

'Forget it,' she snorted. 'I'm not hiding, and that's that.'

Tom barely had time to respond, or to rue the dreadful luck he had had so far that day, when a voice behind them froze him to the spot.

'Michael, is that you?' asked a girl's voice.

Tom closed his eyes and refused to turn around. He could hear the audible gasps from Jake and Molly.

When the voice drew nearer, the tone changed. 'Oh, my God, it's you, isn't it?' spat the girl with contempt.

'Oh, no!' muttered Tom.

The very last person he wanted to see at that precise moment was Rachel Trump.

Chapter Eight

The Gathering Storm

'Get out of my way, you freak,' snarled Rachel, and burst through Jake and Tom.

But then she froze, open mouthed, when she saw Molly standing awkwardly in front of her. She mouthed several words that failed to come out.

'Hi,' said Molly, unable to believe her own eyes, and staring in spite of herself.

'Who are you?' asked Rachel at last.

Tom stepped forward and grabbed Molly's arm, turning her away from Rachel's gaze. 'No one, Rachel,' he said. 'No one at all. Just a friend.'

Molly now had her back to Rachel but was still craning her neck over her shoulder to stare at her double.

'She looks just like me,' she mumbled to Tom.

'Yes, I know. It's amazing, isn't it? Now come on, we've got to go.'

'What are you up to, Paget?' demanded Rachel.

She reached out a hand which Tom quickly intercepted.

'Don't touch her,' he yelled.

'Let go of me, you creep!' hissed Rachel, and grabbed his arm with her free hand.

Maybe it was completely irrational, but a little voice in Tom's head kept telling him that he had to stop the two girls from touching one another at all costs. It was the same feeling that had drawn him to *Morladron House*, so he knew it had to be important somehow. So in his desperation to avoid them

115

touching, Tom struggled free from Rachel's grip with more force than he had intended. And as he did so, Rachel slipped and fell heavily against the corridor wall. Her head rolled from side to side for a second, and then she slumped to the floor, unconscious.

'Oh, great!' sighed Tom.

He dropped to his haunches and rolled her over onto her back. 'She's out cold,' he said, turning to the other two, who were now standing anxiously over him.

'What have you done?' demanded Molly.

'I didn't do anything. It was … her. What am I going to do now?'

'Well,' began Jake, 'why don't you undress her, and give her clothes to Molly for now, so she could be Rachel …'

Horrified, Tom and Molly looked at him and said in unison: 'Jake!'

'Sorry,' he mumbled sheepishly. 'Yeah. Bad idea, sorry.'

'We can't just leave her here,' said Molly.

Then they heard footsteps echoing down the corridor behind them.

'What's going on here?' demanded a male teacher.

Tom sprang to his feet and positioned himself between the teacher and Molly. 'Ah … sir. It's Rachel Trump. She's fallen over and I think she's knocked herself out.'

'Let's have a look,' said the teacher, and crouched over the stricken girl.

He slapped her face gently a couple of times until a slight groan emanated from her mouth.

'She's fine,' he said. 'I'll take her to the nurse. She may need to go to hospital for a check-up. You can't be too careful these days. You three run along to class. I'll take it from here.'

And with that, he hauled the groggy Rachel to her feet and then picked her up in his arms when he realised she was incapable of walking.

At that moment, Mrs Tyler, the French teacher, turned up with a sheaf of papers tucked under one arm. 'What's happened here?' she asked.

'Don't worry. I've got it in hand, Doris,' replied the other teacher, his voice straining with the burden in his arms. Whereupon he staggered off down the corridor.

'Right, you three,' said Mrs Tyler. 'Come along. Let's go and learn some French.'

Whilst Mrs Tyler took the register, the unlikely trio sat at the front of the classroom and had to endure a barrage of bemused looks and a constant ripple of whispered comments. They sat in silence, self-conscious and as still as statues. Yet as uncomfortable as it was, Tom knew the real problems were still to come, starting with Mrs Tyler's French lesson.

He turned to Molly and said quietly: 'Try to remember that you're Rachel now. She's not as bright as you. In fact, she's pretty stupid to be honest. And maybe take your glasses off and let your hair down, so you look more like her ...'

Molly gave him a withering look and pointedly left her glasses and ponytail just as they were. But before she could utter a word, Mrs Tyler spoke up to settle down the class.

Then Tom's thumping heart sank when the teacher said with a perplexed look on her face: 'Rachel? Didn't I just see you outside in the corridor?'

Molly glanced uncertainly at Tom and then cleared her throat. 'No, Miss. That weren't me. I dunno who it was,' she said, in an affected accent, which Tom could only describe as a poor attempt at cockney. Tom did not need to look to know that every pair of eyes in the room was now firmly fixed on Molly.

Before Tom could whisper anything, Mrs Tyler resumed. 'I see. And where's your uniform?'

Tom closed his eyes for a moment and sighed to himself. Just what else was going to go wrong? Molly had come through to his world the previous evening, so was still dressed in her after-school casual clothes. At least she was not going to be caned, he thought.

'Oh, sorry, Miss. I spilt some fink on it this mornin'.'

Mrs Tyler's face was a picture. The bizarre accent coming out of Rachel's mouth, more than her answers, had rendered her momentarily speechless. Whispers and the odd giggle rippled around the classroom.

'What are you doing?' whispered Tom, when the teacher's attention was at last off Molly.

'What do you mean?' she whispered back sourly.

'Your … stupid accent. I said Rachel was thick. I didn't say … she was trying to be in EastEnders.'

'This isn't easy, you know,' protested Molly, her face reddening with annoyance and embarrassment in equal measure.

'Just try to be yourself. And just don't say too much.'

'I'm doing my best,' she snapped, and sat back with her arms folded. 'I can't wait till I go back and get out of this stu–'

'Rachel Trump,' barked Mrs Tyler. 'As usual you have plenty to say for yourself.'

This time Molly gave a thin smile but said nothing.

'Well,' continued the teacher, 'perhaps you could start off the lesson today and entertain us with your French.'

Tom was unsure whether to laugh or cry.

'So, Rachel, why not start by telling us what you did last night. *Qu'est-ce que tu as fait hier soir?*'

Hurriedly, Tom began to whisper, trying not to move his lips: 'Rachel isn't–'

'Tom Paget!' cut in Mrs Tyler. 'No helping her, please.'

Molly swallowed hard and then said: 'Er … *Hier soir je me suis allée à la plage pour voir mes amis.*'

The sound of a pin dropping to the floor would have been deafening in the silence that followed. The class was paralysed and open-mouthed, none more so than Mrs Tyler who managed to compose herself first. 'Er … well done … Rachel. That was excellent. I … w-well done!'

Tom closed his eyes, put his head in his hands and sighed: 'Why me?'

Jake leant over and whispered. 'She's certainly not Rachel, is she? Sorry, I ever doubted you.'

Tom could do nothing but smile weakly and shake his head. The end of the lesson could not come soon enough.

It was hard not to stare out of the window. Not that there was much to stare at from the first floor, other than the car park and the playground below. But the history teacher was standing at the front of the class droning on about something that, in normal circumstances, Tom might have found interesting. These were, however, anything but normal circumstances.

He had already inquired about Rachel and been told that she was fine and resting at home. No doubt, she was already plotting her revenge on Tom and pleading with her family to let her out so she could exact it.

Beside him, Molly shifted in her seat and fidgeted with her pen with a look of utter boredom, which would not have looked out of place on Rachel's vacuous face. Yet Molly was clearly bored out of her mind due to the fact that there was no point in taking notes about a history that was largely unfamiliar and irrelevant to her. Besides, she could not ask questions for fear of arousing any further suspicion, and it was that, thought Tom, that must have been really frustrating for such an avid learner as her.

Whilst Tom was repeatedly going over in his mind the extraordinary events of that morning, a dark cloud drifted across the hitherto cloudless sky and blotted out the sun with an abruptness that drew his eyes upwards. More and more massive clouds began to swirl into existence, like giant puffs from an invisible chimney. As he watched, spellbound, the remaining patches of blue sky became fewer and fewer, smaller and smaller. An eerie half-light descended over the town, causing streetlamps to pop on, car headlights to begin piercing the gloom.

Tom tapped Molly on the arm to draw her attention to the unfolding scene, but the approaching storm had already pulled her out of her boredom.

A blinding flash of lightning caused them both to close their eyes and look away. Barely had their sight recovered, when a deafening crash of thunder exploded above them and roared on for several seconds until they feared the classroom windows would shatter. Taken aback, the teacher fell silent whilst his students began excitedly muttering their surprise.

Outside, the light was fading with every blink of the eye, dusk moving into night in no time at all. A gusting wind began wrestling with the line of trees on the school perimeter and then overturned a dustbin with a loud clatter of metal on concrete. A spiralling eddy of rubbish grew out of the spilt contents of the bin and moved across the playground like a spectre, before collapsing suddenly, as if the ghost had been cut down.

The first heavy drops of rain tapped at the classroom windows.

'Great,' said Tom. 'We're going to get wet going back to the house.'

A vivid streak of lightning burst out of the charcoal-grey sky and struck one of the tall trees on the other side of the playground, instantly igniting it into a dazzling ball of fire. Only a few seconds later, the fire fizzled out as abruptly as it had begun, and nothing but the blackened silhouette of a trunk remained, denuded of branches and leaves.

And then the bell rang to signify the start of the lunch break. Knowing they didn't have long to get to *Morladron House*, Tom and Molly hurried out of the classroom and down the stairs. Tom managed to borrow an umbrella from a friend, and then out they stepped into the gathering gloom.

'We can't go out in this,' protested Molly, as she looked up at the sky, knowing that a deluge was imminent.

'Do you really want to stay in this world?' replied Tom. 'Because if we don't go now, you could well be stranded here for ever.'

The resigned look with which she responded gave Tom his answer. She evidently had no desire to stay in his world a minute longer than was absolutely necessary.

With lightning bolts exploding around them at regular intervals, and the blustery wind tugging at the umbrella under which they cowered, they hurried out of the school grounds and down into the town. Heavy raindrops patted the umbrella, as if a higher power were toying with them, delaying the inevitable moment when the heavens would open and the pair of them would get soaked.

More lightning, more thunder: the brightest flashes of light, the loudest explosions of noise Tom had ever experienced. The tempo of the spattering of raindrops increased slowly, until, just as the bridge in the centre of the town came into view, the anticipated torrent of rain began with a roar. Instantly, a thick film of agitated water spread over the roads and pavements and gardens. Tom struggled under the force of the water pressing down on the umbrella. But still they pushed on towards the bridge.

A sudden, jagged fork of lightning struck the road to their right, only a short stone's throw from their feet. Dozens of tiny worm-like sparks danced across the water, which boiled like a witch's cauldron for several seconds. Barely had they regained their balance from the shock, when another white crack of lightning exploded to their left. Then, a few paces before them, another flashed, as thick as the trunk of an ancient oak tree. The water all around them was hissing and sparking with energy, threatening to devour them at any moment.

Fearing another imminent strike and reacting entirely on instinct, Tom pointed at the bridge in front of them and yelled at Molly beside him to run. The force of the rain on the umbrella was unrelenting, deafening, rendering speech almost impossible even when their heads were virtually touching.

Water was cascading down a flight of steps that led down to a towpath along the river's edge below, a river that had already swollen appreciably and was flowing as violently as it only ever did after a winter storm, and never, in Tom's experience, in June.

After splashing down the steps, they turned to their right and came to a halt under the shelter of the bridge, their shoes and trousers drenched, their hearts pounding as if they had been running for miles.

Tom closed the umbrella and shook a thousand droplets of water into the river beside him. He then turned and looked back out into the storm just as lightning lit up the low-lying cloud, momentarily giving form to the bulging, swirling mass that was hanging over his town like thick smoke from a giant, polluting factory.

His memory was jogged; he recalled the accounts he had read in Molly's school library only the day before. 'The Great Storm,' he muttered to himself.

'What?' said Molly, still panting, her cheeks red.

'This has something to do with your being here.'

'What are you talking about?' she demanded, wiping her glasses. 'It's just a thunderstorm. I don't know about here, but we get thunderstorms all the time where I come from,' she added.

Agitated, Tom ignored her mockery and said: 'How can you say that? Have you ever seen lightning behave like that?' He gestured with his hands to emphasis his point. 'It felt like something was trying to get us.'

'That's ridiculous,' scoffed Molly, with an exaggerated twist of her face. She was having to shout to make herself heard above the roar of the rain that assaulted the bridge above. 'We're wasting time.' And with that, she grabbed the umbrella from his grasp and snapped it open once more. 'Come on.'

Tom glanced at the muddy, swirling mass of the river beside them as it swept an increasing amount of debris towards the sea. A giant branch tumbled past, followed by a cardboard box and a tyre. He could see the river was close to bursting its banks, so he knew they had to move.

'Okay,' he said. 'But this time we'll run – all the way.'

And so run they did. Back up the steps, across the bridge and up the roads on the far side of the valley, each with a hand on the shaft of the umbrella, trying in vain to keep dry. The streets were narrow and deserted and dark, and torrents of water flowed along the gutters, carrying mud and rubbish down towards the river. And still the thunder rumbled on, like some fierce giant causing devastation nearby.

A lightning bolt struck a chimney above them, and before they knew what was happening, bricks were flying down all around them, smashing into puddles like small meteorites. Tom tripped and nearly fell face first into the road. In trying to regain his balance, he had ripped the umbrella from Molly's hand, and then a gust of wind pulled it inside out, before wrenching it from his hand. It flew off down the road like a caged bird that had just been released. So now their heads were soaking, too, and moments later, Tom could feel his torso go cold and numb and wet.

But he grabbed Molly's hand with no protest from her, and on they went, splashing along the roads, shutting out the discomfort, knowing they had to get back to the house and the mirror.

Running uphill was taking its toll. They stopped briefly under a large tree to catch their breath and to wipe their faces and their hair. They exchanged an uneasy glance before pressing on, past the shops and the smaller terraced houses with no front gardens, and up towards the larger houses with their larger plots, where the ground finally began to level out.

And then, as they passed a large front garden, there was a flash and a mighty bang. The next thing Tom knew he was lying face down on a lawn, and there he would have stayed had the unrelenting rain not continued to pummel his back and stir him back to consciousness. The very instant he remembered who he was and where he was, he rolled over and sat up, anxious to check that Molly was okay. No sooner had he wiped the rain from his face than it was drenched again, so he shielded his eyes with a hand instead.

A short distance away from him, a large patch of the lawn that he was on was charred and smoking. And Molly was nowhere to be seen. He thought his heart was going to stop beating, his breathing to cease. This could not be happening.

'No!' he yelled, and began scrambling around on all fours, desperately looking for her, any sign of her, whilst a part of him seemed to know she must have been struck, must have been vaporised by the lightning.

Tears mixed with the rain on his face. He stood up and began frantically searching every bush in the garden, refusing to give up on her, oblivious to the unforgiving rain that clawed at his face.

Another shaft of lightning struck nearby. And in the momentary pool of light it cast, he saw her, curled up awkwardly near a tree, unconscious but alive. Tears of pain turned to tears of sheer relief. He raced towards her, skidded down onto his knees across the sodden grass, wiped away a matted clump of wet hair from her face and then shook her soaking body until she stirred. He wanted to hug her, to hold her, to tell her how he felt, but time was against him. Instead, he hauled her to her feet before she had fully regained consciousness and dragged her along until the strength returned to her legs and they were able to run once more towards *Morladron House*.

At last, they were standing before the gates to the house on the hill, the storm still raging all around them, their bodies soaked to the skin. They scrambled over the gates, ran around the back and finally entered the dark and lifeless house. They fumbled through the dark, using the frequent bursts of lightning to help them navigate until finally, they were standing in the old bedroom. Tom held Molly's still dripping hand and pressed his other palm to the mirror.

Instantaneously, they were through, and the abrupt silence in the void was as striking as the thunder had been ear-splitting. With his hand still in Molly's, Tom turned to her and whispered: 'I thought I'd lost you for a minute.'

Her dripping face smiled weakly but warmly at him. She wiped her free hand across her face and quickly realised she had lost her glasses.

'What kept you?' boomed a familiar voice. Michael strode purposefully towards them.

'The weather,' replied Tom, wiping his own face.

Michael looked down at their holding of hands and smiled. 'Did you have fun?'

Quickly and guiltily, they released their grip.

'Anyway,' sniffed Michael, arrogantly, indifferently, 'I'd love to stay and chat but let's get going, shall we? Rachel and I are going to bunk off this afternoon,' he added, with a gleeful grin.

'You're doing what?' protested Tom. 'You'll get me into trouble.'

'Hey,' said Michael, stabbing a finger into Tom's chest. 'You've had all the fun so far today. Now it's my turn.' He then looked at his wet finger and said: 'Good grief. You're soaking. What've you been doing?'

'Yeah, listen, Michael …' began Tom, and intended warning his look-alike about what had just happened, and how their travelling was, perhaps, unleashing dangerous forces about which they knew nothing. But when he saw Michael's disinterested face, he thought better of it. Since even Molly was sceptical, he decided to leave that discussion for another time.

'So,' resumed Michael, 'I was thinking we'd come back at eight o'clock this evening. If that's okay with you, of course,' he added with a smirk. 'I think you still owe me, after getting me into trouble last week.'

'Er, if you were hoping to see Rachel, I'm afraid she was sent home this morning after banging her head. I heard the doctors told her to rest at home for the rest of the day.'

'Oh, great,' sighed Michael. 'So there's no real point me going through today at all, is there?'

Molly gasped. 'Well, other than to check she's all right. You could always do that, if it's not too inconvenient for you?' She glared at him.

Tom expected Michael to respond with aggression, but instead he looked sheepish and muttered: 'Well, yeah, I suppose.' He coughed nervously. 'Okay, let's say four o'clock then. I can make football practice that way.'

'Oh, you're just so romantic, aren't you?' mocked Molly.

Once they had hurriedly dried themselves in Michael's house, Tom went to find some dry clothes, which he hoped Michael would not mind his borrowing, and Molly ran off to her house to change into her dry school uniform. After changing clothes in a matter of minutes, Tom hurried outside to meet up with Molly down the road.

It was as warm and sunny in Molly's world as it had been in Tom's less than an hour before, and after only a few minutes, Tom was sweating uncomfortably under the blazer, which he had made a concerted effort not to forget this time. It was hard to think that he had been soaked to the skin not so very long ago and now he was sweating. It felt like a completely different day already.

With only a few minutes to go before the end of the lunch break, Tom and Molly met up and headed off to school. At least they did not have as far to go this time since Molly's and Michael's respective houses were closer to the school than Tom's was in his world.

'What did you say to your parents about last night?' asked Tom, as they strode along, just short of jogging pace.

'Oh, they're both at work now. I've got that conversation to look forward to later this evening,' replied Molly, rolling her eyes. 'Anyway, why do you care?' she snapped, but then immediately looked repentant. 'Sorry. Sorry, I can't get used to you not being Paget, I mean Michael Paget. I don't understand how you and Michael can be so different.'

'That's how it seems to work,' replied Tom, and then he chuckled. 'You, for example – you're a right cow in my world.'

They both laughed.

'You and Michael really don't get on, do you?' continued Tom.

Molly's face seemed to cloud over. 'The boy's an idiot.'

'Oh, I'm sure he's not that bad.'

Molly turned to look at him through the new pair of glasses she was now wearing. 'You really don't know what he's like, do you?'

The comment and the look she gave him made Tom feel uncomfortable. He decided to change the subject quickly. 'Well, anyway. I need to tell him about what happened today. Somehow we caused that.'

'What, the storm?' asked Molly, surprised. Tom nodded. 'No. I told you earlier, Tom – that was just a thunderstorm.'

'You can't tell me that was a normal storm. It wasn't natural. I've never seen anything like that before.'

'These things happen,' shrugged Molly. 'I've seen some pretty bad storms before.'

'What about the Great Storm, here in your Porthgarrick, fourteen years ago? That never happened in my Porthgarrick. And suddenly, today, we had that bad storm. That's too much of a coincidence.'

'Listen, Tom. I don't know much about the Great Storm, but what I do know is that people were killed. There were tornadoes and all sorts. There was nothing like that today.'

'I know it had something to do with you – with us – being there. I can feel it.'

Molly sighed. 'You and Michael have swapped several times already, right? Well nothing happened on any of those occasions, did it?'

'Perhaps that's because we've never stayed long enough. Look, I know I can't explain it, but ...' He felt the lump in his throat that always came when his mother entered his thoughts. But at last, he felt he could tell Molly everything. He told her about his mother's unexplained death, and how his grandfather had disappeared at the same time. Yet in Michael's world they were both still very much alive but estranged from the family. And he explained how all these events had happened fourteen years ago, at the time of the Great Storm, and how he was fast beginning to think that there were too many coincidences in all this, and that it was all somehow linked together. And he told her he could never rest until he had the answers.

'Michael's father,' he went on, 'seems genuine enough. I really don't think he knows anything. But maybe Michael's grandfather does. I need to find where he is.'

Having listened patiently and attentively, Molly smiled a sympathetic smile. 'Tom, I'll help you any way I can. But you must realise our worlds are very different, from what I've seen. They may look identical, but people, places, events – they're all different. You may not find your answers here.'

'I know. But something tells me that I will.'

This time Molly simply smiled again.

As they neared the school, Tom caught sight of another of the giant, animated posters of a smartly dressed Ed Sheeran waving to a crowd.

'Why do you have posters of Ed Sheeran everywhere?' he asked.

Molly immediately looked puzzled. 'Who? Do you mean Christopher Sheeran?'

Of course, thought Tom. Ed Sheeran would be known by his middle name in this world. 'Yes, I guess that must be him. What does he do in this world?'

'You mean you don't know?' she asked, her voice full of astonishment. She glanced at her watch and across at the almost empty playground at the front of the school. 'We don't have time now, but I'll tell you later.'

Once again, Tom found himself staring out of the window in

the middle of a lesson, brooding over the events of an extremely eventful day. It was an odd feeling of déjà vu, as if the morning had never really happened, or had perhaps just been a dream, or even a premonition. His mind was a tangled mess of thoughts, of threads of thoughts, which shot off at tangents to one another, leaving him confused and tired and unable to resolve anything at all.

He heard the teacher at the front of the class calling a name, but it was several seconds before he registered that she was calling *his* name.

'Yeah? Sorry, um, sorry?' he stammered, shaking himself back to the present.

The young teacher eyed him with impatience. 'Welcome back, Paget. Glad you could join us. Now would you kindly tell the class what you know about Christopher Sheeran?'

Tom laughed ironically, remembering Molly's parting promise to him earlier that afternoon, but his smile quickly evaporated before the heat of the teacher's furious glower. He suddenly remembered he was in a politics class and he knew absolutely nothing about politics in his own world, let alone in Michael's.

'I … um … er … I don't know.'

'You don't know?' retorted the teacher, to a backdrop of sniggers in the class. 'Of course you do. Come on, tell us: what does he do?'

'He's … a singer?' he said, with the greatest of hesitation, knowing it was almost certainly wrong but not knowing what else to say.

'A what?' demanded the teacher.

'A singer. You know, *I'm in love with the shape of you,*' he said quietly, not daring to sing the tune. The class erupted with a mix of gasps and giggles.

'I beg your pardon?' snarled the teacher.

'I'm sorry … um … I guess he's not a singer then.'

'Right!' snapped the teacher. 'I've had enough of your insolence, Paget. You do not try to crack jokes in my class, do you understand? You have just earned yourself a detention.'

Tom's heart sank, his mouth opened, but nothing would come out.

'You can jolly well stay behind until four-thirty this evening,' continued the teacher, and then began scribbling in a notebook. 'Report to Miss Doomsday after school.'

'But … I can't. I've … I've …'

'That's enough, Paget. Any more from you, and you'll be staying on till five o'clock.'

Chapter Nine

Detention

In the few minutes between lessons, Tom fought his way through the crowded corridor towards Molly. Frantically, he called out her name until she heard him and turned around. When he caught up with her, he pulled her to one side. 'You have to help me,' he pleaded.

'What?' she replied. She looked startled, then concerned. 'What's happened?'

'I've been given detention …'

'Oh, right.' She rolled her eyes, as if to say she thought he was being over-dramatic, and began walking along the corridor again. 'What have you been doing this time?'

'You don't understand,' continued Tom. 'I've got detention after school – today.'

She gave him a puzzled glance across her shoulder, clearly still not grasping the desperation that Tom felt.

'I'm meant to be meeting Michael at four this afternoon, remember? If I don't turn up, I'm stranded here.'

'Well, I'm sure Michael will wait for you.'

'Molly, we have to …' A couple of Molly's friends appeared, eyeing Tom suspiciously but still uncomfortably close, forcing Tom to continue in an urgent whisper. 'We have to touch the mirror at exactly the same time, otherwise nothing happens. If I don't get back at four, I could be stuck here for ever.'

Molly stopped again and stared into his eyes, reading his obvious agitation. 'Tom, if you don't go to detention, Michael will get into serious trouble.' She glanced down at the bandage on his hand. 'You of all people should know that by now.'

'I know, but what choice do I have? I can't stay here.'

Molly frowned. 'Well, in that case, just don't turn up. I guess it's only Michael. Why should either of us worry if he gets into trouble?'

'Molly, that's not the problem,' returned Tom, trying not to raise his voice with irritation. 'My last lesson today is with Miss Doomsday, so even if I wanted to run off I couldn't. You've got to help me.'

Molly looked deeply into his eyes and sighed. 'Oh, Tom.'

The bell rang and the end of the school day had arrived. No one moved or even uttered a sound, such was the fear Miss Doomsday instilled into her charges.

After a brief and deliberate pause, she cleared her throat and stood up. Once she had reminded everyone of the homework she had already set them, she said: 'Right, you may all now leave.' She quickly scanned a list on her desk. 'Except of course for Paget and Trego. You two can stay behind.'

Tom's heart sank even lower than it already was, for he still had no escape plan. Anxiously, he stared at and fiddled with his pen, whilst the rest of the class stood up and cast furtive glances in his direction.

Sean McBean's large frame suddenly loomed over Tom. He leant over and whispered in a menacing voice: 'Don't even think of not turning up. I'll be watching.'

Tom opened his mouth to try to explain that he had to escape, for Michael's sake as much as for his own. But Sean's baleful scowl had already turned and marched off towards the door. He would never have listened, anyway, mused Tom.

Presently, the room was empty save for Miss Doomsday, standing fiercely at the front, the girl Trego and himself. The teacher gathered up her books and folders and said: 'Right. You two come with me.'

There was only option left for Tom. 'Sorry, Miss Doomsday. Could I possibly go to the toilet first? I won't be long,' he asked, in the most courteous voice he could muster.

Perhaps she was caught off-guard by such unexpected politeness from Michael Paget, for Miss Doomsday frowned and then consented to his request.

Desperately trying not to be unduly hasty, Tom hurried out of the door and rushed down the corridor. He turned a corner and was about to break into one final, desperate sprint for the main entrance, when he bumped straight into Sean McBean, flanked by two of his mindless cronies.

'Where do you think you're going?' asked Sean, in his slow and aggressive voice. But before Tom could answer, he added: 'I do believe you have a detention to go to, don't you?' And he grabbed Tom's left arm in a vice-like grip.

'Sean, listen to me,' said Tom. 'If I don't get back for four o'clock this afternoon, Michael won't be able to come back. And neither of us wants that, do we?'

'Nice try, loser. If you don't go with Doomsday, Michael gets into trouble, and I don't want *that.*'

'If you don't let me go, Michael won't be around to get into trouble, you idiot. He'll have to stay where he is, possibly for ever.'

'What are you on about?'

Tom studied Sean's blank expression, and it was then that he realised that Michael's friend had no idea what he was talking about. Michael had clearly not told him everything, had only used Tom's own idea of pretending that they were cousins who swapped lives now and then, and nothing more. In which case, Tom had no hope of convincing Sean to let him go. He tried to wriggle free from the boy's grip, to no avail. And faced with the brute's two friends as well, escape was impossible.

'Now turn around,' ordered Sean. 'And let's go back, shall we?'

'You're making a big mistake,' muttered Tom through gritted teeth.

'Of course I am,' replied Sean coldly, and promptly spun his captive around and shoved him in the back, forcing him to stumble a couple of steps down the corridor.

Tom was running out of options. He could have risked running in the opposite direction and would have been confident of outrunning the three thugs behind him, but he knew Miss Doomsday was lurking ahead somewhere nearby.

As Tom was marched down the corridor, Molly and a group of her friends appeared in front of the boys. Her eyes flitted between Tom and Sean, who gave her a brief, vindictive smile. She and Tom then exchanged a look of anguish, before Miss Doomsday reappeared and added Tom to the line of half a dozen dejected pupils already trailing behind her, their heads bowed like condemned prisoners.

The group was taken to the school library and introduced to a table overflowing with piles of books. The pupils were informed they would be spending the next hour returning the books to their rightful place on the shelves and generally tidying up the library. And whilst they set about their task under the watchful eye of Miss Doomsday and one other teacher, Tom found himself wondering what trivial misdemeanours this group of boys and girls had committed to deserve their punishment. After all, if the school meted out a caning for forgetting to wear one's blazer, detention must have been reserved for what were considered lesser offences. And then the thought of being stuck for ever in this crazy world filled him with dread.

As he wandered down an aisle between bookshelves with a pile of books teetering in his arms, he looked out of the window and gazed longingly at the sun-drenched playing field outside, where a group of students were limbering up in preparation for a game of cricket. Slowly, he placed the books down on the windowsill, glanced around to ensure no one was watching and then tried to open the window. He pulled and pulled at the catch, until his heart sank quickly with the realisation that it was firmly locked. He looked at his watch. Time was running out.

He placed the books onto their respective shelves and then returned to the centre of the room to gather his next pile. When the library door opened with an unusually loud bang, he looked up and saw Molly enter the room, offering an immediate apology for the noise. The teachers paid her only cursory attention, for she was obviously a regular visitor. Slowly, and clearly trying not to arouse suspicion, she moved towards Tom and then slipped a small note into his hand as she passed him. Surreptitiously, he glanced at the note, which told him to meet her outside by the tennis courts in two minutes. As soon as he had read the note, he looked up, puzzled, but Molly had already moved away with her back to him. What was she up to? And how did she expect him to get outside?

His confused mind was still trying to unravel the puzzle

when he saw Molly deliberately collide with a boy who was attempting to carry a particularly large pile of books towards the bookshelves. The books flew in all directions, clattering to the floor, and Molly flung herself down in overly dramatic fashion whilst the boy froze like a statue.

'You complete fool!' she yelled, and as she looked up from the floor, she caught Tom's eyes for a brief moment, and seemed to indicate with a deliberate widening of her eyes for him to go, to flee the room.

He looked at the two teachers, whose attention was firmly focused on Molly and the scattering of books all around her, and seized his moment. He was out of the room in a flash, not bothering to look behind him, and headed straight for the tennis courts, even though they were at the back of the school and instinct told him it was the wrong direction in which to go. Once he arrived next to a court, he halted and then began pacing anxiously up and down, glancing at the children playing, wary of the teachers close by instructing them. Why was he meeting her here, out in the open? It was madness.

Only a minute or two later, though it had felt like ten, Molly appeared, breathless and red-faced.

'What are you doing?' asked Tom.

'Saving your skin,' she said, and quickly seized his upper arm without slowing her stride and dragged him along with her. 'If you'd gone straight out the main entrance, they'd have seen you,' she continued. 'They won't expect you to come this way.' Tom could only smile at her. 'I'm not just a pretty face, you know,' she grinned.

She took him to a line of trees at the back of the school, and after checking there was no one around, they dipped through a small hole in the fence behind the trees and into a farmer's field. From there, they circled around the school and were soon back on the roads, heading for Michael's house.

'I guess you know who Christopher Sheeran is now,' said Molly, as they walked along in the afternoon sunshine.

'Well, I gathered he's your Prime minister,' smiled Tom. 'In my world he's a very famous singer. Funny really.'

'There's nothing funny about our Prime minister,' replied Molly solemnly. 'The man's a fascist pig.'

Tom laughed. The idea was still too weird to comprehend. 'Well, I guess plenty of people must like him if they voted for him.'

'Voted?' spluttered Molly. 'What do you mean *voted*? No one voted for him. There haven't been elections in this country since well before I was born. We've been living under martial law for years. People get arrested and disappear all the time.'

'Really? I guess that explains a lot. Our worlds are just so different, aren't they?'

For a moment, Molly was lost in thought, before she asked: 'So you can vote in your world?'

'Once you're eighteen, yeah.'

'I wish I could vote. Perhaps I should come and live in your world,' she laughed.

'I'd like that,' muttered Tom. 'But I think we already know that could never happen.'

'You still think I somehow caused that storm, don't you?'

'Yeah,' replied Tom. 'I'm afraid I do.' He had known this conversation was coming, and now it was about to start, he felt dejected. 'Listen, Molly. This is starting to get out of hand, this travelling back and forth between worlds.'

'You can't stop now,' said Molly, her wide eyes betraying her disappointment. A disappointment he had almost wanted to see, but now that he had seen it, it made him feel even more disconsolate.

'Too much is going wrong,' continued Tom. 'There've been too many near misses.'

'It's still early days, Tom,' persisted Molly, full of encouragement. 'You're still just getting used to coming here. Once you get the hang of things in this world you'll fit in fine.'

'It's not just me and Michael getting one another into trouble. It's what happened earlier today, with that storm. We're playing with something we don't understand. It's too dangerous, too much can go wrong. What if one of us causes something terrible to happen?'

Molly suddenly looked dejected herself. 'So, you're not coming back?' she asked quietly.

'I don't know, Molly,' he replied, shaking his head. 'Of course I want to keep coming back, but …'

'You could always stay here,' she said without looking across at Tom. 'You could just miss the appointment with Michael … and not go back.'

The words just hung silently in the air for what felt like an age. After a moment, Molly sniffed nervously, embarrassed that she had uttered such a suggestion. Tom felt uncomfortable and guilty because, for a second or two, he had been tempted, excited by the idea.

Tom finally broke the awkward silence. 'I can't. There's Jake and my other friends. And as bad as my dad is, he is still my dad. I've always hoped he would change one day, and I'll get to know him better. And I guess he's the only one who can tell me what happened to my mum.'

Molly did not reply. Tom was afraid to look at her in case there were tears in her eyes, and yet equally afraid to look in case there were none.

'Besides,' he concluded, 'this isn't my world. I don't belong here. We have no idea what would happen if I stayed.'

'I know,' said Molly at last, her voice strong and business-like. 'I was only joking.'

For a moment, he thought he had detected something in her voice that indicated that she was not joking. Or was it just wishful thinking? Part of him almost wanted her to break down and beg him to stay. But he knew her well enough already to know she would never do that. Besides, even if she had pleaded with him to stay, he knew it was the wrong thing to do.

'I'm sorry,' he said quietly. 'I was hoping we could have become friends. But it's just too dangerous.'

'You must do what you must do,' she replied evenly.

Now he really did think he could tell she was disappointed. 'I'll talk to Michael, but I'm not sure when I'll be able to come through again.'

'Well, in that case,' she said matter-of-factly, and came to a halt. She held out a delicate hand. 'I wish you all the best, Thomas Paget. It's been fun.' She was smiling bravely, yet, although he could tell she was trying to hide an emotion, he could not tell whether it was anger, disappointment or sadness.

He shook her hand, even though he wanted to hug her instead, and smiled wistfully back at her. Now he had a lump in his throat.

'If you do come again,' she continued, 'you know where I am. Look me up.' And after one last smile, she spun on her heels and walked off.

At least there was no time to dwell on the sadness of the

moment, for Tom only had a few minutes left in which to get back to the house.

A short while later, he was standing once more in the void facing Michael.

'You're late,' said Michael curtly. 'You're always late. I was standing with my hand on that stupid mirror for over a minute.'

'Sorry, Michael,' replied Tom, his mind elsewhere. 'How's Rachel?'

'She's fine. But she says it was your fault she fell over.'

'It was an accident.'

'Yeah. That's what I said to her.' Michael's face broke into a grin. 'You know what girls are like.'

It was not the reaction Tom had expected. Michael was unpredictable, and it unnerved him more and more.

'Listen, Michael.' Tom cleared his throat nervously. 'I think we need to stop doing this. For the time being at least,' he added when he saw Michael's growing frown.

'What do you mean? Just when things are starting to get exciting?'

'We still don't really understand any of this, do we?' Tom then recounted what had happened earlier in the day, how the storm had struck from nowhere, how he believed they were somehow responsible.

'You're paranoid,' scoffed Michael. 'What's the matter with you?'

'Maybe I am. But maybe we're just too young for this. Perhaps we should come back when we're older, come back and study it.'

'I'm not interested in studying it,' snapped Michael. But then he fell silent and seemed to be lost in thought for a moment until, to Tom's surprise, he said: 'Maybe you're right. I tell you what: why don't we have tomorrow back in our own worlds and then meet again on Friday. It'll give us time to think things over. We can then discuss it again, and if you still feel the same way, we can sort out what to do in the future.'

Tom had expected more of a fight from Michael, but maybe he, too, was beginning to see the dangers of what they were doing. Perhaps his double was not as despicable as Molly tried to make out. It was going to make his decision whether to leave it all behind that little bit harder to make. And then there was Molly. Could he really leave her behind?

As if reading his thoughts, Michael gave him a knowing look and said: 'We're stuck, you and I. You want to keep seeing Molly, and I want to keep seeing Rachel.'

'I guess you're right,' mumbled Tom.

Moments later, Tom was back in his own world, where it was sunny once again, as if the morning's storm had taken place in an entirely different world, and for a brief moment, Tom hesitated by the mirror. The thought suddenly entered his mind that he should turn around and smash the mirror to pieces and walk away from the house for good. The thought grew and grew, until he was on the verge of acting upon it. But then something stopped him. He just could not quite bring himself to destroy it. He only hoped he would not regret it.

Friday morning soon came around, and the two weeks of wall-to-wall sunshine in Molly's world showed no sign of coming to an end. Indeed, she had watched the forecast over breakfast, and the weatherman had said the heat wave was set to continue for the next few days. At least the weekend was just around the corner, so there would be some respite from

---

sweltering in a wretched school uniform.

Molly was in her bedroom, getting ready for school when she heard the doorbell ring. A few seconds later, her mother called up the stairs to her. 'Molly, it's for you.'

Puzzled, she asked who it was.

'He says he's a friend of yours,' replied her mother. 'He says his name is Tom.'

In her haste to get down the stairs, Molly nearly stumbled. Once at the bottom, she saw Tom standing in the open doorway, with his usual scruffy hair and that perpetual look of concern on his face. He was fidgeting nervously, playing with his still bandaged right hand, stroking his chin and his hair. He then looked anxiously over his shoulder back outside a couple of times before he spotted Molly coming towards him.

'Molly, I need your help,' he whispered in a hushed, urgent tone, as she approached.

Molly smiled in response. 'You always do.' She found it hard to contain the excitement she felt at seeing him again. 'What's up this time?'

Tom glanced anxiously at his watch. 'I don't have time to explain. Please come with me, I need you.' And he beckoned her outside.

Molly pulled the mobile phone from out of her pocket and looked at the time on the display. 'Tom, do you know what time it is? We've got to go to school soon.'

'Exactly. There's no time. Come on, please.'

'Wait. What is this all about?'

Tom looked passed her, back into the house, and then quickly behind himself. 'It's Michael. He … I can't explain here, can I?' he added impatiently.

Molly sighed, beginning to feel a little irritated herself. But

144

Tom was looking at her with those pleading eyes and was obviously very anxious about something. Reluctantly, she shouted to her parents that she was going out for a short while, and after closing the front door, she followed Tom out into the street.

Tom was already running down the road. He turned around and cried out: 'Hurry up, please!'

She started to run after him. 'Where are we going?' she called out, panting.

'There's no time,' he insisted, and waved her on with a hand behind his back.

She struggled to keep up with his pace, but could see the anxiety on his face, and felt herself becoming more and more uneasy in turn. After several lung-bursting minutes, they arrived at Michael's house. He ushered her through the front door and up the stairs, past the room where she knew the mirror was stored and into what she assumed was his bedroom.

Once inside, Tom stopped and turned around to face her as she entered the room. Behind her, the door swung shut, and she caught sight of the strange cheval mirror in the corner of the room next to his bed. Straightaway, she knew something was wrong. She spun round, and there against the wall, where the open door had been hiding him, stood Sean McBean.

Molly flashed around to look at Tom. 'What the ...?' she muttered but didn't know what to ask.

Tom was staring at her with a smirk growing across his face. 'That was almost too easy,' he said quietly, cruelly, and began unravelling the bandage on his right hand. With obvious relish, he held up his palm to show her there was no scarring there at all.

145

Immediately, she felt a sick, tightening knot twist in her stomach. She had been tricked by Michael. She was about to call out when she felt a large hand press against her mouth, and another envelop her shoulders from behind, until she was unable to move or make a sound.

Chapter Ten

Grandpa Sam

As soon as Tom had reappeared in the void, his heart sank and he instantly wished he had destroyed the mirror as he had contemplated doing less than two days earlier. For standing in front of him, a short distance away, were Michael and the thickset figure of Sean McBean.

'Oh, no!' he muttered to himself, then strode forward with purpose. 'Michael, what are you doing?'

'I just thought I'd have a bit of fun,' grinned Michael, 'just in case this is our last time.'

'Don't be a fool,' snapped Tom. 'I told you, it's too dangerous to bring other people.'

'Don't be so dramatic,' replied Michael, his voice and his face full of disdain. 'Anyway, you brought your girlfriend with you last time. It's only fair I bring someone with me this time.'

'You don't know what you're doing, Michael.' Tom glared at his look-alike and noticed how similar they looked, more so than before. Michael had left his hair unkempt, and his shirt and trousers and his unpolished black shoes were identical to Tom's, were not as smart as Tom was used to seeing on Michael. Maybe he was becoming paranoid, but it looked like Michael was trying to impersonate him more closely than ever before.

'I'm sorry,' resumed Tom. 'But I can't let you do this.'

'It'll be fine,' insisted Michael, and grabbed Tom's upper arm. 'You owe me,' he glowered. 'You ran away from detention and got me into more trouble ...'

'I'm sorry. But I had no choice.' Tom shook off Michael's grip with a violent swing of his arm and took a step backwards to avoid being seized again. He could feel the anger rising rapidly inside him. The boy was a fool, just as Molly had said. 'We wouldn't be here now, having this conversation, if I hadn't,' he added, seething.

Michael's face was florid with rage. 'You're missing the point,' he yelled. 'If you hadn't got into trouble in the first place you wouldn't have got detention. I'm lucky I didn't get caned when you ran away. Instead, I've got detention every day for the next week. So you can start by doing tonight's for me.'

Tom was in no mood to concede any ground in this particular argument. 'This is exactly why we should stop all of this. It's getting out of hand. Let's go back to our own worlds now and forget we ever found this stupid mirror.'

Sean, who hitherto had remained unusually quiet, suddenly darted forward and tried to grab Tom, but the latter saw him coming and stepped quickly to one side. Clearly still unsure on his feet on the narrow pathway, Sean remained rooted to the spot and instead turned his outstretched hand into an accusatory, pointed finger. 'You don't seem to understand,' he said. 'We're not giving you a choice. Now get me out of this stupid place ...'

'No, *you* don't understand,' replied Tom, with his own aggressive finger. 'You're going nowhere unless I agree to it. This only works if Michael and I work together.'

Just when the tension between Tom and the other two seemed to be reaching boiling point, seemed to be heading for an inevitable scuffle, Michael's face broke into that malicious grin that Tom was starting to loathe and fear in equal measure.

'Oh, Tom,' he said calmly. 'We've tried to be reasonable. But I thought you might be like this, so I took out an insurance policy, just in case.'

Michael's sudden serenity made Tom feel instantly uncomfortable. 'What do you mean?'

Michael stood to one side and pointed to the rear of his mirror behind him. 'Come and have a look,' he said serenely.

With a growing sense of unease, Tom moved slowly towards the blurred rectangle hanging in the air at the end of the rainbow path. As ever, the window looking into Michael's house was a distorted mass of shapes and shimmering colours. Tom could just about make out furniture in the room and a blob of light in the background from a window.

'Take a good look,' said Michael, and silently tapped the portal to his world.

Tom drew closer and peered into the rectangle. His eyes began to make out more shapes: a bed, a desk. And a figure huddled on the floor. A girl with dark hair and a gag in her mouth, and large, terrified eyes staring at him through small, stylish glasses.

Tom gasped. He turned sharply to Michael. 'What are you doing? Let her go.' And he grabbed Michael by the scruff.

Michael brushed him off. 'Now, now. Calm down. That's no way to get your girlfriend free, is it?'

'Let her go now, before—'

'Before you what?' snarled Michael. 'Like you said earlier: nothing happens unless we work together. If you let me and Sean go into your world, you can free Molly yourself. It's as simple as that.'

Tom looked back at the blurred image of Molly writhing on

the floor. He knew he was helpless, that Michael had out-manoeuvred him. He felt sick.

'If you want,' continued Michael smugly, 'we can wait here all day. We're in no rush. But the sooner we go through, the sooner you can free the lovely Molly. It's up to you.'

'You have no idea what you're doing,' said Tom, struggling to contain his temper.

'Wrong! I know exactly what I'm doing,' retorted Michael.

Tom now had a straight and terrible choice between Jake and Molly. Which one should he help? Yet it had to be Molly. She was in immediate and obvious trouble. But maybe there was a chance he could help both. 'Okay,' he said abruptly. 'But come back at Midday, like we did the other day.'

'Absolutely not,' said Michael, and dismissed the suggestion with a wave of his hand. 'I was thinking more of ten o'clock tonight. That way you can do today's detention for me ...'

'No way,' replied Tom, shaking his head.

Michael prodded him in the chest with a finger. 'You are in no position to tell us what to do. We're coming back at ten o'clock, and that's that. The longer we stay here, the longer poor Molly has to lie on the floor, all tied up. Poor Molly.' He turned towards Sean, and the two boys laughed. He then stepped away from Tom, and walked backwards towards the rear of Tom's mirror, keeping his piercing gaze on Tom as he moved. 'Your move, Tom,' he whispered. 'Your move.'

Tom knew he had been backed into a corner. He felt sick to the pit of his stomach, knowing the only thing he could do now was to help Molly, and to somehow shut from his mind any thought of what might happen to Jake. He returned the unrelenting gaze from Michael and Sean, whose faces scrutinised him with a mix of disdain and self-satisfaction, before turning around and placing his hand on the shimmering image of Michael's bedroom. There was a comment followed by a laugh from Michael, but Tom's focus was elsewhere.

A few seconds later, he was standing in the bedroom looking down at Molly who was bound and gagged on the floor. She stared up at him with eyes full of anger and fear. He quickly crouched down and began untying the gag at the back of her head.

'Oh, Molly,' he said. 'I'm so sorry. This is all my fault.'

As soon as the gag was loose, she spat it away from her mouth with a jolt of her head. 'Who is it this time – Michael or Tom?' she demanded.

'Molly, it's me,' was all Tom could say, and began hurriedly untying the rope around her hands and legs. But Molly continued to eye him suspiciously. 'What happened?' he asked.

The moment the ropes were loose, Molly quickly shook them off as if they were snakes. 'Michael pretended to be you,' she replied, and then stood up. 'He said you needed my help.'

Tom apologised profusely once more, but he could tell she was still not entirely convinced he was who he said he was.

'Anyway, I thought you weren't coming back again,' she added.

'Michael said we should swap one last time, and like a fool I agreed. I'm so sorry. I never knew he planned to do this. He kidnapped you because he knew it was the only way I would let him take Sean with him.' He then turned around and grabbed the heavy wooden frame at the top of the mirror and stared at it, full of exasperation. 'This stupid mirror. I sometimes wish I had never found it.'

'We're going to be late for school,' said Molly, glancing at her watch.

'I'm not going,' replied Tom, still staring at the mirror. In fact, his gaze was so intense he was staring through the mirror, wishing he could somehow see the other side and the mischief Michael and Sean were already plotting in his world.

Molly moved urgently towards him, jolting him from his reverie. 'Tom, you have to,' she said. 'You of all people know what this world is like. If you get caught outside of school, you'll be arrested and punished.'

He looked at her reflection in the mirror and immediately saw her hard, sceptical expression melt away, to be replaced by the wide-eyed, concerned face he knew. She had obviously now accepted that he really was Tom and not Michael.

He turned to face her. 'Molly, Michael has gone into my world with Sean. God knows what they'll get up to. And what if there's another storm because of them.'

Molly rolled her eyes and seemed to mumble: 'Not again!'

'Listen,' continued Tom, undaunted by her scepticism. 'Jake told me that as soon as we came back here last time, the storm stopped almost straightaway.'

'Yes, but storms do that, they come and go. It's not unusual.'

'That storm was. It was in the news. People caught it on their mobile phones. The clouds appeared out of thin air over Porthgarrick, and nowhere else in the country that day. It must have been due to our being there. Now that Michael and Sean have gone through, Jake and everyone else I know is in danger. Maybe the whole of Porthgarrick is in danger. If I get back tonight and find that people have died because of all this,

I'll never be able to forgive myself. I have to try to get back.'

Molly sighed. 'Even if that were true, there is no way through on your own ... is there?'

Tom turned back to face the mirror and ran a finger around the intricate wooden carvings around the frame, wishing there was something as simple as a symbol to decipher, a button to push, that would miraculously transport him back to his world. 'I don't know,' he muttered. 'If only I knew how it worked.'

Molly came over and stood shoulder to shoulder with him, both of them staring at the mirror. 'Where did it come from in the first place?' she asked.

'I have no idea,' he mumbled.

'But how did it come to be in your family,' persisted Molly. 'Somebody must know something.'

'My father won't say ...' He paused with a sudden realisation. A wave of excitement welled up inside him. 'Michael's grandpa must know something,' he said, turning quickly to Molly. 'All this has happened before, I'm sure of it.'

'Has it?' asked Molly.

'Think about it,' persisted Tom excitedly. 'The mirror was in his house. And the Great Storm in this world happened when he was still living there. He must know something. My grandpa disappeared when I was a baby, but Michael's grandfather is still alive.' He moved towards the door. 'I have to find him. Come on. Michael's dad is still at home. We'll ask him where Michael's grandfather is.'

Tom hurried downstairs and into the kitchen, with a bemused Molly trailing in his wake.

'Ah, Michael,' said Michael's father, as soon as Tom entered the kitchen. His grave tone suggested he was not happy. 'You and I need to have a word,' he continued, and then stared angrily at Tom, apparently oblivious to Molly in the background. 'I will not have you talking to your mother like that, do you hear me? I don't care what you think – she is now your mother. And you will treat her with the respect she deserves.' His face had turned red and his fists were clenched.

For a second or two, Tom forgot where he was and flinched in anticipation of his father's striking him once more. But the man was not Tom's father, and nothing more than those stern words came from him. Michael had clearly upset his parents that morning, which would complicate matters, for Tom needed Michael's father on his side.

'Sorry,' he said, in his best contrite voice. 'I'm really sorry. I really am.'

Michael's father opened his mouth, but nothing seemed to come out. He looked across to his wife, but she, too, looked as taken-aback as he was. Both parents were evidently lost for words. Whether his apology was so unlike Michael as to be suspicious did not worry Tom at all. He needed Michael's father's help, and the only way to do that was to apologise unreservedly, and thereby hope to relieve the tension, even if he had no idea what he was apologising for.

'Sorry, Mum,' continued Tom, turning to Michael's stepmother. 'What I said was unforgivable. I didn't mean it, and I'm really sorry for any offence I caused you. I've been under a lot of pressure recently, but that's no excuse.'

For a few uncomfortable seconds, she stared at him with a stony expression before her face suddenly brightened into a smile. 'Apology accepted,' she said.

Tom sighed with relief.

'Who's your friend?' continued Michael's stepmother with

a nod towards Molly. 'And where's Sean?'

'Oh, er, Sean's already gone to school. And this,' said Tom, bringing an uncomfortable Molly forward, 'is my friend Molly.'

Whilst Michael's parents and Molly exchanged brief but polite greetings, Tom sniffed impatiently. He could see Michael's father was getting ready to go to work, and he needed his answers quickly.

'Dad?' he said, stepping forward. 'Where's grandpa living these days? Grandpa Tranter, that is.'

'Grandpa Tranter?' chuckled Michael's father. 'He's in a prison for the mentally deranged.'

'Mathew!' admonished his wife.

'Well, it might not be called that. But that's exactly what it is.'

'Why is he there?' pressed Tom.

'He tried to kidnap you when you were a baby. But he was arrested and thrown in prison. After that, he kept prattling on about parallel dimensions and travelling to other worlds and other insane stuff ...'

Tom's heart leapt in his chest. He shot an excited look across to Molly, who returned the look, open-mouthed.

'After a few years,' resumed Michael's father, 'he was taken out of prison and moved to what they laughingly call a psychiatric home.'

'So, where is he now?' persisted Tom, struggling to contain his excitement.

'Remind me tonight,' replied Michael's father, and put on his smart jacket. 'I'll give you the address and we can pop over for a visit if you're really that interested. But I warn you, he's totally bonkers. He'll tell you all these ridiculous stories about

Morladron House and the Smugglers' Tunnel and heaven knows what …' He picked up a bunch of car keys from a bowl and bent down to pick up a briefcase.

'The Smugglers' Tunnel?' said Mrs Paget. 'I don't remember hearing about that one before.'

'Well, sounds like I've got a few stories to tell you all this evening, then,' laughed Mr Paget.

But for Tom, the evening was no good. There was no time to wait. Jake was in danger. 'No,' he said suddenly. 'I need to know now.'

'I beg your pardon!' Michael's father flashed an angry look at him.

Molly quickly stepped forward. 'What Tom means, Mr Paget,' she began, glaring briefly at Tom, 'is that we need the information for a school project. We should have done it last night, but we forgot. If you could just tell us so we can write it down, then Tom won't get into trouble.'

Tom smiled to himself. He could have kissed her.

Michael's father gave Molly a quizzical look. 'Right, I see,' he said rubbing his chin, and then paused for a moment. 'Who's Tom?'

Tom's heart sank. Molly blushed. 'Oh,' she laughed affectedly. 'I mean Michael. I always call him Tom. I prefer his middle name Tom, you see.'

Michael's father looked completely mystified, but then shrugged his shoulders and said: 'I see. Well, your grandfather is in the Royal Porthgarrick Psychiatric Institute. It's that big house on the outskirts of town, overlooking the river.' He then glanced at his watch. 'Anyway, you two had better get going to school. I don't want another meeting with that psychopathic headmaster of yours.'

After an exchange of smiles all round, Michael's father left through a side door that led into the garage, whilst Tom and Molly hurried back out into the hallway. Tom had no intention of collecting Michael's blazer and school bag this time and headed for the front door instead. As soon as they heard Michael's father drive off, they went out into the street.

Tom looked at his watch. 'Molly, you've got to get to school,' he said, as they walked along.

'Don't be daft,' she said. 'I'm coming with you.'

Tom stopped and grabbed her arm. 'No, Molly. I can't let you get into trouble on my account …'

'Look, Tom. You need my help. How are you going to get to this institute without me to show you where it is? Besides,' she grinned warmly, 'I'll never get to school in time now unless I run. And it's too hot to run.' Tom opened his mouth to protest further, but Molly held up a hand. 'I'm not discussing it any further. I'm coming with you and that's that. I'll worry about tomorrow, tomorrow. Now, come on. We're wasting time.' She started walking again and then fished out her mobile phone from her black trousers. 'I'll phone my parents now and tell them I'm going straight to school. Otherwise, they'll wonder where I am.' Before Tom could speak, she had pressed a button and was speaking into the handset.

Of course, he was glad she was coming along, even if he was worried about the consequences for her. There was, however, no denying the fact: he really did need her help.

As they hurried along the streets of Porthgarrick, trying to keep out of sight as best they could whenever someone wandered past, Molly told him she knew where the institute was, since she and her family had driven past it on numerous occasions. He was content to follow her lead. After all, this was

157

her world now, and she knew all the back roads and shortcuts and the places where police officers were likely to be patrolling. And whenever he expressed his fear that she might get into trouble, she quickly dismissed his concerns, saying she had never been in trouble before, and would invent some story to convince her parents to help her.

Finally, after nearly an hour's walking, they arrived at a bright and colourful sign that read *Royal Porthgarrick Psychiatric Institute.* They peered through the gate and saw a large mansion house with a tarmac driveway and a front garden so over-grown with oak trees that the house was almost completely in shadow, even on such a sunny day.

Tom wrapped his hands around two bars in the wrought-iron gates. He had only removed the bandage on his right hand that morning and the cold metal pressed uncomfortably against his scar. 'Great,' he said. 'How do we get in now?'

To his astonishment, Molly walked up to the intercom and pushed the button. 'You've just got to be confident,' she said matter-of-factly. When a gruff voice answered, she said: 'We've got an appointment with Mr Tranter.' And then a side gate whirred open to let them through. 'See. Simple.' And she smiled.

They walked up the driveway and into the main entrance. Behind a polished mahogany desk sat a large, middle-aged woman, wearing a permanently morose expression.

'Good morning,' said Tom, as confidently as he could, even though his heart was pounding faster by the second. 'We've come to see Mr Tranter.'

'Do you have an appointment?' demanded the woman, without looking up from her computer screen.

'No, but I'm his grandson.'

'You can't see anyone without an appointment,' continued the woman.

'Okay,' said Tom, trying to keep his composure. 'Can I make an appointment for today?'

'You need to phone.'

Tom sighed impatiently and had to grit his teeth to stop himself from losing his temper.

Molly stepped forward and tugged his shirt. 'It's okay, Tom,' she smiled. 'We'll come back another day.'

'No, it's not okay–'

'Yes, it is,' interrupted Molly, and gave the woman a broad smile when she looked up at them. 'Come on, Tom. We need to go now.' And she pulled him away from the reception desk.

'What are you playing at?' asked Tom, as they headed outside once more.

'There was no way she was going to let you see him,' she insisted. 'If we'd got nasty, she would have called security. Remember what it's like in this world.' She pulled him around the side of the house. 'Besides, I saw through a window that all the inmates are outside on the terrace at the back of the house. Do you know what your grandpa looks like?'

'Well, I've seen photos. But they were taken years ago. My grandpa disappeared when I was a baby.'

'Well,' said Molly brightly. 'We'll just have to make it up, won't we?'

At the back of the house was a long terrace, which overlooked an extensive garden with a well-manicured lawn and immaculately tended trees and shrubs. Dozens of elderly people were dotted around both the terrace and the lawn, some talking in small groups over a cup of morning coffee, others wandering around the grounds or reclining in chairs on

John D. Fennell

their own. Amongst them moved half a dozen white-uniformed nurses, buzzing from one individual to the next, like bees collecting pollen from a garden full of flowers.

Carefully watching the nurses, Molly bent over to ask the first man they came across, who was sitting on his own reading a newspaper. But they got nothing but gibberish from the man who was clearly mad. They moved on to a woman nearby who pointed at a man in the distance, who was meandering around the garden on his own in a long coat, which must have been stifling in the heat of the mid-morning sun. His head was hunched forward over his chest, and his hands were clasped together behind his back, making it apparent he was deep in thought. As they drew near, Tom began to think the man did look familiar.

'Excuse me,' said Tom quietly. 'Sorry, but are you Mr Tranter?'

Slowly, the man looked up and studied Tom with a distant, tortured look in his eyes. Immediately, Tom could tell he had found his man. With thin, greying hair he must have been in his sixties, but looked younger and fitter than Tom had expected.

'Sam,' mumbled the man. 'Call me Sam.'

'Well, actually,' said Tom nervously. 'I probably shouldn't call you Sam because–'

'Tom?' said the man suddenly, when he scrutinised Tom's face more closely. 'Is that you, Tom? What are you doing here?'

Tom was flabbergasted. 'What?' He glanced around at Molly, before adding: 'I ... you mean, Michael, don't you?'

'You're not Michael,' scoffed the man gruffly. 'Michael's not here. He's in the other world.' And abruptly he changed direction and walked off, leaving Tom and Molly to stare at one another, motionless and dumbstruck.

Chapter Eleven

Revelations

Tom and Molly exchanged a look of sheer astonishment. 'Grandpa, wait!' said Tom, trotting after the man. 'What do you mean? Why am I not Michael?'

Sam stopped and looked Tom up and down suspiciously. 'You don't belong here,' he said finally with a sniff. 'You have to go back to your world.'

'But how do you know I'm not in the right world?'

'Questions, questions. You're just like your father. He never did believe me when I told him.'

'Told him what, Mr Tranter?' asked Molly.

Sam studied her with his dark eyes, eyes so active and alive they seemed to move faster than his aging mind could think. His face creased into a brief smile. 'Your girlfriend, is she?' he asked. 'Very pretty.'

'Well …'

Sam looked back and forth at the pair of them and then chuckled at their embarrassment. 'Of course, she should be Michael's girlfriend really. You shouldn't be here at all.' And with that, he turned and strode off once more, the bottom of his long coat trailing behind him.

Bursting with questions, Tom and Molly darted after him once again. A nurse in a white uniform glided into Tom's eyeline, but to his relief she stopped and bent over an old man reclining in a chair and paid the young visitors no attention.

'Grandpa, I'm not who you think I am,' began Tom again, ignoring Sam's confusion between him and Michael. 'I found the mirror. The mirror in *Morladron House,* and came here from another world.' For the first time, he did not expect to be ridiculed for coming out with such a statement.

Sam stopped and gave Tom a cold stare. 'I see. Humouring me now, are we?' he replied, and a displeased frown grew across his forehead. 'How's your mother these days?'

Tom gritted his teeth, swallowed hard. 'My mother is dead.' Just uttering the sentence choked him up.

'Your mother's not dead,' snorted Sam. 'Michael's mother is dead, not yours.'

Tom gasped. Michael's grandpa knew, knew that one mother was dead and another alive, even if he had mixed up the names. Instantly, he sensed he was about to find out what had happened all those years ago, and the thought filled him with both terror and excitement.

'Grandpa,' said Tom, and touched Sam on the arm, arresting his attention.

The man looked down contemptuously at the spot on his coat where Tom had touched him and then gave him a piercing glare.

Undeterred, Tom went on: 'Tell me what happened. I need to know. What happened when I was a baby?'

'Who sent you? I suppose it was more stupid quacks, was it? They just want to hear my stories and then laugh at me again. Is that why you're here: just to have a good laugh at a sad old man?'

'I promise you – no one sent us,' insisted Tom, deciding to change tack. 'Look, I know I'm in the wrong world. But I want to get back to my own world, but I don't understand what happened or how I can do that.'

Sam's piercing eyes bored into Tom's, as if trying to read

his mind.

'Please, Mr Tranter, help us,' urged Molly in the background.

'The moment you laugh, the moment I detect so much as a smirk,' said Sam with a threatening finger, 'I'll stop.'

Tom was so full of raging, conflicting emotions he could not even smile, let alone laugh.

'Come with me,' said Sam at last, and beckoned them to follow him to a spot at the edge of the lawn, until they were well and truly out of earshot of everyone else in the garden, although Tom suspected that all the other patients had probably heard his story many times already.

'There's a mirror in my house,' he began quietly, looking warily over their shoulders, and then casting a glance behind him into the bushes and shrubs, as if suspecting that someone may have been lurking there, eavesdropping on the group. 'Well, it used to be my house until they took it away from me. And then Tom's wretched father moved the mirror out of the house as well. The mirror belongs in the house, do you hear me?' he said, and dug a finger into Tom's chest. 'Anyway, the mirror used to be in my old house.'

'You mean *Morladron House*, Mr Tranter?' asked Molly.

'Of course I mean *Morladron House*. What other houses did I used to own?' A brief flash of anger spread across his face, before disappearing behind his disturbed but enthusiastic face. 'That house has belonged in our family for generations, for hundreds of years, as far back as anyone can remember. I inherited it from my father and lived there with my dear wife for many happy years. My wife was German, you know–'

'So where did the mirror come from?' asked Tom impatiently.

'Ah, the mirror,' replied Sam with a glint in his eye, as if the mirror had not even been mentioned hitherto. 'It's been in the family almost as long as the house. There are so many legends and stories about that mirror. Some say it was a gift from a strange supernatural traveller. Others say it was brought back by pirates in the sixteenth century, who had found it in a mystical land in Central America. No one knows for sure. But one thing we do know,' he continued, drawing his two listeners in closer with barely-contained glee in his face, 'is that the mirror allows you to travel to another world …' Eyes and mouth wide, he paused for dramatic effect, clearly expecting his listeners to be shocked and amazed at the revelation.

'We know,' said Tom quickly and in a near-whisper, such was his excitement. 'We've been through the mirror.'

Sam drew back with immediate indignation. 'Impossible!' he roared, causing Tom to hurriedly look behind him in case someone had heard the bellowing voice. 'You need the key.'

'What key?' asked Molly in a hushed voice.

'Do you want me to tell this story or not?' hissed Sam.

'Sorry, Grandpa,' said Tom, appeasing the man with a hand on his arm. 'Please go on. We won't interrupt anymore,' he added, glancing at Molly beside him.

Sam narrowed his eyes and studied the two of them suspiciously. 'Very well,' he said quietly. 'Where was I? Oh, yes, the mirror. Members from your family and from my family have been travelling through the mirror for hundreds of years…'

Tom opened his mouth to ask a question, but when Sam glared at him, he thought better of it.

'Our two worlds are identical in many ways, yet at the same time totally different in so many others. Geographically speaking, they are the exact mirror image of one another; even historically the two worlds have followed uncannily similar paths. It is the people who are different,' he added, wagging an over-dramatic finger. 'If someone is an angel in one world, they are a devil in the other. But of course, most of us are neither angels nor devils, we are somewhere in between. So it follows that the opposite of most average people, is another average person. And so it was that when our two families began to travel between the two worlds, they found a balance, a way to co-exist in harmony.'

Tom could immediately tell that Sam had told his story countless times before. The words sounded so rehearsed, like the lines from a book, read by an accomplished Shakespearian actor. Scarcely daring to move, Tom and Molly hung on his every word.

'According to the stories told by our families, the first travellers who went back and forth did so for fun, but then, increasingly, to make money. Selfish men, on both sides, sought to exploit the miracle of the mirror to increase nothing more than their own wealth.

'Then around two hundred years ago, a man came from your world into this, a man so evil and full of greed that he nearly started a war. Fortunately, he was stopped in time; but members of our two families were so shaken by what had happened that they met and resolved to never again allow the mirror to be used for personal gain.

'From that moment on, family members were educated and trained for years, and only those who were deemed stable enough were allowed to travel through the mirror. If anyone failed the rigorous testing, they were never even told about the mirror.

'In this way, our families began to use the mirror for purely altruistic purposes. They exchanged information on science, politics, philosophy – anything that could improve either of our two worlds. But if ever a truly great man or woman came into the family, full of unselfish ideas and enthusiasm, we immediately alerted the opposite family, in case their alter ego turned out to be a devil. And in this way, for two hundred years, it all worked well.'

Sam lowered his gaze, and a shadow seemed to creep across his features, obscuring the sparkling excitement that had only moments earlier lit up his face.

'Then it was my turn,' he continued, but now in a sombre tone. 'And the turn of your grandfather, Bill, my equivalent in the other world. In the beginning, if anything, it was I who was the devil, the one who needed the education, and Bill who was the angel. But eventually, I grew up to be, in my father's eyes at least, an upright member of society. So he showed me the secrets of the mirror, and I was introduced to Bill, and we got on like a house on fire. We took over the mantel from our respective fathers and began travelling all the time, exchanging knowledge and revelling in the idea that we were helping to improve humanity in our respective worlds.

'But as time went on, this world,' continued Sam, and spread his arms wide to emphasis his point, 'began to improve at a greater rate than Bill's, where wars and political corruption began to spread out of control. Bill became restless. He wanted to bring his family into my world for their safety. But that, as our two families have known for hundreds of years, is not possible. You see, the mirror holds a terrible and deadly secret. It is not a mystical secret as such, but some strange law of physics, which meant that Bill and I could not coexist in the same world for long, because we are effectively the same person. And the same person cannot exist twice in one world. The natural balance is upset, a storm is unleashed and the world, or nature, or whatever it is, tries to spit out one of the two people, like an angry beast with indigestion.'

It was exactly what Tom had feared had happened when Molly's trip to his world had ended in that terrible storm. He could not contain himself, since he now knew for sure that Jake was in danger. 'Which one does the world try to spit out?' he asked urgently.

'Ah,' said Sam gravely. 'As I said, there is no mystical force behind this. God is not controlling it. It is only physics, or so we surmise. The world does not know which person does not belong, so both people are attacked simultaneously and with equal ferocity, until one is killed, it matters not which, and the status quo is thus restored.'

'But how long do you have, before the attacks begin?' continued Tom, once again glancing across at Molly, who stood, mouth wide open in amazement.

'Bill and I tried to study the phenomenon,' resumed Sam, stroking his chin. 'But we found there was no pattern. Sometimes, we could stay in the same world for only a couple of hours before the storms came, other times ten or twelve hours. It is as unpredictable as the weather itself. There was simply no way to predict how long we had each time. We just had to keep a close eye on the skies and make sure we never strayed too far from the mirror.'

'So what happened, Mr Tranter?' asked Molly. 'Between you and Bill, I mean.'

'Well, Bill became increasingly disillusioned with his own world. When his grandson was born – you,' said Sam, and prodded Tom with a reproaching finger, 'he became a desperate man. One day, he brought his daughter, your mother, and you into this world with him and demanded that I in turn go and fetch my daughter and grandchild. He insisted, at gunpoint, that all three of us should swap places and go to live in his world. I tried to reason with him, but before long this town was enveloped in the most terrible storm this world has ever known. The Great Storm they called it. But there was nothing great about it. A bolt of lightning killed Bill in the grounds of *Morladron House*. It so easily could have been me, but fate chose him instead. But before I could stop her, your mother and you were in my car and drove off. I tried to follow you, but the weather was so terrible that I lost sight of the car. So I went to my own daughter's house and took her and my grandson with me. I wanted to take them to safety, to the other world, until such time as I could find you and your mother and restore things to the way they should have been.'

Tears were pouring down Sam's face, and his voice was faltering with emotion. Tom wiped his own face and found a flood of tears there, too. For he knew what was coming, had suddenly realised who he was, even if Sam had yet to accept whom he was talking to.

'But,' continued Sam, by now staring into space, into a point distant in his memory, yet clearly so painful even after fourteen years, 'my daughter was killed before I could take her to safety.' He put his head in his hands and wept for a moment, before regaining a degree of composure. 'I grabbed Michael and took him through the mirror to your world and left him with your father, who knows nothing of the mirror. I then came back here to try to sort everything out ...'

'Oh, my goodness!' exclaimed Molly, as she too had

realised what the old man was saying. 'Tom … you were born in this world.'

'I was born here,' repeated Tom. The words stuck in his constricted throat. He stared at Molly, shaking.

'Impossible,' snapped Sam, regaining his earlier anger in a flash. 'I've told you before – that is impossible.'

Tom grabbed his grandfather by the shoulder and peered into the man's eyes. 'Grandpa, it's me,' he insisted. 'Two weeks ago, the boy in this world and I accidentally discovered the mirror, and we've been swapping places ever since.' Tom could see the angry scepticism in the man's face, so he pressed on as fast as he could. 'The boy you call Tom is in the other world at this moment. This is my world.'

'Michael?' said Sam, suddenly softening his hard exterior. 'Is that really you?'

'Well, all this time, I thought my name was Tom, but yes, it's me, your real grandson.'

The scepticism dropped from Sam's face and suddenly, he enveloped Tom in an immense bear hug. Tom was not sure whether to laugh or cry. This revelation was too overwhelming to comprehend in such a short space of time. The realisation that he was not who he thought he was, felt like a blow to the solar plexus. He could barely breathe, felt light-headed. The man whom he believed to be his father was not his father after all but Michael's. And at last, he knew what had happened to his mother, his real mother.

'I thought I would never see you again,' said Sam, releasing his grip and wiping away the tears, tears no longer of sorrow but of joy. 'When Bill's daughter and grandson turned up some days later, I tried to take the child back to his world and bring you back here, but I was stopped before I could swap you back. You see, your father knows nothing of the mirror. I tried to explain everything to him, but he refused to believe me, said I had lost my mind. He had me arrested for kidnapping the child, and I was sent to prison. Your father eventually sold my house and most of its contents, but because your mother had always loved the mirror, he took it back to your house with him, unaware of what it can do.'

'What happened to the boy's mother?' asked Molly, her own face full of tears.

'She pretended to be my daughter and started living with your father,' he said, looking back at Tom. 'But your mother was such an angel, which meant this impostor was the opposite. Your father couldn't understand why the woman he had married, the woman he loved, had suddenly changed overnight. They tried to make it work, but soon found they were totally incompatible. After a few months, they separated and filed for divorce. Your father got custody of the child because by now the woman was so unstable. She left the country and went to live in France, I believe.'

'How did my mum die?' asked Tom.

Sam's face was instantly sad once more. 'We were chased by a tornado. I never saw it take my darling Katie, but it must have swallowed her.'

Tom's head sank. At least he knew now, and that was something, something he had always wanted to know. Molly put a comforting hand on his shoulder.

Finally, he looked up, knowing there were still other important questions to ask. 'Grandpa,' he said, his voice still quavering. 'How did you manage to travel between the two worlds?'

'I used the key of course,' he replied. 'There is a medallion, a small mirror attached to a chain. The traveller wears it around the neck and faces the main mirror. With one hand, you touch the reflection of the small mirror in the large mirror, and you are then transported through to the other side.'

'But something that important you'd have to keep in a safe place, wouldn't you?' asked Molly, clearly trying to prise the information from Sam without arousing his suspicions.

'Indeed it is. I kept it in my safe under the floorboards, where I'm sure it is still well and truly hidden to this day,' said Sam. But then a look of puzzlement crossed over his face, a look that swiftly morphed into a suspicious frown. 'But you must know this already. How else could you have travelled through the mirror?'

'There is another way,' replied Tom. 'You just have to–'

'You're lying!' boomed Sam suddenly. 'You've deceived me, haven't you?' Tom's protests were drowned out by Sam's angry voice. 'I see what you're up to. You're not really Michael at all. You just wanted to learn where the key is kept, so you can use if for yourselves.'

'No, Grandpa. Honestly. We–'

'Enough of your lies. Do you take me for a fool?'

'Is everything all right, Mr Tranter?' asked a nurse, who had crept up behind Tom and Molly without their realising.

'Yes, I'm fine,' said Sam sternly. 'My two young visitors were just leaving.'

Before Tom could say another word, Sam had turned his back on them and was striding off towards the house.

'Come on, you two,' said the nurse, putting a gentle hand on one of each of their shoulders. 'It's time to go. Mr Tranter needs his rest. Who are you by the way?'

Tom wiped away another tear, before replying: 'I'm his

grandson.'

'I'm bored,' said Sean, and shook the chain-link fence, through which he had hooked his fingers.

Michael simply sniffed and continued staring through the fence at the playground beyond. Groups of schoolchildren, bathed in sunshine, were milling about chatting or playing games. In the distance, Michael could just about make out Rachel standing with her friends and talking in her habitually sassy manner. He had already been over to see her, but he had done such a good job of looking like Tom that she had dismissed him from her presence with a flea in his ear. He could have stayed to convince her otherwise, but he was starting to lose interest in her. After all, he was probably never going to see her again, so what was the point?

So what was he going to do now? The original plan had been to get hold of Jake McBean before he made it to school, tie him up and then let Sean impersonate him for the day. But Jake had managed to get to school before they found him, no doubt tipped off by Tom, who must have told him he, Tom, would not be there that day. So now they were stuck. Sean could not go into the school without raising too many questions, because two Jake McBeans would have been hard to explain away. His plans were scuppered. What could they do now?

But then it dawned on him. Of course, it was obvious. He turned to face Sean. 'Do you know what the word "impunity" means?' he asked, with a growing smirk.

'Of course I do,' replied Sean.

'But do you know what it means for us?'

'What are you talking about?'

John D. Fennell

'Sean, we can do absolutely anything today. Anything at all – with impunity. This world is nowhere near as strict as ours. There aren't police and soldiers on every street corner. We can steal and vandalise, and as long as we don't get caught before we get back tonight, Tom will take the blame and we escape punishment without a problem.'

'Sounds great. What are we going to do then?' asked Sean.

'Oh, come on!' exclaimed Michael. 'Where's your imagination? I said we can do anything, anything at all. And more importantly, we can get away with it.'

'You mean like, burn down the school?' suggested Sean, his face breaking into a grin.

'Now you're talking,' replied Michael. 'I like that. I like that a lot. We can set fire to this stupid school, and Tom gets the blame. I think that should make me and him about even, don't you think?'

'Well, if we're going to do that,' said Sean, looking up at the sky, 'we should start soon, before those clouds bring any rain.'

Michael followed his friend's gaze upwards into the sky and saw a dark cloud forming overhead. As they watched, it grew rapidly, like a large blob of ink spreading on a sheet of paper.

174

Chapter Twelve

The Medallion

'So, do I call you Tom or Michael now?' asked Molly with a hesitant smile.

Tom simply chuckled meekly. It was all too much to take in; he didn't know what to think. However, for the moment, only one thing mattered. 'Jake's in danger,' he said at length. 'We have to get back to my world.'

Even if, strictly speaking, it was no longer his world, it was the place where he had grown up, where his friends lived. And his friends were in danger.

The remainder of their hurried walk back to *Morladron House* was spent discussing where they might find the medallion. In the end, Tom was convinced it must have been kept in the same room as the mirror had been. As long as the house was identical to the one in his world, he was sure they would find it.

As they approached the house, he felt the heat of the midday sun on his face, and yet he shivered when he thought about what might have been happening at that precise moment back home. What if the storm had already arrived? What if Jake was already …? It was no way to think. He had to remain positive. Sam had said that sometimes there were ten or twelve hours before the storm hit. Indeed, when Molly had come through to his world a few days earlier, it had been a long time before anything had happened.

He clung to that hope, as they rushed around to the back of the house and clambered through a similar hole to the one he knew in his world, and entered a musty and dark room.

Inside, it was just like the *Morladron House* that by now Tom knew so well: all the windows were boarded up, such that only occasional shafts of dust-filled light filtered into the interior. Downstairs, most of the furniture had long since been removed, but when they raced up the creaking wooden staircase and checked the rooms upstairs, the occasional relic of a bygone age remained silently in place: here a large wardrobe or dresser, there an old wooden bed or a table – dark, lifeless shapes, long forgotten and gathering dust. Threadbare or moth-eaten rugs still covered most of the wooden floors, and Tom was sure that one of them was concealing the safe he so desperately sought.

At last, he found the room he thought corresponded to the one that contained the mirror in his world. Full of excitement and trepidation in equal measure, he cast aside a rickety old chair and heaved the rug away into a corner. The resulting pall of dust made them both cough. But the floorboards beneath were bare, solid planks of wood, as long as the room itself. No sign of a hidden section, no sign of a safe.

They tried another room with no luck. Then another and still nothing.

'It has to be here,' said Tom in frustration.

Molly paused. 'Wait!' she said. 'This house is the mirror image of your one, isn't it?' Tom agreed, slightly confused. 'Then we should be looking at the other end of the landing.'

Before Molly could utter another word, Tom tore out of the room and along the landing. Of course, he thought, it was a simple mistake to make in the dark. He burst into a room that he calculated to be the one, and sure enough above him was the same small hole in the roof, letting in a shaft of sunlight, dazzling like a golden pillar in the middle of the room. He and Molly pulled up the large rug, and there it was, in the floor, a short section of floorboard, close to the patch of sunlight. Tom sank to his knees and pulled up the piece of wood to reveal the metal fascia of a safe. He brushed away a thin layer of dust and saw the small digital display screen above a keypad with numbers and letters arranged as on a push-button telephone, only back-to-front.

'The combination!' gasped Tom. 'We don't know what the combination is.' His heart sank.

Molly knelt beside him. 'Try Paget or Tranter.'

Tom punched in the numbers that corresponded to the letters of the two names. The word *error* appeared after both attempts. 'Oh, no!' he said. 'I don't believe this.'

Molly sighed heavily. 'Okay,' she said, trying to sound calm. 'Let's think about this.'

She paused in thought, whilst Tom tried Thomas and then Michael, again to no avail.

'My darling Katie,' she said suddenly.

'I beg your pardon?'

'Your mother's name. Your grandfather clearly adored his daughter. Try Katie.'

Tom hurriedly typed in the name. *Error.*

Then he looked more closely at the screen. 'Wait,' he said. 'I think it has to be a six-digit number.'

'Okay,' said Molly slowly but thinking quickly. 'Katie … Kate … Kathy … Ah, try Kathie with a c and a k.'

A brief moment of anticipation was followed by the sinking feeling of disappointment when the same error message reappeared. Tom said nothing but gave Molly a look of dejection.

She stared blankly back at him, her mind still buzzing. 'Ooh, ooh,' she said at last, with such excitement it made Tom smile. She was clearly enjoying the challenge. 'Your grandpa said his wife was German – try Katrin.'

Tom typed it in. And then there was a whirring, and the front of the safe began to lift at one side.

'Yes!' said Molly, and clapped her hands together with glee.

Tom reached inside, rummaged around the shoebox-sized safe, fished out several envelopes and sheets of paper, which he cast aside on the dusty floor. But then, right at the bottom of the safe, he saw an object wrapped in an old piece of cloth. Slowly, he took it out, filling with excitement, knowing this was it, he had at last found the key his grandfather had mentioned. Holding it in one hand, he peeled back the corners of the cloth with the other hand to reveal the object, while Molly edged ever closer. At once, a thick metal chain cascaded out of the cloth until one end spilt onto the floor, revealing the face of a small mirror. The circular medallion was a little bigger than Tom's palm and just as thick as his hand. Framing it was a chunky wooden border with tiny, intricate carvings of the same weird faces and geometric shapes that adorned the two full-sized mirrors. It was immediately apparent that the medallion belonged to the mirrors, had been made by the same people, centuries earlier. In the centre was a small round mirror that reflected the image of Tom's face, full of wide-eyed wonder.

After only a couple of seconds, Tom carefully curled up the chain onto the face of the mirror and wrapped the object back inside the cloth. 'Right,' he said. 'Let's get back.'

With a spring in their steps, they rushed back outside into the hot sunshine and hurried back to Michael's house as fast as they could. Desperately hoping there would be no one at home, Tom opened and then closed the front door as quietly as he could. As he crept up the stairs with Molly behind him, they heard the smash of breaking glass coming from the rear of the house.

Molly froze to the spot. 'What was that?' she asked.

'No idea,' said Tom, barely slowing down. 'We don't have time to check. Come on.'

He darted into Michael's bedroom and walked up to the mirror, his heart pounding with expectation and fear. He saw Molly's reflection move up behind him. 'Right,' he said, unwrapping the medallion. 'Let's see how this works.' He then paused and turned round to face Molly. 'Molly, I should go alone–'

'No way!' she replied, with a look of horror.

'It's too dangerous ...'

Molly opened her mouth and was about to argue further when there was a crash and a bang from the room next door. Heavy, muffled footfalls could be heard moving about. Tom and Molly looked at one another with disquiet.

'What was that?' whispered Molly. Tom shook his head, straining his ears. 'Someone's in the house.'

'It's probably Michael's stepmother,' said Tom, and turned back to face the mirror. Carefully, he unravelled the chain and hung it around his neck. 'Stay here. I'll try not to be too long.'

'Tom!' protested Molly.

But before another word was uttered, there was a violent bang on the bedroom door. Tom and Molly jumped out of their skins and spun round just in time to see the door fly open. In walked Sam, brandishing a piece of metal tubing in both hands as if it were a samurai sword. His demented face was set with a crazed mix of anger and determination. With bared teeth and a growl, he rushed towards Tom, his weapon rising higher and higher above his head as he moved.

'Grandpa, what are you doing?' yelled Tom, as he instinctively raised his arms in front of his face.

But the only answer Sam gave was to swing the pipe down with all his might. Tom and Molly were split apart as they dived onto the carpet in opposite directions, just as the metal tubing crashed into the mirror above them with a sickening screech of metal on glass. In an instant, Tom forgot the danger to himself, jerked his head round, fearing the mirror had been damaged. But before he could sigh his relief at seeing it still intact, his grandfather swung down hard onto the mirror once more with a grunt.

The moment Tom realised that Sam had been trying to strike the mirror and not him, he scrambled to his knees and held up an arm as his grandfather raised the metal pipe once again. 'No, Grandpa!' he cried. 'I have to get back.'

Sam's eyes were wide and crazed. 'No!' he bellowed. 'This mirror has to be destroyed.' And he struck it hard anew.

As he reached over his head in preparation for another blow, Molly grabbed the pipe from behind, while Tom rose to his feet and tried to grab his arms.

'Wait, Grandpa,' pleaded Tom. 'My friends are in danger. I have to get back.'

'No, no, no!' replied Sam, and with a violent swing he shook loose Molly's grip. He then shoved Tom in the chest and sent him reeling backwards onto the bed. 'This thing has caused too much pain and suffering. I will not allow it to be used again,' he added, and struck the mirror once more.

Tom winced, expecting the mirror to shatter into a

thousand irreparable pieces at any moment, and with it would disappear the only way to save Jake and his Porthgarrick.

'No!' shouted Tom and Molly in unison, as the pipe thumped against the wooden frame. But Sam could not hear them in his frenzied state.

Tom leapt forwards to try to thwart the man's next attack, but Sam was too quick and too strong for him. This time, however, the pipe struck the mirror with such force that it rebounded back and hit Sam on his own forehead. For a moment, he froze, then his eyes rolled in their sockets before he suddenly collapsed in a heap on the bedroom floor.

Molly rushed forward to check the supine figure. 'He's out cold,' she said.

But Tom had already turned away and was examining the mirror. Aside from a few dents in the wooden frame, which could possibly have been there already, there was no obvious damage, much to his relief. He then spun round to check on his grandfather.

'He's all right,' said Molly. 'But we can't leave him here.'

'Come on,' replied Tom, and grabbed the man's arms. 'We'll take him downstairs. Michael's mum will be home soon. She can deal with him.'

And so they dragged him awkwardly onto the landing and then down the stairs and left him slumped in an armchair in the lounge, looking as though he were simply having an afternoon nap.

'What happens if he wakes up,' said Molly, looking down at the unconscious figure, 'and attacks the mirror again?'

'That's why you have to stay here–'

'Oh, no way,' protested Molly vehemently. 'We've discussed this already. And I'm coming with you, whether you like it or not.'

'But–'

'Well,' said Molly, folding her arms and glaring at Tom through her small glasses. 'We can stand here and waste time arguing, or we can go and save Jake.' The look she gave him defied him to contradict her.

'Okay,' he said, shrugging his shoulders. 'Let's go.'

They bounded back up the stairs and re-entered the bedroom. Tom slipped the medallion over his neck and stood looking at his reflection in the mirror.

'Right, you ready?' he asked Molly, who stood behind him and then placed a hand on his shoulder. As soon as she nodded, he reached out a hand and touched the reflection of the small mirror dangling in front of his chest.

Instantly, the maggot-like sparks appeared and danced up his outstretched hand. For several seconds, he felt light-headed.

And then there they were, standing in the dark room in *Morladron House*, having somehow by-passed the void altogether. Tom blinked and flashed a look upwards at the sky through the small hole in the roof. When he saw clear blue sky, he let out an audible sigh of relief. His greatest fear had been that they would arrive in the middle of an almighty thunderstorm.

Molly followed his upward gaze. 'I think we're okay,' she said.

'Let's hope so. Come on,' he replied and headed for the doorway. A horrible thought entered his head: what if they were too late and the storm had been and gone already? His mind was a blur. He removed the heavy medallion from around his neck, stuffed it into a trouser pocket and forced himself to focus on the present.

They rushed outside and into the lane that led back down into the town.

Tom stopped dead in his tracks, felt his throat go dry and his heart rate increase tenfold. Before them, hanging over the town below, was a massive cloud, swelling and growing blacker with every terrifying moment they watched it. It hung low and menacing, like an upside-down island rising out of the sea of blue sky around it. Directly above them, the sun still shone bright and strong, but only a long stone's throw in front of them the ground was in shadow, a huge expanding shadow that was spreading inexorably across more and more of the town.

No words were needed. They simply ran down the lane, driven by the adrenaline that coursed through their veins, and unable to avert their gaze from the mass of cloud above. Already, they could feel the wind picking up as they descended into the valley, and an onrush of thoughts flooded into Tom's mind, terrible thoughts of lightning bolts and tornadoes and the devastation inflicted upon the other Porthgarrick not so many years previously.

Even though his lungs were bursting, Tom found the stamina from somewhere to keep running, running into the town and across the bridge and on towards the school. Behind him, he could tell Molly was struggling to keep up, but at least in his world there was no imminent danger of arrest as there had been in Molly's earlier, so he could afford to let her slip behind and know she would be safe.

When they were still several minutes away from the school, Tom skidded to a halt. In front of him, above a line of trees, he could see a pall of smoke rising upwards and merging with the black cloud. Even in the gathering gloom, he could see it was coming from the area where his school was. A streetlamp popped on nearby, and he felt a drop of rain strike his reddened face. And so on he ran.

When at last, he reached the perimeter fence that ran around the school, he saw pupils streaming out of the front gate, clustered in small groups, exchanging excitable, agitated conversations. He stopped and peered through the fence at the playground beyond, where it seemed that half of the school was still amassed in large groups. Teachers were hurriedly taking registers and then, once completed, dismissing their charges out of the school. To the right of the playground, a bright red fire engine was parked next to two large, smouldering rubbish bins that had been placed next to the science block. The wall above the bins was now smeared with a large expanse of soot.

Still gasping for breath, Tom stopped a small knot of boys who were coming towards him, grins on their faces, arms waving as they shared a joke. 'What is going on?' he wheezed.

When the boys saw who it was, they stopped instantly and stared open-mouthed, saying nothing for a second or two, allowing Tom to catch his breath still further.

Eventually, one of them spoke. 'Someone started a fire next to the science block … they said it was you.'

Tom cursed under his breath as he heard footsteps behind him.

'Nice glasses, Rachel,' added the boy with a smirk, and then the group wandered off, faces screwed with puzzled smiles.

Tom turned around and saw Molly bending over, gasping for air. He placed an encouraging hand on her back.

'What are we going to do now?' she said between gasps.

'If we can't find Michael and Sean,' he began, 'we'll just take Jake back to your world till we figure out what to do.'

So they pressed forward through the sea of pupils pouring out of the gates, ignoring the funny looks and muttered comments, and scanning each face in the hope of seeing Jake. As they finally reached the playground, the few lights still on in the school were glowing bright in the murk, and more and more spots of rain could be felt in the wind.

Even though Tom had been anticipating it for several minutes, the first explosion of lightning and thunder made him start with a heart-stopping shiver. Instinctively, his eyes were drawn upwards to the swirling mass of black cloud above, which writhed like a living entity, so close that Tom felt that if he climbed onto the roof of the main school building, he could have reached up and touched it.

'Tom!' cried a boy's voice. 'What the hell are you doing here?'

Tom turned to his right and saw Jake rushing towards him, his face a picture of surprise. 'Jake,' he said, and his heart leapt for joy. 'It's good to see you. We have to get you out of here,' he then added with urgency.

'What are you talking about?'

Molly came to join them. 'Look!' she cried.

Tom's head spun round to his left, and followed the line of her finger, which was pointing to the left of the school. There in the shadows, at the opposite end of the school to where the fire engine and firefighters were, he could see two figures skulking low to the ground, one slender, the other tall but stocky with a shock of blond hair.

'It's Michael and Sean,' said Molly. 'I'm sure of it.'

For a moment or two, Tom studied the two figures moving

in their suspicious manner, and then he was off, sprinting towards them as fast as his legs could carry him. A teacher called after him, demanding he return at once to the playground, but the words struck deaf ears. When Molly and Jake ran after their friend, the teacher fired her words at them also and then gave pursuit when they, too, ignored her commands.

A jagged streak of lightning crashed to earth nearby, startling Tom, temporarily blinding him, causing him to briefly slow his pace. But even as the thunder echoed around him, he had recovered and was hurtling once more towards the two boys who were still lurking in the shadows, apparently unaware of his approach.

As Michael and Sean disappeared around a corner, Tom raced after them and then, when he rounded the corner, staggered to an abrupt halt to avoid colliding with the well-built frame of Sean.

Michael, just in front of Sean, spun round and his jaw dropped. A plastic bag he had been carrying fell to the ground, spilling matches and lighter fuel and crunched up pieces of newspaper onto the concrete. 'What are *you* doing here?' he demanded. His face was astonished, shocked, angry. 'How–?'

'Never mind how I got here,' said Tom, his anger overcoming his breathlessness. 'What exactly are *you* doing? We agreed not to get one another into trouble ...'

Like a pouncing cobra, Sean reached out a hand and grabbed Tom by the scruff of his shirt. He then thrust him backwards against the sidewall of a building. 'You're a fine one talking about getting people into trouble. You little–'

'You great fool!' snarled Tom, flailing his arms around in an attempt to release Sean's grip. 'You have no idea what's going on here …'

Michael moved forward and seized Tom as well. 'How about you shut up,' he demanded, his face millimetres from Tom's, 'and tell us how on earth you got back here.'

Tom ceased his futile attempt to break free from Sean and stared back at his look-alike. 'Listen to me, Michael,' he pleaded. 'This weather, this thunderstorm,' and he raised his eyes up to the blackened heavens, 'is being caused by us. You have to go back, both of you – now! Before it gets worse.'

'Let him go,' yelled a breathless Molly, as she came round the corner.

A moment later, Jake appeared, red-faced, puffing and then angry when he saw Tom pinned to the wall. 'Let go of him,' he demanded, in an aggressive tone such as Tom had never before heard him use.

'What?' yelled Michael. 'You two as well? What is going on here?' But then he raised a threatening finger. 'Keep out of this, both of you.'

Before anyone spoke another word, the clatter of footsteps rose above the sound of the gathering wind, billowing through the nearby trees, a pounding of boots only seconds away.

A flash of concern flickered across Michael's eyes. 'Sean,' he said urgently. 'We gotta go.'

Wasting no time, Sean threw Tom onto the ground with a snort and a glare and ran after Michael, who had already turned and fled, leaving the spilt contents of his bag on the ground. Molly and Jake rushed over to check that Tom was all right, but with nothing more than his pride bruised, he was about to spring back onto his feet to go after the fleeing duo when a male teacher appeared from around the corner, flanked by two burly firefighters in their dark uniforms and bright yellow helmets.

A violent thunderbolt burst overhead, and the raindrops grew larger, more frequent.

'Paget!' growled the teacher. 'Stay there.'

'But Mr Williams,' protested Jake. 'Those are the two you want,' and he pointed after the two boys who could still be seen sprinting away from the scene.

'Yes, quick!' added Molly. 'They're getting away.'

Without a moment's hesitation, the two firefighters darted after the two boys, while Tom rose gingerly to his feet, his eyes following the chase. He saw the two boys split up and disappear out of sight, a fireman in pursuit of each one.

His mind was racing. As much as Michael and Sean deserved to be caught for what they had done, their capture would cause more problems than it would solve. And the only immediate option left was to get Jake to safety until they could come up with a different plan.

'Right, Paget,' said the teacher, and placed a heavy hand on Tom's shoulder. 'You're coming with me.' Tom was about to speak when the teacher hurriedly continued: 'And before you say anything, I saw you light that fire, so don't try to deny it.'

'N-no, you've got it wrong,' stammered Tom.

'He's right,' said Jake. 'It wasn't him.'

Tom shook the hand from his shoulder. 'I'm sorry, sir,' he said evenly. 'I can't come with you. I have to go.'

'I beg your pardon!' replied the man, his face turning pink. 'You, young man, are coming with me to see the headmaster.'

'I can't.'

'Tom,' said Molly, moving forward to intercede. 'Don't get yourself into trouble over this. We'll bear witness that you didn't do anything, that you weren't even here.'

'Molly, we have to go back. Look up there,' he said, pointing to the threatening mass of cloud above. Then, as if helping to emphasise his point, a bolt of lightning sparked into the ground nearby, blinding their eyes, pounding their eardrums. 'Come on,' he yelled. 'We don't have long.'

Frozen with indecision, Molly and Jake did not respond straightaway, causing Tom to pause for a second too long. For just then, another teacher appeared alongside his colleague. Before Tom knew what was happening, he had a teacher at each shoulder, and both of his arms were being pinioned behind his back. The harder he struggled, the harder they gripped his arms. And then yet another teacher arrived, followed by another firefighter. Molly and Jake were being ushered away, told to go back to the playground, in spite of their urgent protests. Tom's mind was a horrible blank, full of nothing but panic. It was all happening far too quickly for him to think what to do.

And then at last, a thought came into his mind, the only option now left. 'Okay, okay,' he said, finally releasing the tension in his arms, hoping it would give him the breathing space he needed. The two teachers began marching him towards the school. Molly and Jake were receding backwards away from him, their anxious eyes barely leaving his for a second. The distance between Tom and his two friends grew and grew.

The heavens opened, the spattering of raindrops turning into a deafening deluge in the blink of an eye. Lightning arced across the sky.

He felt the grip on this left arm slacken a fraction. He waited another second or two, then violently shook free his arm. Knowing he would have no more than a couple of seconds to react, he plunged his freed hand into his trouser pocket and plucked out the medallion. While the teacher on his left fought to regain control of his left arm, Tom threw the object with all his might towards Jake, who was still peering at him through the vertical rods of rain that fell between them.

'Jake!' he yelled. 'Catch!'

The glistening medallion flew through the air, bombarded by heavy raindrops as it went, its chain trailing behind it like the tail of a comet. A wide-eyed Jake stepped forward, steadied himself and took the catch, as Tom knew he would.

'Molly!' screamed Tom. 'Take Jake back with you.'

The two startled teachers restraining Tom were too intent on regaining control of their charge to register what he had just done, what he had just said. And with Jake staring blankly at the medallion in both his large hands, Molly tugged his sleeve and pulled him further away from his friend.

As Tom was marched towards the school, he glanced over his shoulder just in time to see Molly and Jake disappear into the crowds of children leaving the school.

Chapter Thirteen

Whirlwinds

It was now as black as night, and the heavy rain stung her face and her hands and her arms. And it made her shiver when she remembered what had happened only two days previously. Molly's whole body was shaking, shaking from the drenching rain that pelted her body, and shaking from the anxiety she felt for herself and for Tom. As they were carried out of the school grounds amidst the torrent of pupils, she grabbed hold of Jake and pulled him under the shelter of a tree.

When they could see one another without having to constantly wipe the water from their eyes, Jake glowered at her. 'Are you going to tell me what's going on?' he demanded. 'Tom's not supposed to be here today. And what the hell is this?' he asked, holding up the dripping medallion.

And so, stumbling over the words in her haste to get across the urgency of their predicament, Molly told him everything, everything that had happened so far that day and everything that Sam had told them about the mirror, about the medallion and about the cause of the storm that was raging above them.

'So, you're saying everyone with a double in this world is now in danger?' asked Jake, horrified, the fear in his eyes a perfect reflection of Molly's own feelings.

'Yes, exactly,' replied Molly, removing her glasses and wiping away yet more droplets of rain with a finger.

'Well, that means me, you and Tom.'

'I know.'

'And Tom just told you to take me back to your world for safety?'

'Yes, he did. But–'

'Well, I'm sorry, but I'm not going,' said Jake. 'We have to help Tom. I'm not leaving him here while I just run away – he's my best mate.'

'I have no intention of just abandoning him either,' retorted Molly. She was suddenly cross that he would even suggest such a thing. 'He's my friend, too.'

'Yeah, I've noticed!' replied Jake, with a hint of bitterness in his voice. He looked away and ran a hand across his forehead and eyes, as much in thought as to wipe away the water.

There was an uncomfortable silence between them, filled with the pounding of the rain on the leaves above and the road nearby. A flash of lightning momentarily lit up the street, bathing it in light as bright as day, before the darkness returned, softened only by the hazy, orange glow of rain-spattered streetlamps.

When the deafening rumble of thunder had abated, Molly said calmly: 'Look. The only thing we can do now is try to find Michael and Sean and take them back with us.'

'And just how are we going to do that?' asked Jake, spreading his hands wide in exasperation. 'They could be anywhere.'

'Now that they're in trouble and being hunted, I think they'll go back to the house and try to find out how we came through without Michael touching the mirror. All we can do is go back to the house and wait for them to turn up.'

'Aye,' sighed Jake, guilt in his eyes. 'I guess you're right. I'm sorry for getting angry. It's hard for me to look at you and not think you're Rachel.'

Molly gave him a wry smile. 'I have the same problem with you and that brute Sean.'

Tom paced up and down as best he could within the confines of the small office, backwards and forwards between the small window at one end of the long, thin room and the door at the other, and past the two immensely cluttered desks in the middle. The police were on their way, they had told him; he was to wait where he was until they did. But waiting was the last thing on earth he wanted to be doing. Outside, the thunderstorm was intensifying with, it seemed, every passing moment, and the heavy rain roared louder and louder on the roof and on the ground like the sound of a great river in flood.

When he spun sharply on his heels and headed towards the window once more, a vivid flash of light erupted outside, briefly illuminating the playing field and the line of trees beyond. The resulting roar of thunder seemed to shake the entire building and rattled the metal window frame. Tom thumped one of the desks when his eyes and ears had recovered. Precious time was being wasted. Before long, people would start dying: Jake or Sean, Molly or Rachel, himself or Michael. And if the Great Storm was anything to go by, others would die too, innocent people who knew nothing, had done nothing. And it would all be his fault.

The door burst open and in walked the squat figure of Mrs Meadow, her face as grim as the clouds outside.

'Hi,' said Tom meekly. But if he thought for one moment his favourite teacher was going to be a soft touch, her angry face told him otherwise.

'So, Tom. Are you going to tell me what on earth is going on?' she said, folding her arms and boring her eyes into his.

Tom sighed and opened his mouth a couple of times, but he simply had no idea what he was going to say, how he was going to explain all this in such a way that she might believe a word he said.

'Frankly, Tom, your behaviour today has been despicable. I am very, very disappointed in you.'

Tom averted his gaze and ran his fingers wearily through his still damp hair.

'Have you really got nothing to say for yourself?' continued Mrs Meadow. 'I know you've got issues at home, but there is no excuse for this behaviour.'

'Oh, Mrs Meadow,' he said finally, wearily. 'You wouldn't believe me if I told you.'

'Try me.'

He sighed again. 'Someone has been impersonating me.' He had no choice but to withhold some of the truth, otherwise she would have dismissed his fantastical story out of hand.

'Oh, really?' replied the teacher, before the anger returned to her face in a flash. 'I can't believe *you* of all people are behaving like this. After all I've done for you in the past, you try to treat me like a fool–'

'I promise you, Mrs Meadow – it wasn't me, I swear to you.'

'Mr Williams saw you in broad daylight. Are you saying he's lying?'

'No, he's not lying. At least, he thinks he saw me. This other kid looks just like me.' He watched as a frown creased across her face. 'Look, you've always been really good to me, and I've always appreciated that. So why would I repay you by lying? I have no reason to. Does setting fire to the school really sound like something I would try to do? And what else did Mr

Williams say? That he saw a big blond kid helping me? Well, the only big, blond kid in this school is Jake McBean, my best mate. And the same Jake McBean who wouldn't hurt a fly, let alone try to burn down the school.'

'You're either a very good liar–'

'I promise you, it was not me,' persisted Tom. 'And you have to help me get out of here to find the real culprit.'

'That's never going to happen, Tom,' replied Mrs Meadow.

'Come with me,' continued Tom. 'Chain me to your car if you like, so I can't escape. But I have to find this boy.'

Mrs Meadow studied him for a moment with a furrowed brow, clearly weighing up the information he had just given her. And he thought he saw a flicker of uncertainty in her eyes.

When another explosion of white light filled the room, his head swung instinctively back towards the window. He turned in time to see another giant fork of lightning arc downwards from the impenetrable, black sky, saw it split into jagged fingers as it approached the ground, striking the playing field in several places at once. Only a second or two later, more massive streaks attacked the ground. And in the brief moments of blinding illumination they afforded, he saw it: a massive funnel of whirling cloud and debris, which extended from the ground to the blackness above, like a giant pillar that was straining to hold up the thick blanket of cloud. Slowly, it seemed, it snaked a haphazard but inexorable path towards the school, towards him, gouging a furrow through the ground as it approached.

Terror spread through his body in an instant like a rampant virus, a paralysing terror that froze his body and his mind for a few agonising seconds. He then placed two hands on the pane of glass and strained to get a clearer look, desperately hoping he had been mistaken. But the tornado was still there, now nothing more than a huge silhouette in the darkness, but nonetheless still there, weaving its way towards him.

He turned back to face Mrs Meadow just as the office door flew open once more. Before he could say a word, his father was standing in the doorway with his scruffy overalls on, his face angry and set to explode.

'I don't believe this,' muttered Tom. It seemed everything that day was conspiring against him.

'What the hell have you been doing now?' demanded his father and brushed past Mrs Meadow as though she were nothing more than a hat stand. 'You're doing this on purpose, aren't you?' he continued, wagging a finger in Tom's face. 'Just to show me up ...'

'Mr Paget!' bellowed Mrs Meadow in a voice that reminded Tom of her double, Miss Doomsday. 'Please calm down.'

'This has nothing to do with you,' he retorted over his shoulder, fists clenching.

But Mrs Meadow was not the sort of woman to be browbeaten that easily. 'On the contrary,' she insisted, 'it has everything to do with me.'

Tom's father turned and glared at the teacher. 'Your headmaster called me here. So if you don't mind, I'll deal with this now. He's my son.'

For a brief moment, Tom felt the urge to shout out the words 'You are not my real father!', but it was not the right time to confront that particular issue. 'Dad,' he said instead, 'we don't have much time for this. We have to get out of here.' His heart was beating faster than he thought it was possible to do, so fast it seemed it would explode in his chest at any moment.

'You,' snarled his father, spinning around angrily, 'you, my boy, are not going anywhere.'

'Mr Paget,' resumed Mrs Meadow. 'We did not call you here to punish your son …'

And then the ground began to shake, and the roaring of the rain abruptly disappeared behind the roaring of the advancing tornado.

While the two adults were stunned into silence, Tom stepped between them and said, shouting above the noise: 'Listen to me. While you two are busy arguing, there's a great big tornado out there heading this way. And it's trying to kill me!'

'What are you talking about?' his father seemed to mouth, though the sound was inaudible above the approaching din.

Ignoring the comment, Tom darted towards the door, hoping to arrest the attention of the two adults and lure them out of the room and away from immediate danger. But when he reached the doorway, he stopped and turned around, and to his horror he saw both of them standing like statues, staring out of the window at the blackness beyond. His father was even shuffling towards the window, curiosity drawing him towards the gathering noise.

The walls began to shake. A book fell off a shelf and a tin of pencils clattered onto the floor.

Mrs Meadow was closest to Tom, so he grabbed her arm and tugged her until she turned to glare at him indignantly, as if she had just been awoken from a deep sleep.

Just then, the window shattered and seemed to be sucked outwards into the darkness. In the next moment, the far end of the room vanished before their eyes in a swirl of flying debris, and in its place was a wall of what looked like black smoke, blurred with the high velocity of its sideways rotation. Every scrap of paper on the desks, every book on the shelves were sucked towards it. Moments later, a book flew out of the twister towards them at great speed, as if spat out by an angry beast, and narrowly missed Tom's ducking head.

He pushed Mrs Meadow unceremoniously out of the way so that she moved behind him, and rushed back into the room towards his father who stood motionless, transfixed by what he was seeing. Tom seized him and spun him around to look into his face, but his shouted words were swallowed by the roar of the twister.

At that instant, the power was cut, plunging the room into darkness, and only then did his father react with a sudden desire to flee. So they ran for their lives, with the massive tornado breathing down their necks.

Outside the room, Mrs Meadow was frantically beckoning to them to follow her out of the building. But Tom had no need to see her anguished face to know there was danger behind him, for he could feel the monster's breath on his skin, tugging at his shirt and his hair, could hear the building being wrenched apart and the roar of the twister itself assaulting his eardrums, almost calling his name.

Once in the large entrance hall, he thought he heard a scream behind him, somehow rising above the surrounding din. He spun around as his father sprinted past him, and saw a male teacher sprawled across the floor, clutching a leg. Immediately behind the stricken teacher rose the giant plume of black smoke, a vortex almost as wide as the room itself, rotating faster than the naked eye could register, carving a way through the building, tearing it in two, ripping apart bricks and metal and glass with the ease of an electric saw slicing

198

through a block of soft wood. Fragments of the building, large and small, were being drawn into the belly of the beast, adding to its terrible power. Then, as if it had gorged on too much of the building at once, some of the fragments were being spat out at great velocity, arrows of debris flying in all directions, crashing into walls and smashing windows and doors.

Tom ran a couple of paces towards the teacher who was reaching out with a hand towards him, his face contorted with fear. But an instant later, the man had disappeared, devoured by the tornado. Knowing there was nothing more he could do, Tom ran, ran for his life as the vortex rumbled towards him at its own pace, as if taunting him, knowing it would eventually capture him no matter what he did or how fast he ran.

He raced through the main entrance and back outside into the torrential rain. Ahead of him, his father was sprinting away, rapidly disappearing into the gloom, abandoning his son. As Tom ran, his eyes scanned the playground and the car park, until he saw Mrs Meadow, jogging as best she could towards her car. Tom had been left to fend for himself. He was alone.

And it was then that he stumbled and fell onto his front with a splash. At once, a multitude of heavy raindrops pummelled into his body like the fingers of an angry mob trying to pin him to the ground. He hauled himself to his knees, scrambled a pace forward, before falling awkwardly once more onto the rain-soaked concrete. Behind him, he heard another explosion of masonry, and moments later, fragments of glass and brick rained down on him, exploding in the water all around.

Just when he felt that time was running out, a pair of dazzling headlights rapidly drew closer. The car's approach was silent amidst the cacophony of deafening sounds around him. Turning sharply as it approached him, the car came to an abrupt halt, spraying him with yet more water. The passenger door flew open, nearly striking him in the head, but when he looked up and peered inside, he could see Mrs Meadow sitting at the wheel, calling to him, noiselessly it seemed, beckoning to him with an urgent hand. He scrambled to his feet and leapt inside the car. Barely had he landed on the seat when the vehicle sped off towards the school's front gate.

Tom could not resist craning his neck for a look behind. The tornado had burst through the other side of the main school building but was now beginning to recede into the distance as they drove away. Behind it, and utterly dwarfed by the towering maelstrom in front, the building had been severed in two and now stood dark and lifeless.

Molly was convinced the rain had eased a fraction, perhaps even that the thunder was no longer quite so loud. And that could surely only mean one thing: one of the six doubles causing the storm had been killed. What if it was Tom?

Just when the thought began to terrify her, there was a flash of lightning and a clap of thunder as violent as anything that had preceded it, and yet in a strange way the thunderbolt comforted her. Perhaps no one had died after all.

In order to seek temporary respite from the storm and to catch their breath, she and Jake rushed under a bus shelter and flopped onto the narrow seats with their backs to the road. Rain was pouring off the glass roof and onto the pavement in front of them like a waterfall. She felt the uncomfortable press of her mobile phone against her leg and reached into her pocket and took it out. Straightaway, she felt the urge to phone someone: a friend, her mum, her dad, just someone familiar to talk to, to comfort her. But this was not her world. There was no signal on her phone, and even if there had been, there was no one to ring. She felt so terribly afraid. She felt like throwing her useless phone away, but instead she put it away in her pocket.

'We can't afford to stop here for long,' she said.

Jake mumbled a response, then added: 'So, you're nice then, are you? Is that how it works?'

'Well, I like to think so, yes.'

'This is so weird,' smiled Jake wryly.

'Jake!' snapped Molly. 'Will you focus!'

'Er … yes, sorry.'

For a few seconds, there was nothing but the beating of the rain on the shelter's roof and the constant spattering of droplets on the pavement. Until a large, soaking-wet figure appeared under the shelter in front of them.

'You two!' it said bitterly.

'Sean!' said Molly and leapt to her feet, initially surprised then wary. 'Where's Michael?'

'How should I know?' yelled Sean. He ran a hand through his soaking blond hair and shook the drips away. 'We got separated.'

'We have to find him. All of this,' continued Molly, waving a hand vaguely at the weather, 'is being caused by all of us being here in the wrong place – you, me and Michael. We have to go back straightaway before someone is killed.'

Sean laughed a mocking, mirthless laugh. 'You expect me to believe that rubbish? It's just a freak storm. Probably due to global warming or something.'

'It's true, Sean. We–'

'I don't care about your stupid little stories,' snarled Sean. 'All I want to know is how you got here, and how you're going to take me back with you.'

'You don't understand, Sean,' insisted Molly defiantly. 'We have to find Michael as well.'

'No!' yelled Sean, and stabbed a large finger towards her. '*You* don't understand. You are taking me back – now!'

Staring up into his cold eyes, Molly was about to shout her reply when Jake came over and put a gentle hand on her shoulder. 'It's okay, Molly,' he said in a voice that was as quiet and unthreatening as his look-alike's was hostile. 'Come on, let's take you and Sean back now. I can then come back and look for Michael and Tom.'

She wanted to argue at them both, but she knew Jake was right. There were currently six of them causing the storm, so it was imperative they reduced that number as quickly as possible.

Sean glared at Jake with a mix of suspicion and disquiet, before addressing Molly once more: 'I suggest you listen to your friend.'

'Come on, then,' sighed Molly, and stormed off into the rain without further ado.

So the trio hurried down into the town, at first trying to dart under trees, bus shelters and shop fronts whenever they could, but soon realising they were so wet already it hardly mattered anymore. With thunder and lightning still exploding around them, they crossed the bridge in the centre of the town. No sooner had they reached the other side than a bolt of lightning forked into the ground so close to where they were walking that they were all thrown to the ground.

Sean was the first to rise to his feet and stormed across to

Molly and Jake, rage written across his dripping face. 'I've had enough of this,' he bellowed. 'Tell me how to get back.' And he seized Molly by the scruff, hauling her to her feet. She struggled and cursed at him, but he was simply too strong for her.

Jake wiped the rain from his face and stood next to Molly. 'Leave her alone,' he demanded.

'Or what?' said Sean, raindrops spitting from his lips as his voice boomed.

Jake was frozen to the spot, indecision written across his face.

'Look at you,' continued Sean. 'You're pathetic. I know how this works. You're the opposite of me. That means you're weak and spineless. You're a disgrace to the name of McBean.'

'Is that right?' mumbled Jake coldly. And then without warning, he seized one of Sean's arms and began twisting it behind his back. Molly was immediately released as Sean took a swing at Jake, who avoided the punch by swaying backwards out of harm's way, but in doing so, had to release his grip on Sean's arm.

As the two well-built boys squared up to one another, looking like identical twins, Molly noticed the rain suddenly lessen its intensity. Instantly, her eyes were drawn away from the scuffle and into the distance towards the far bank of the river. There she could see thin wisps of smoke that seemed to be rising up into the air from nowhere, weaving around one another like courting swallows, shimmering, distorting the twinkle of lights from the town behind them like a heat haze.

Sean swore vehemently at Jake. Punches were flung, missing their mark. But Molly's gaze was not averted for one second. She watched as the wisps of smoke entwined

203

themselves together, grew thicker and thicker until they formed one large spinning pall of black smoke, wobbling uncertainly around its axis. It began to grow before her eyes, spinning faster and faster, gaining density and height and width, seemingly with every revolution it took, until it had grown into a writhing, gyrating whirlwind, taller than any building in Porthgarrick.

The two boys collided and began wrestling in front of her eyeline, wrenching her out of her trance. 'Stop it, you two!' she yelled. 'We don't have time for this.'

With a grunt of exhaustion, Sean ignored her, his face distorted with rage as he attempted to get Jake into a headlock. For a moment, Molly thought she saw tiny sparks appear all along the arms of the two boys as they wrestled. But they vanished in the blink of an eye, as one boy pushed the other away.

Across the river, the tornado was growing, reaching high into the sky until its top disappeared in the murky cloud, as though drawing its power from the black mass above. And slowly, it began to advance, swallowing a car and a bench and a streetlamp, with such ease that they might have been nothing more than tiny pieces of litter. It crept over the side of the wharf and plunged into the river, transforming in an instant into a giant waterspout, sucking the water up towards the sky.

With a clang of metal on concrete the medallion fell from Jake's pocket onto the pavement.

Puzzled, Sean looked down at the coiled chain between them. 'What's that?' he demanded. Jake bent down to pick it up, but Sean got there first. After only a cursory glance at the object, he declared: 'It's this, isn't it? You used this to get here.'

Without replying, Jake lunged forward to try to seize it back. The two boys collided and fell onto a grass bank that sloped down to the river's edge.

Molly ran forward to help retrieve the medallion. Jake and Sean were on the sodden ground, each with a piece of the mirror's chain in their hands, tugging it back and forth. Molly slid down the bank and grabbed a piece of the chain, which dangled between the two boys. Curses were exchanged, but words were now useless, since the roar from the waterspout was growing louder by the second.

As the tussle continued, Molly caught sight of the waterspout spinning ever larger across the river towards them, a giant, writhing funnel of liquid silver. It ripped through a line of small fishing boats, the first of which exploded in a bouquet of tiny wooden fragments. A second boat was drawn up inside the spout as easily as if it were a toy, before being spat out across the river towards them. It flew low over the children's heads and crashed into a line of cars at the top of the grassy bank, collapsing on impact, sending planks of wood in all directions.

Molly flung herself to the ground as a section of boat, as large as a man, came spinning towards her. She covered her head with her arms and expected the wood to crash into her at any moment. Instead, she heard it whistle over her head, missing her by what felt like millimetres.

She rolled onto her back. Then she noticed Jake was lying face down next to her, dazed and barely moving, a plank of wood lying across him. Further down the bank, towards the river's edge, Sean was lying in a crumpled heap with a large section of boat covering his torso. He groaned and tried to lift the wood but seemed too weak and too stunned to summon the necessary strength.

Molly looked up. Behind Sean the waterspout was roaring towards the riverbank. Hurriedly, she hauled herself to her knees, more concerned for the medallion than for Sean. By now, Jake had regained his senses. He slid further down the bank on his knees towards Sean. On the grass he found the medallion, picked it up and threw it across to Molly.

She yelled at him to run away, but her words were drowned out by the roar of the waterspout. Jake scrambled further down the bank towards Sean and with all his might he tried to heave the fragment of hull off his look-alike, just as the waterspout came ashore and morphed once more into a tornado. Sean was now wide awake and aware of the impending danger, his face terrified. The two boys wrestled with the wood, but one end of it had been fired into the moist ground and refused to budge.

Though Jake seemed to barely notice, the tornado was now only five metres from where they were, billowing his shirt, ruffling his blond hair. Then it was four metres, three metres. Molly scrambled down the bank, pulled Jake's shirt as hard as she could, such that he fell onto his back. And at that very moment, Sean disappeared with a silent scream into the heart of the whirlwind.

Molly pulled Jake to his feet, and together they clambered on all fours up the muddy, wet bank and back onto the pavement. Without daring to look back, they ran around the wreckage of the other boat and sprinted up the road.

Molly was terrified, running for her life. At least Jake was no longer a target. But *she* most definitely still was.

Chapter Fourteen

No Way Back

Even at full speed, the windscreen wipers on Mrs
Meadow's car were struggling to cope with the volume
of rain pouring down the glass. To Tom's eyes, the road
ahead seemed nothing more than a few smears of light against
a backdrop of black. Not that his attention was focused
outside, but rather on figuring out what he was going to do
next.

'I'll take you back to my house for now,' said Mrs Meadow,
her voice raised so as to be heard above the drumming of the
rain on the car roof.

A burst of forked lightning momentarily lit up the road
ahead.

'No!' said Tom. 'You've got to take me back to *Morladron
House.*'

'Do I?' replied the teacher, taken aback. 'Why on earth do
you want to go there?'

'The boy who's been impersonating me has gone there.'

'Listen, Tom,' sighed Mrs Meadow. 'What you did today
was wrong. But after what just happened at the school it
hardly matters anymore. We'll deal with it another time.' She
paused for a moment, concentrating intently on her driving. 'I
suppose at least your actions meant the school was virtually
empty when that tornado hit.'

Tom bit his lip with frustration. 'You don't understand. I
have to get back to the house.'

'I'm sure you do,' replied Mrs Meadow. 'But not in this

weather.'

It was hard to keep his impatience in check. Time was running out for him and his friends. He had to find a way to convince the teacher to take him to the house. In his head, he ran through every excuse he could think of, but each one sounded just as unbelievable, just as lame, as the actual truth itself. So he soon concluded that the only answer was to tell the truth and hope she would believe at least some part of it.

'I have to go back to *Morladron House*,' he began calmly, 'because this weather, this storm, is being caused by me.'

'I see,' replied Mrs Meadow somewhat surprised, as if talking to a small child. 'Just like that tornado was trying to kill you, I suppose.' She glanced across at him and nodded sagely. 'Yes, I heard you say that, Tom, when we were in the office. Really! What has got into you these last couple of days?'

'It's true,' he said despondently, realising just how absurd his last statement must have sounded.

'Even you've not been that naughty,' smiled Mrs Meadow.

In front of the car, no further away than the length of two or three cars, a vivid fork of lightning struck the road, causing Mrs Meadow to brake sharply. Moments later, however, when the darkness had returned, she accelerated down the road again.

'Come on, Mrs Meadow,' said Tom with renewed urgency. 'Think about it. This is no ordinary storm. We've just seen the school destroyed by a tornado. I may not be as wise and as well travelled as you are, but even I know that sort of thing just does not happen, certainly not here in Cornwall. And please don't try to tell me it's due to global warming.'

'Well, I'll grant you, it is a bit freakish.' She glanced across at Tom and began to look concerned at the obvious earnestness in his face. 'Okay, Tom. So tell me: what has this got to do with you?'

Tom hesitated, knowing that what he was about to say would sound preposterous. Yet what choice did he have? 'The boy who looks like me comes from a parallel world. And basically, we're not supposed to both be here at the same time.'

'Oh, really,' said Mrs Meadow. 'And have you been to this parallel world?'

'Yes, several times.'

Her face said it all. She frowned and shook her head almost imperceptibly. 'Honestly, Tom,' she mumbled.

'I'm telling the truth,' insisted Tom. He sat sullenly for a moment before resuming. 'Your maiden name is Doomsday, isn't it?'

Mrs Meadow flashed him a look of complete shock. 'What? How on earth did you know that?'

'Because I've met you in the parallel world. You still work at the school, but you're not married. So, you're known as Miss Doomsday.'

She smiled doubtfully. 'You could have found out my maiden name. I don't know how, but you could have.'

'Mrs Meadow,' said Tom impatiently, 'even if I went to all that trouble of finding out your maiden name, why would I bother? Just on the off chance that one day I might try to convince you I'd been to a parallel world? That's ridiculous, and you know it.'

For what felt like several minutes, but was probably no more than a few seconds, Mrs Meadow drove the car in silence. Until suddenly, she said: 'Okay, okay! I'll take you to that house. Heaven only knows why you've come up with this ludicrous story, but I'll go along with it for now. You must have your reasons. And, I suppose, until today, I've never had any reason not to trust you.' With that, she pulled abruptly into a driveway to turn the car around.

With lightning still erupting around the car at regular intervals, they splashed their way back into the town. At one point, they caught sight of the massive tornado that had earlier torn through the school, as it apparently meandered aimlessly in a field. At least by initially heading out of Porthgarrick, thought Tom, they had, for the time being, lured the twister away from the town.

A short while later, they arrived in the centre of the town. Even though the rain had eased a little, visibility was still poor. As they drove cautiously across the bridge, the swollen river raging beneath them, a clutch of flashing blue lights grabbed Tom's attention. Through the rain and the gloom, he could just make out a fire engine, perhaps an ambulance too, on the opposite side of the river. As they drew nearer, he saw to his left the wreckage of a fishing boat perched upside down on a pair of crumpled cars. The fire engine and the ambulance were parked nearby, but their attention was not on the boat or the cars. Behind the vehicles stood the remains of a terraced house, the end of which was missing, as though it had been sawn clean off. Fearing what he would see, Tom's eyes followed the line of destruction up the side of the valley, until he saw another tornado climbing up the hill. It was significantly smaller than the one which had hit the school, but the devastation it had wrought was no less terrible. Trees had been uprooted and tossed aside like twigs, cars thrown about like cardboard boxes. It had not yet reached halfway up the far side of the valley, but there was no doubt in Tom's mind where it was heading.

When they had crossed the bridge, Mrs Meadow brought the car abruptly to a halt. The road to their left was blocked by a mixture of debris, the fire engine and ambulance and by people generally running around in a hurry.

She glanced across at the blocked road and then up at the twister in the distance and said: 'Well, that settles that. We'll have to go back to my house after all.'

Without saying a word, Tom opened the car door and planted a foot on the wet road.

'What are you doing?' demanded Mrs Meadow. 'Get back in the car.'

Whilst still seated in the passenger seat, Tom turned around to face her and replied: 'If you won't take me, I'll walk there.'

'Don't be a fool, Tom. Can't you see what's going on up there? It's too dangerous. Now get back in the car this instant.'

'I can stop this,' insisted Tom through gritted teeth. 'But I have to get up to that house.'

'Have you gone mad …?'

Tom turned his back on her and stepped outside. The rain poured onto his head and his shoulders, and the wind blew his sodden shirt against his cold skin, making him shiver uncomfortably. But he had meant what he had just said: he would walk if he had to.

'Get back in the car,' barked Mrs Meadow, leaning across the passenger seat, fear in her eyes as much as anger.

Tom paused a moment then bent down to peer into the car. 'Only if you take me to *Morladron House*,' he said.

'Okay, just get in.'

He climbed in and closed the door behind him.

Mrs Meadow put the car into gear with an angry thrust and turned right, away from the devastation. 'I'll take you the back way,' she said, barely able to disguise the irritation in her voice. 'What is this all about?' she then demanded, her patience cracking.

'If I don't get back up there soon,' replied Tom, pointing up at the top of the valley, 'more people are going to die. I have to stop this.'

'You're really beginning to scare me now, Tom. Stop talking like that. Just how do you intend to stop this? No one can control the weather. That's ridiculous.'

'It's complicated,' replied Tom. He knew it was pointless trying to explain any further. Besides, now that he had seen the destruction wrought by the tornado on the town, he could barely think of anything else but getting back to *Morladron House*. And if Michael and Sean were not there, he would return with Molly to her world and take Jake with him until they figured out what to do. But that was assuming Molly and Jake were there with the medallion, and more importantly, assuming that his two friends were still alive.

He sighed to himself. How could he have let this happen? He had already seen one of his teachers killed before his eyes. If more people died how could he ever forgive himself? Ultimately, this was all his fault.

They sat in awkward silence, as Mrs Meadow negotiated the web of narrow streets that flowed with gushing water, water that seemed as impatient to find a path down to the river as Tom was to get up to the old house. Parts of the town were now in total darkness, the power no doubt extinguished by the tornado. So, when they turned down such a darkened street, the next bolt of lightning was all the more blinding, all the more terrifying.

At last, they were on the narrow country lane that led to

Morladron House, with trees and tall hedges on either side, silhouetted in the gloom, standing guard phantom-like over the road. Tom's eyes were fixed impatiently on the smudges of light on the road cast by the headlights, until, without warning, the way ahead seemed to vanish abruptly. Mrs Meadow slowed the car to a stop, for there in front of them, lying across the road, was a giant oak tree, felled by the storm, blocking their route to the house. Straightaway, Tom knew there was no choice but to finish his journey on foot. He flung open the car door, letting in the buffeting wind and the rain.

Even Mrs Meadow seemed to have realised there was no stopping him this time. 'Wait!' she cried. 'There's an umbrella in the boot. And a torch.'

But Tom was already outside, ignoring the wind and the rain, and grappling with the branches of the fallen tree, desperate to find a way through.

Molly was soaked to the skin, exhausted and terrified. She had not dared to look behind her for what felt like ages, just in case the tornado was still creeping after her as she jogged along. But at least she could still hear Jake behind her, with his heavy footfalls and his breathless puffing. All around her, it was pitch black, with only the regular bursts of lightning to light the way ahead.

For a moment, she stopped in the road and bent down holding her knees. Just as she looked back up, the roots and branches of a giant fork of lightning cracked across the sky. And as the light exploded before her, she saw the silhouette of *Morladron House* a short distance away. When she turned around, she could just make out the large and somehow comforting frame of Jake only a few paces away. 'Hurry up,

Jake,' she cried out. 'We're nearly there.'

Jake stopped in front of her and bent over gasping for air, unable to speak.

'Come on, Jake,' she urged again. 'We can't afford to wait.'

'Hang on,' wheezed Jake, and reached out a hand onto her shoulder.

While he caught his breath, she fished out the medallion from her pocket and ran her fingers across the weird wooden frame, across the smooth glass. Just what on earth had she got herself mixed up in?

Still barely able to breathe, let alone speak, Jake righted himself and said: 'Come on.' And they began walking the last few metres up to the house. 'So how does that thing work?' he asked after a pause, pointing at the medallion.

'You just wear it around your neck and then touch its reflection in the big mirror, and that's it. You just go through to the other side. We only found it this morning.'

'Oh, right. But–'

'Jake, Molly!' cried a voice behind them.

They both started and spun round in the same motion. Just behind them approached a figure as bedraggled as they were, emerging out of the gloom.

'Tom!' they exclaimed in unison.

He glanced nervously behind him and said: 'Yes. Come on.'

'But how did you get out?' asked Molly.

'Come on!' he insisted, and ran past them towards the house. 'I'll tell you later. We don't have time.'

Molly and Jake needed no second bidding, and turned and ran after him, arriving moments later outside the house. A large tree inside the grounds of the old house had been felled by the storm and had flattened a section of the perimeter hedge, thus affording them much quicker access to the driveway. The trio clambered into the front garden, ran around to the back of the house, stumbled their way in the dark through the overgrown rear garden, pulled away the loose boards from the window and climbed into the house.

Inside was filled with the sound, smell and feel of dripping water. Feeling their way along the walls, they shuffled through the house and into the hallway where shafts of dazzling light momentarily exploded all around them when a bolt of lightning landed nearby. Up the rickety stairs they ran, along the landing and finally into the room that they had all thought they might never see again. Water was pouring through the hole in the roof and spattering noisily onto the large rug in the centre of the room, as if a water pipe had burst. Then, when the storm unleashed yet another thunderbolt, the flash of light poured through the hole as well, and a jagged crack of lightning briefly appeared reflected in the face of the mirror, like the flash from a camera.

Molly watched Tom stride over to the mirror, hold it between his two hands and then suddenly spin round to face them. 'Right,' he said impatiently. 'Where is it, that thing, whatever it is?'

'You mean the medallion?' said Molly, and took out the object from her trousers.

'Yes, that's it …'

'Wait!' cried Jake from the doorway.

Molly turned to look at him and was surprised to see him undoing the wrist strap on his watch. But before she could ask what he was up to, he removed his watch and flung it across to Tom.

'Catch!' said Jake. And Molly followed the arc of the metal

watch across the room and into Tom's outstretched hand. 'Good catch,' continued Jake, an odd tone in his voice.

'What are you two doing?' she demanded. 'We don't have time for games.'

But neither boy said a word. Instead they glared motionless at one another for a moment, before Tom flung the watch back at Jake's feet.

'You're right-handed,' said Jake. 'You're Michael …'

'What …?' said a startled Molly.

But instead of responding to either of them, the boy suddenly leapt towards Molly, grabbed the medallion from her hand and then pushed her backwards onto the floor, before she had had time to ascertain for herself who it was. As she lay on her back, momentarily winded, she watched as her assailant turned around to face the mirror, then as Jake came running towards him, rugby tackled him to the floor, and the medallion jangled across the floorboards.

Molly scrambled across the floor on all fours towards the medallion, but Michael had already pushed Jake aside, had jumped to his feet. He snatched the object from in front of her nose, pushed her head away with a hand. She let out a squeal of pain and frustration.

Then she heard footsteps and voices downstairs. A faint flash of light swept across the floor, too weak to be lightning. The voices grew louder. 'Molly! Jake!' said one of the voices. Footsteps were creaking urgently up the staircase.

Jake was on his feet again, squaring up to Michael.

'Michael, wait!' cried Molly. 'We both have to go back, you and me. We can stop all this.'

But he simply swore at her, pushed Jake away once more and turned to face the mirror.

The flash of a torch appeared in the doorway.

'Michael!' cried Tom, and ran into the room, an arm outstretched. 'No!'

But Michael reached out a hand, touched the reflection in the large mirror and vanished before their eyes. Tom stood stock still in the centre of the room, the torch beam shining on the mirror, and nothing but the spattering water in the corner of the room to break the silence. 'Oh, no!' he muttered finally.

Molly and Jake rushed towards him, shook him gently from his paralysis. 'Tom, you're okay,' said Molly, unsure what to say in the circumstances.

'How did he know how to get through the mirror?' asked Tom.

There was a pause, then Jake turned to Molly and said: 'He must have overheard us outside.' Then he turned back to Tom. 'Molly was explaining to me how it works.'

'What's going on in here?' inquired a voice behind them. And in walked Mrs Meadow, puffing and leaning on a closed umbrella in the doorway.

But the trio scarcely even registered her appearance.

'Did you find Sean?' asked Tom.

'He's dead,' replied Molly, glancing at Jake, and then lowering her eyes.

'Still,' began Jake brightly, 'at least the weather should improve now that Sean and Michael have gone.'

Tom sighed heavily. 'You're forgetting Molly,' he said. 'The weather won't stop till Molly or Rachel is dead. And now we have no way to take Molly back to her world.'

Chapter Fifteen

The Hunt for Michael

Lightning seemed to explode all around the house. Three, four, five simultaneous bolts besieged the building, bolts that were brighter and louder than any others hitherto.

When the assault had subsided, Mrs Meadow moved into the room towards the startled trio. 'Is somebody going to tell me what on earth is going on here?' Tom was about to respond when the teacher continued: 'Let me guess - it's complicated!'

'You could say that,' smiled Tom weakly.

'Tom,' urged Molly. 'What are we going to do?'

'What if we destroy the mirror?' suggested Jake. 'Maybe that would break the magic, or whatever it is that causes all this.'

'This has nothing to do with magic,' replied Tom. 'Besides, we don't know how to destroy the mirror.' He thought back to his grandfather's failed assault on the mirror back in Molly's world. 'It's a lot stronger than it looks. And even if we did manage to destroy it, we don't know that that would make any difference. Anyway, we don't have long.'

'Right,' said Mrs Meadow and stepped in between the three of them. 'Whatever nonsense is going on here can wait till the weather gets better. Now come on you three, let's get you out of here…'

'Why did you bring her here?' asked Molly sourly.

Tom was about to answer when Mrs Meadow glowered at Molly and said: 'Tom did not bring me here, Rachel. I brought *him* here. Now–'

'My name is Molly, *not* Rachel.'

'I'm sure it is, young lady. We can go and discuss this with your parents, if you like.'

'Mrs Meadow,' cried Tom, with such authority that the room immediately fell silent. 'Rachel is already at home with her parents. This is Molly Trump, Rachel's equivalent in the parallel world I just told you about. And if we don't get her back to her world soon, she is going to die. It's as simple as that.'

Molly emitted an audible gasp. Tom had not meant to spell it out quite so brutally, but there it was. Whether Mrs Meadow chose to believe him or not, was now immaterial.

'Maybe it would work with any old mirror,' suggested Jake.

'No,' said Tom, downcast. 'My grandpa said it had to be that special one. He called it a key.'

'Maybe,' resumed Mrs Meadow, looking increasingly agitated, 'we should go and have a chat with the police about all this…'

Tom looked at Mrs Meadow, who was wearing the most sceptical of frowns across her round face, and said: 'I don't wish to be rude, but we're not going anywhere until Molly is safe. By all means you go, if you must, but we're staying.'

'Oh, Tom!' said Molly, suddenly excitable. 'Your grandfather seemed surprised when you told him you had travelled through the mirror without using the medallion.'

'Yeah, well, so?' replied Tom, thankful for the excuse to look away from Mrs Meadow's disapproving face.

Molly's face, by contrast, was as bright and wide-eyed as he had ever seen it. Tom began to feel excited, sensing she had realised something, something that might just save the day.

'Well,' she went on, 'that means they must have travelled between the two worlds without touching the mirrors in the way you and Michael were doing. They must have only used the medallion …'

Jake's face fell. 'Which Michael now has,' he said.

'But, but don't you see? Your grandpa said they *both* travelled back and forth between worlds, he *and* the other grandfather. And the only way you could do that–'

'Is if they both had a medallion,' said Tom, his throat bursting with excitement. 'Molly, you're a genius.' And he lunged forward and hugged her, before suddenly feeling very self-conscious and quickly releasing her.

Molly, in turn, looked startled, but still wore a broad grin.

'I knew we brought you along for a reason,' laughed Jake.

'Goodness! You really aren't Rachel, are you?' mumbled a bemused Mrs Meadow.

'But where is the medallion?' asked Jake.

Tom and Molly were still looking at one another, eyes wide, their minds racing.

'It must be under the rug, in a safe,' said Tom. 'Quick.' And they leapt to one end of the rug and began rolling it up. Jake came to help them whilst a bewildered Mrs Meadow stepped aside and looked on in stunned silence.

And there it was: an identical loose section of wooden floorboard in the identical spot to the one in Molly's world. Fumbling in his eagerness, Tom prised it up and shone the torch down at the near-identical safe in the floor, the only difference being that the numbers on the keypad were not in reverse. Without a moment's hesitation, Tom punched in the numbers that corresponded to KATRIN. But immediately, an error message appeared.

Looking over his shoulder, Molly had seen what had happened and said: 'It won't be the same. It'll be your mother's name – I mean, the woman you thought was your mother, the woman from this world.'

Tom was instantly crestfallen. 'I don't know her name,' he said. 'My dad would never even tell me her name.'

'I don't believe this ...' said Jake, almost in a whisper. 'We've got this far–'

'Your father never even told you your mother's name?' said Mrs Meadow, moving forward to see what they were all looking at.

'No,' replied Tom. 'Anyway, she wasn't my mother. My real mother lived there.' And he pointed at the mirror.

'Anna,' added Mrs Meadow quietly. 'Your mother's name was Anna.'

'How did you know that?' asked Molly.

'This is a small town. Everyone knows just about everyone else. I got to know your parents years ago, Tom. Everybody did. They weren't popular people. I never could work out how two such selfish and unloving parents as they were, could produce someone like you.'

Tom smiled briefly at her before returning to the safe. 'We need a six-letter version of Anna,' he said.

But try as they might they could not come up with a name that worked. Even Mrs Meadow began to offer suggestions. After several failed attempts, Tom slapped the floor in frustration and slowly looked up at Molly, willing her to have another brainwave. She returned his look, but seemed to be focused on a point far, far behind him.

Once more lightning flashed, thunder roared and the house shook. But no one even flinched, so focused were they on trying to solve the puzzle.

'It has to be German,' Molly cried at last. 'Your mother, your real mother, had a German name, so this one must have had one, too. So what about … Hannah?'

Tom typed it in, scarcely daring to hope. But this time the safe whirred and began to open. 'Yes!' said the three teenagers in unison.

Inside the safe, Tom found a similar bundle of papers on top of an object wrapped in an old piece of cloth. When he unravelled it, an identical medallion appeared which he held aloft in triumph. Without wasting any further time, the three friends moved in front of the mirror. Tom was about to place the chain over his head when Molly gripped his arm.

'Wait!' she said. 'Jake and I can go through and find Michael on our own. That way we don't have to worry about the weather trying to kill you.'

'You're kidding, right?' replied Tom. 'I'm not staying here. The sooner we find Michael and get that medallion back the better.'

Molly smiled back at him. 'Okay, but just remember those words when you next suggest to me that *I* stay behind.'

'Agreed,' replied Tom, and then placed the chain around his neck.

He was about to proceed when Mrs Meadow forced a cough to gain their attention. 'Excuse me,' she said. 'Just what are you three doing?'

Tom turned round to face her. 'We're about to, er … disappear. As soon as we're gone, the weather will start to improve almost straightaway. But I promise you, we'll be back later.'

'Sorry? You're going where?'

'You'll see,' smiled Tom, and then turned to Molly and Jake, offering them each a hand. 'Hold tight,' he instructed them, and with that he turned back to face the mirror. Molly and Jake grabbed his proffered hands, and after a deep breath to calm his nerves, Tom reached out the hand holding Molly's, and touched the reflection of the medallion in the mirror.

Tom had expected to reappear in Michael's bedroom, with warm sunshine pouring through the windows and birds twittering gaily outside. But instead, there was nothing but an eerie greyness all around, and the ground was shaking, whilst a rumbling sound assaulted his ears. As Molly and Jake gasped their surprise and fear, Tom instinctively held out a hand to steady himself. His hand immediately touched warm metal.

'We're inside a van,' he said, and his eyes began to quickly take in their surroundings. They were sandwiched in a narrow space between the vehicle's rear doors and a pile of large cardboard boxes against which the mirror was resting upright and incongruous. A bright sunny day was straining to seep through a crack at their feet under the double doors at the rear of the van.

Without warning, the van seemed to go round a bend at speed. Jake was flung heavily against the side wall, Tom fell on Jake, Molly fell on Tom, and they all ended up in a heap on the floor.

'What the heck is going on?' asked Jake, as they all scrambled awkwardly back to their feet.

'I don't know,' replied Tom. 'The mirror was supposed to be in Michael's bedroom, but someone is moving it.'

'Maybe it's Michael,' said Jake. 'After all, he only came

223

through a short while ago.'

'Michael's only fourteen,' scoffed Molly. 'He can't drive.'

'Oh, no!' said Tom. 'What if it's my grandpa? He couldn't destroy it, so he's going to move it.'

But before they could speculate any further, the whine of the van's electric engine changed pitch, and the trio were flung against the doors. The van was tilting upwards and Tom realised they were being taken uphill. He tried to picture in his mind where they might be heading, tried straining his ears to listen for clues as to their location. He was sure they had just gone through the town centre, and now he was equally convinced that they were speeding up the side of the valley. The intended destination became more and more obvious to him. 'He's taking us to *Morladron House*,' he said.

'But why go there?' asked Molly.

'I don't know,' replied Tom. 'But remember, the poor chap has lost his marbles. He probably thinks it's safer there.'

'Is this van electric?' asked Jake, scratching his blond hair.

'Yeah,' replied Tom. 'All the vehicles in this world are electric.'

'Cool,' replied Jake with a smile. 'That's really cool.'

'Believe me,' said Tom, wistfully rubbing his right hand. 'Not everything in this world is cool.'

For several minutes more, they were thrown this way and that, until eventually the angle of incline began to decrease, together with the speed of the van.

'We must be nearly there,' said Molly nervously. 'What are we going to do now?'

'If it's just an old man, I'm sure we can overpower him and just run off,' suggested Jake.

'We don't know for sure it is my grandpa,' said Tom. 'And

he might not be alone.'

'Why don't we just go back through the mirror and come back in a few minutes?' proposed Molly.

'Yeah, but how would we know when it was safe to come back?' countered Tom. 'No. Come on, we'll hide.' He began to move some of the boxes to one side. 'There must be enough room back here for us.'

The van came to a halt and the motor fell silent. A moment later, they heard the driver's door open and then slam shut, but by this time, they had managed to secrete themselves behind the boxes. The rear doors sprang open, and dazzling sunshine poured in. Shielding his eyes, Tom peered around a box and saw his grandfather climb into the van and begin struggling to manoeuvre the bulky mirror, a determined look on his face. Eventually, he dragged it out of the van and into a wheelbarrow.

When he moved out of sight, with a squeak of the barrow's wheel, Molly turned to Tom. 'You were right,' she whispered.

'So we can just overpower him, then?' murmured Jake.

'No!' replied Tom. 'I don't want to risk hurting him. As long as we check where he puts the mirror, we can come back later.'

Cautiously, they slunk out of the back of the van, crouched down and peered out from under one of the gaping rear doors. They could see Sam standing in front of the large metal gates in front of *Morladron House* and looking furtively in all directions. Once he had satisfied himself he was not being watched, he then proceeded, with the aid of a pair of bolt cutters, to cut through the chain that was locking the two gates together, and entered the grounds of the house. Without exchanging a single word, the three friends followed the hunched figure and his squeaking wheelbarrow as he made for the front door. After producing a set of keys, he opened the door and disappeared inside with the mirror still perched precariously on the barrow.

Tom instructed the other two to remain outside while he followed his grandfather into the house. He peered tentatively around a doorway and watched as the man dragged the mirror up the dusty and creaking stairs with a series of grunts and hauled it into a room off the landing. After waiting a couple of minutes, Tom was as satisfied as he could be that Sam was not going to move the mirror anymore, and he made a mental note of the room into which he had taken it. He then hurried back outside.

'Right. Let's go and find Michael,' he said, moving purposefully past the startled Molly and Jake who were sitting on the doorstep.

As they hurried after him, Jake asked: 'But how are we going to find him? Where are we going to look?'

'He'll go home … eventually,' replied Tom. 'If he's not there already.' He then removed the medallion from around his neck and stuffed it into his trouser pocket. They would have to walk back through the town, and the last thing he wanted was to attract any unnecessary attention.

Molly ran up beside him as he strode down the lane. 'Tom, if the weather starts to turn again, promise me you'll go back straightaway,' she said.

'Okay, but we have to get that medallion off him. We can't have him running around with it.'

'Yeah, and we can't have you dead and half the town destroyed,' replied Molly. 'If it gets dangerous, Jake and I can go after Michael. After all, he can't go back to your world, can he? He doesn't know where the mirror is now.'

'Okay, okay. Point taken,' conceded Tom, without wanting to catch her eye. For he knew that he would find it just about impossible to walk away and leave Molly and Jake to deal with Michael, even if the weather turned against him. He alone was responsible for what was happening, so he alone had to make sure it could never happen again.

Jake sidled up on his other side. 'So, Molly says you're really Michael,' he said. 'And that Michael is really you.'

Tom smiled wryly. He had almost forgotten what he had learnt earlier that day. It already seemed such a long time ago. 'That's about right, yeah,' he said.

'So you were born in this world and he was born in my world?' continued Jake. Tom agreed. 'But you can't coexist in the same world, otherwise the weather turns bad?' Again, Tom nodded. 'I knew I should have stayed in bed this morning,' he chuckled, scratching his head. Then after a pause he added: 'What exactly are we going to do when we find Michael?'

'Take the medallion off him,' replied Molly.

'And then what?' persisted Jake.

'Well, I guess you and I go home and take both medallions with us,' returned Tom, with a shrug of his shoulders.

Just then an electric car hummed past them. Jake watched the car in awe, before returning his gaze back to his friends. 'You're going to destroy the medallions, aren't you?' he said, after the vehicle had receded out of sight.

For a moment, without breaking his stride, Tom contemplated the wide-eyed, excitable face of his friend. 'You know what?' he said eventually. 'You're right. I think I will destroy them … if I can.'

Jake came to an abrupt halt in the middle of the road. 'Hang on, guys,' he said loudly. 'Don't you think we should think about this?'

Tom stopped and stared at him. 'Come on, Jake. We don't have time.'

Jake spread his arms out in supplication. 'But there's so much we could learn from this place. Think of all the stuff we could learn, all the good we could do.'

'People have died, Jake,' said Tom. 'Because of what Michael and I have been doing, people have died. And I cannot – I will not – allow that to happen again.'

'Oh, but Tom,' continued Jake. 'Think what we could do.'

'Others have tried in the past to make this work and failed. The mirror changes people, makes them greedy and selfish. People will always end up dying because of it.'

Molly glowered at Jake with such a piercing glare that he had to avert his gaze, and when he realised what Tom was saying, he stared at his feet in contrition instead. 'Look, Tom. I'm sorry. I forgot about your mother. I'm still trying to get my head around all this.'

Tom patted his friend on the shoulder. 'We all are, mate.'

They were about to walk on when Jake spoke again. 'But … if I understand correctly, your being here is not only endangering you and Michael but also this town, and we have now saved Molly by returning her back here. So why don't you and I just go back home? We don't need to be here anymore.'

Tom moved impatiently towards his friend. 'Jake, we have to get that medallion off Michael–'

'But why?' demanded Jake.

'Because if we don't, he could travel back and forth between our two worlds at any time of night or day, and cause who knows what chaos ...'

'He's not stable,' added Molly, lending weight to her argument by waving her hands about dramatically. 'Remember, he's the opposite of Tom: he's selfish, he's arrogant, he's ... he's ... dangerous.'

'Okay,' conceded Jake. 'I'm sorry. I ... this is all a bit ... I don't know ...'

'Come on, Jake,' said Tom, waving his hand. 'We have to find him before he does anything stupid.' And with that, he turned and resumed his walk down the road. Molly hurriedly joined him.

'What did you mean he's dangerous?' he asked, turning to her. 'Are you saying I'm not dangerous?' he grinned.

Molly smiled coyly back at him. 'I'm sure you'd like to think you're dangerous. But trust me, you're nothing like Michael.'

By the time they arrived back at Michael's house, thick black clouds were already beginning to bubble up over Porthgarrick. With his eyes glancing nervously to the heavens, Tom popped inside, leaving Molly and Jake to skulk under a large tree on the opposite side of the road. Minutes later, he reappeared looking up to the sky as anxiously as before. This time, however, he was sporting a garish red football shirt and carrying an umbrella.

'He's not back home yet,' he said, as he rejoined his friends under the tree.

'Nice shirt!' exclaimed Jake.

'This is so that next time you can tell the difference between me and Michael,' he replied, and handed Molly the umbrella. 'And this is so we don't get wet again,' he grinned.

229

'Tom,' she frowned in reply, 'it's not going to come to that this time. *You* are going back before that happens.' And she meant it, too. She would drag him back if she had to.

'We've got a few more minutes,' replied Tom, casting an apprehensive glance up at the gathering storm.

A polythene bag crackled past them in a hurry, buffeted along the street by a wind that had not been there moments earlier. Above them, the dark clouds were devouring the remaining patches of blue sky with apparent relish, and the three friends knew the first peal of thunder and the first drops of rain would not be far behind.

Jake put a hand on Tom's shoulder. 'Tom, you should get going.'

'Just another five minutes,' replied Tom, as he looked up and down the street, hoping that Michael would turn up at any moment.

The image of Sean being sucked in by the tornado and disappearing into oblivion flashed across Molly's mind, taking away her breath for a chilling moment. She was not about to let the same fate befall Tom. She grabbed him firmly by the arm. 'Tom,' she urged. 'You're going *now*. Even if you run, it'll take you fifteen minutes to get back to *Morladron House*. That's just too long.'

Tom looked into her eyes and then at Jake and sighed his frustration.

'Don't worry,' said Jake. 'We'll get him.'

'Okay,' muttered Tom at last.

But then, suddenly, there he was, striding down the street, as bold as brass, blissfully unaware that he was being watched. As Michael approached his house, he stopped and peered up at the foreboding sky, and a look of complete consternation spread across his face. No doubt only moments earlier, he had been supremely confident that Tom was unable to follow him, that he alone held the key to travelling back and forth between the two worlds; but now that confidence had apparently sunk without trace.

One by one, the last rays of sunshine were snuffed out, and in response to the gathering gloom, the streetlamps began to spring into life. Before Molly could react, Tom had sprung from her grip and was racing across the road towards his doppelgänger. The moment Michael set eyes on him, he tried to turn and flee, but Tom had already closed his arms around the boy's upper arms.

'What are you doing, you idiot?' yelled Michael, shaking himself violently. 'Let go of me!'

'Give me that medallion,' growled Tom in response.

A spark of lightning flashed to the ground barely a stone's throw from where the boys were wrestling, and the roar of thunder that followed seemed to shake the very ground they were on, the very air they breathed. Molly's heart was pounding out of control as she and Jake rushed across to Tom's assistance. As they neared, she saw Michael wriggle free from Tom's grasp and let out a curse at the top of his faltering voice. Tom lunged forward and grabbed his arm, reissuing his demand for the medallion. But as Molly and Jake moved in to lend a hand, sparks began to fly from Tom's hand, and from the part of Michael's arm he was holding, brilliant white sparks of pure energy. Molly froze to the spot in horror and held out a hand to stop Jake moving any closer.

Apparently oblivious to what was happening, the two boys continued to struggle. Michael was throwing punches and kicks, resorting to more and more violent means in an attempt

231

to shake loose his attacker, forcing Tom to duck and weave to avoid being hit. And every time they came into contact for more than a second or two, the sparks returned; crackling shards of static, brighter, larger every time.

Cautiously, Jake inched his way towards them, anxious to help his friend yet wary of the strange phenomenon. But as he did so, a jagged arm of electricity sprang from the point where Tom was wrestling with Michael's arm, and touched a spot in the road only four or five metres away. Less than a second later, it moved and touched a different spot nearby. Then it moved again, striking the ground like the lashing tentacle of some giant beast, causing Molly and Jake to stumble backwards, reeling from the shock. Molly screamed out a warning to Tom, but by then the two boys had separated once more, and the tentacle had abruptly vanished as though at the flick of a switch.

Horrified, Molly was moving slowly backwards, but she simply could not take her eyes off Tom. His eyes were narrowed, his teeth bared, his attention so focused, so intent on overcoming his opponent, that he had not seen the danger arising every time he touched his look-alike.

Ignoring Michael's shouted curses, Tom lunged at him again and seized an arm. Without warning, a fresh tentacle reached out in the opposite direction and struck a parked car, smashing its windscreen, then denting its bonnet, before retracting out of sight once more.

This time Tom had seen it, had instantly released his grip of Michael's forearm. For a brief moment, he studied his own hands, then the crumpled, smouldering car, then Michael's face. Within a split second, a truce seemed to develop tacitly between them, whilst they exchanged looks of shock and fright.

As they stood facing one another, barely a metre apart, Tom said calmly: 'Michael, look what's happening. This has to end.'

Michael simply scowled at him in return. 'Go home then,' he snarled.

And then the rain came, driving down in sheets, followed by a bolt of lightning, which flew down from the blackness above and struck a tree in a nearby front garden, turning it to a ball of flames in an instant.

A siren wailed into earshot and seemed to draw steadily closer.

'Give me the medallion, Michael,' said Tom, casting only a cursory glance at the flaming tree to his right.

Molly opened the umbrella, and then she and Jake rushed forwards and stood shoulder to shoulder with Tom whilst the rain poured down Michael's reddened face.

'Why should *you* have all the fun?' hissed Michael, returning Tom's glare with interest. Then, making as if to reach out and touch Tom, he made Molly and Jake flinch and take a backward step. Their nervous response made him chuckle. 'Ah, look, Tom. Your little friends are scared.'

The approaching siren rose louder above the beat of the rain on the road, and then a black van pulled into the street behind the three friends, drawing their heads sharply around.

Michael broke the fragile truce. With his look-alike's attention momentarily distracted by the approaching vehicle, he lashed out with a fist, and struck Tom in the face, sending him crashing to the ground and a shower of sparks into the air. Tom had barely landed on the road when Michael turned and fled in the opposite direction.

As the black van, all sleek curves and opaque windows,

purred to a halt outside Michael's house, only a short distance from where Tom was lying, Molly bent over him to shield him with the umbrella. Jake joined her and they helped Tom to sit up.

Vehicle doors rattled open, heavy boots splashed into the road.

'There he is!' said a woman's voice, shrill and menacing. 'The Paget boy is over there.'

A startled Molly looked up. Four policemen had sprung from the van, the rain pouring off their visored helmets, black uniforms and the truncheons in their gloved hands. And behind, under an umbrella, stood the short, stocky figure of Miss Doomsday, her face as grim as the weather above.

'Go after Michael,' said Tom groggily to his friends, the rain washing the blood from his nose.

Molly flashed him a fierce look. 'Don't be silly,' she barked. 'We're not leaving you.'

He grabbed her arm, forcing her eyes to stare into his. 'If you get arrested as well,' he said gravely, 'who's going to rescue me?'

Those heavy black boots were splashing towards the group, and the glare from Miss Doomsday was almost palpable.

Jake put a hand on Molly's shoulder. 'He's right. Come on.'

'Go!' insisted Tom.

Tom released his grip on her arm, and then Jake was pulling her away, but still her eyes had not left his. And then they were running, dashing down the street away from the police officers who were already on top of Tom, seizing his arms, twisting them behind his back, pulling him roughly to his feet.

A short distance ahead, they saw Michael had stopped, was

standing in the middle of the road, ignoring the rain streaming down his face, his eyes fixed firmly on the events outside his house. Molly and Jake caught up with him and turned to watch Tom being hauled into the back of the van by two of the police officers, whilst the remaining two climbed into the driver's cabin. Miss Doomsday climbed in after Tom, and the van doors slammed shut.

Molly turned to Michael whose mouth was just beginning to curl into a smile. 'You've got to help him,' she demanded. 'You've got to go back to his world.'

'I don't think so,' retorted Michael.

'If you don't,' said Jake, moving forwards aggressively, 'one of you is going to get killed.'

'Sorry,' replied Michael. And then without warning, he shoved Jake in the chest with such force that Tom's best friend toppled backwards onto the rain-soaked road. 'It's either him or me. And it ain't gonna be me.'

And before Molly could do a thing, he was away, sprinting down the road and out of sight.

A ferocious bolt of forked lightning struck the roof of a house on the corner of the street, causing a flurry of tiles to clatter down and then shatter on a path. At the same moment, the black police van hummed into life and then set off down the road.

Chapter Sixteen

The Second Great Storm

Stiffly, Jake raised his stocky frame back onto his feet, while the rain pummelled his body remorselessly. He was about to run down the road after Michael when Molly stopped him.

'Wait!' she said, pulling him back under the umbrella. 'We'll never catch him now.'

'Then what are we going to do?' replied Jake, his eyes wide with frustration and fear.

Before Molly could respond, a car turned into the road and pulled up outside Michael's house.

'It's Mr Paget!' cried Molly. 'We have to tell him what's happened.'

'B-but he'll never believe any of what we tell him,' replied Jake.

'Do you have a better idea?' snapped Molly. She turned on her heals and ran with the umbrella towards Michael's father, leaving Jake behind to get soaked once more.

Mr Paget was standing in the road, his jacket pulled over his head, vainly trying to shelter from the relentless rain, and staring down the road at the police vehicle as it hummed away.

'Mr Paget!' yelled Molly, as she drew near. 'Mr Paget.'

He spun round, lowered his jacket and looked at Molly blankly. 'What's going on?' he asked.

Molly was breathless with fear, trying to hold back the panic rising uncontrollably inside her. 'It's your son,' she said.

There was no need, no time, to explain the difference between Tom and Michael. 'Your son's been arrested,' she added, pointing urgently towards the receding van.

'What?' The rain was pouring down Mr Paget's bewildered face.

'That's your son in that police van ...'

Jake moved in beside Molly and ducked his head under the umbrella. 'It's true,' he added.

Mr Paget wiped the water from his eyes, blinked hard and then said: 'Get in.'

It was not what Molly had been expecting. Maybe it was the atrocious weather, but whatever the reason, Michael's father was climbing back into his car and beckoning to Molly and Jake to join him. Without a second thought, they followed him in, Molly into the front passenger seat and Jake into the rear.

The dashboard lit up brightly in the surrounding gloom, and with the headlights on full and the windscreen wipers swinging at maximum speed, the car was in motion once more.

'Tell me what happened?' demanded Mr Paget, without taking his eyes from the road.

Molly swallowed hard. She had no idea how to begin, what to say. How much of the truth should she reveal? How much would he believe? But all that really mattered was finding a way to rescue Tom.

'There ... there's been a terrible misunderstanding,' she began. 'They think he–'

'It's that wretched Miss Doomsday, isn't it?' hissed Mr Paget. 'That woman's got it in for my boy.'

Molly paused for a moment, her mind racing. 'Yes,' she replied slowly. The least she said the better. She just needed him on their side.

'I knew it,' replied Mr Paget, thumping the dashboard. 'Michael can be difficult at times, but it's just his age. Why can't they see that?'

Jake shifted uneasily in the back seat and then leant forward. 'But I don't understand,' he said. 'Why has he been arrested?'

'Yes,' added Mr Paget gravely, glancing across at Molly. 'What exactly has he done this time?'

Molly cursed under her breath. She had been striving to say as little as possible about their situation, and now Jake had gone and backed her into a corner. She turned around and gave him the fiercest of glares, before returning back to Mr Paget. 'He ... didn't go to school today ...'

Mr Paget in turn cursed under his breath.

'You get thrown into the back of a police van for bunking off school?' asked a bewildered Jake.

'Yes, Jake,' replied Molly scarcely able to hide the irritation in her voice. 'Things are different here,' she added without thinking, and immediately winced at her careless remark.

'Then why didn't they arrest you?' persisted Jake.

She would have to thump him if he continued like this. 'They probably couldn't see me under the umbrella,' said Molly tetchily, and shot Jake another withering look.

'Anyway,' continued Mr Paget, 'I'm sure we can clear this up at the police station.'

Just as they turned down another road, a vivid streak of lightning exploded to their right and the resulting peal of thunder shook the car. But when Molly's eyes had recovered from the blinding flash, she could make out, through the blurred windscreen, the black silhouette and the smudged red lights of the police van a short distance in front of them. She breathed a huge sigh of relief.

'What were you and Michael doing out of school, anyway?' asked Mr Paget.

Before Molly even had time to feel uncomfortable, Jake piped up: 'Molly, we have to tell him everything.'

'Jake!' snapped Molly, craning her neck over her shoulder to glare at him.

'Molly, Tom's life is in danger. We don't have time to just go and have a nice cosy chat at the police station. Tom has to go back – now!'

'What's going on?' demanded Mr Paget, with increasing impatience. 'What are you two not telling me?'

'It's nothing important, Mr Paget,' insisted Molly.

'Michael is not your son,' said Jake suddenly, ignoring Molly, leaning forward close to Mr Paget's shoulder. 'Your real son is in that van. And this weather is trying to kill him.'

Several moments of uncomfortable silence followed, in which all they could hear was the persistent rain drumming on the roof.

'What the hell are you talking about?' demanded Mr Paget, and glanced at Jake in the rear-view mirror. 'And I thought your name was Sean, not Jake.'

With a flat palm, Miss Doomsday was making the minutest of adjustments to her pristinely-coiffured black hair whilst staring fixedly at Tom. 'You are in a whole world of trouble, young man,' she said. The meagre light in the back of the van made her features even fiercer and less like Mrs Meadow than ever before.

'I haven't done anything wrong,' mumbled Tom, shifting

uncomfortably on the hard bench with his hands clamped firmly behind his back in a pair of cold handcuffs.

Miss Doomsday looked aghast. 'Firstly, you run away from detention and then today, you fail to turn up to school altogether.' She then slowly shook her head with utter disdain etched across her sullen face. 'That is hardly nothing, Paget.' She spat out his name as if it were a harsh curse.

Tom simply snorted.

'And we know about your little visit to your grandfather in the institute this morning,' continued Miss Doomsday, wagging a finger. 'Now that he's escaped, the police are very keen to question you. Why did you help him escape, Paget? Are you and your grandfather hatching some nefarious plot?'

Instead of speaking, Tom simply responded with a wry smile which seemed to infuriate the teacher even more than if he had argued with her. But he knew there was no point in entering into a quarrel. As long as he was shackled in the back of a windowless police van with two burly guards sitting by the door, his arguing would achieve nothing. So instead, he sat and returned her stare unwaveringly, and became more and more amazed at just how different to Mrs Meadow she was. In place of a kind, pleasant face, there was a stern mask, almost menacing and evil. In a world of opposites, she stood out more than anyone else he had met so far.

'I know you dye your hair,' he found himself saying finally, with no small amount of defiance. Since the situation seemed utterly hopeless, he might as well show the woman he was not afraid and would not be intimidated by her.

Her face reddened with anger, and for a short moment she was speechless until, seething, she returned: 'How dare you …?'

Tom chuckled to himself. It was so unlike him to say such a thing, but he was hardly going to make matters worse. And for a moment, it actually made him feel good to see Miss Doomsday so angry that she was lost for words.

The teacher wittered on some more, but Tom barely registered what she was saying, because by now, his thoughts were elsewhere. The hopelessness of his predicament crept up on him, then began to overwhelm him. It seemed as though his luck had finally run out, as though no one could save him from a fate that was as horrific as it was inevitable. And then, for the briefest of seconds, a thought entered his mind, a thought that immediately filled him full of terrible feelings of guilt. For in that tiny instant, he had prayed for the weather to take Michael and not him.

Realising she had no choice, Molly began her account of the incredible events of the previous fortnight, while a bemused Mr Paget listened intently beside her. Emboldened by his continued silence, she told him everything: how Tom and Michael had been swapping places since discovering what the mirror could do; how the weather had changed when she had travelled to Tom's world; how they had learned the mirror's final, terrible secrets from Sam; and how they had barely escaped from Tom's world with their lives. Scarcely drawing breath, she rattled out the words in her haste to finish the story, lest Mr Paget should interrupt her at any moment with a comment that dismissed her account as madness.

When she had finally finished, an awkward silence hung in the car. Molly could hear nothing but the deep drumming of the rain on the roof, broken only by yet another violent crash of thunder and the sound of her own agitated breathing. She threw a nervous glance out of the windscreen, as much to reassure herself that the van was still in view.

At last, Mr Paget sighed heavily and said: 'Do you honestly expect me to believe that rubbish?'

Although it was exactly the response she had been expecting, the harshness of his tone startled her. 'I promise you, Mr Paget,' she replied, as calmly as she could, 'everything I said is true.'

Jake chimed in with a brief statement of support.

Mr Paget suddenly slammed on the brakes and brought the car to an abrupt and jolting halt. The police van receded into the distance and dissolved into the murk. 'What do you take me for?' he bellowed, turning to stare deeply into Molly's eyes. 'Are you trying to be funny?'

'No, no!' they replied in unison.

'What you two don't seem to realise,' continued Mr Paget, 'is that I've heard all this nonsense before – from Michael's grandfather. I'll tell you what I think happened today: Michael has been asking lots of questions about his grandpa recently, so this morning you and he went to see him. He told you his little story and you decided to have some fun at my expense.'

'Your father-in-law was telling you the truth,' insisted Molly, with a forcefulness that surprised ever her.

'Michael's not even in that van at all, is he?' said Mr Paget.

Molly did not know what to say. It was true: Michael was not in the vehicle. 'Your son is in that van,' she said, wanting to avoid the debate about who was who, desperate to avoid wasting any more time. 'If you believe nothing else, please believe me. He has been arrested. We have to help him.'

'Please, Mr Paget,' added Jake in his habitual soft voice. 'We're running out of time.'

Mr Paget scratched his head and started the car once more. 'Okay. But I warn you, if my son is not in that van, there'll be merry hell to pay.'

Molly was so drained she could not say another word, but simply sighed deeply and sank back into the chair. Through the windscreen she could make out little more than the water-logged road ahead, flanked on either side by sinister, indistinct shapes, which not even the streetlamps were able to illuminate. And every minute or so, the whole scene would flash into life for a brief second or two, revealing houses and trees and cars, lit up by a streak of lightning, crashing to earth a short distance ahead, and reminding her, as if she needed it, that Tom was nearby and in desperate need of their help.

Once more, the scene was dark, patches of grey and black, blurred smudges of faint colour here and there. Two small smears of red light winked into view out of the gloom, and Molly's heart leapt with momentary excitement as she made out the rear of the police van.

But in the next beat of her heart, a blinding flash tore down from the sky directly in front of the car. Immediately, instinctively, Molly screwed her eyes shut, covered them with an arm, but the shimmering image, like a trident cast down by a giant, had already been impressed onto her retinae. Mr Paget, too, had been blinded, had lost control of the car. It slewed across the wet road, crashed into a parked car and skidded back into the middle of the road. Molly could feel the seatbelt straining painfully at her shoulder and the airbag inflating in front of her, before the car juddered to a violent, abrupt halt.

Her first instinct was to open her eyes, but when she did so, the image of the lightning bolt was still there distorting her vision. Behind her, she heard Jake mutter something, and then a rear door flew open, instantly admitting the roar of the rain into the car. Straining to see outside into the pool of light cast by the headlights, which had remained lit, she undid her seatbelt. And then, as her eyesight returned to normal, she saw Jake move into the pool of light. In front of him the police van was in the road, only a short distance away, lying on its side, its bodywork gashed and dented. Jake splashed towards the overturned vehicle, the rain turning his blond hair dark.

Molly was outside in a flash, ignoring the rain pouring down her face, and moved next to Jake who was trying to force open the van's rear doors. At last, one of the doors swung downwards, and a policeman fell out onto the road, unconscious. When Mr Paget arrived on the scene, the three of them peered inside, where a light in the van's roof was flickering on and off. Another policeman was slumped on what had been a wall but was now the floor. Behind him, Tom was lying on his back still attached firmly to the bench, legs now in the air.

'Michael!' exclaimed Mr Paget, and jumped inside.

Tom groaned and barely registered the presence of his real father.

'Don't worry, son,' continued Mr Paget. 'I'll get you out.' Whereupon he clambered over the second guard and began pulling at the handcuffs under Tom's back. As soon as he realised they were not going to come free, he turned to Molly and Jake and asked them urgently to look for the key in the pockets of the police officers.

'What do you think you're doing?' demanded a voice from the back of the van.

When Molly looked up, she saw Miss Doomsday, her hair

dishevelled, rising awkwardly to her feet as if every muscle in her body was aching and stiff. The flickering light in the van gave her features a monstrous look, as if she were a vampire rising from her coffin.

'This boy is under arrest,' continued the teacher, straightening her hair as best she could.

'Yeah. We'll worry about later,' mumbled Mr Paget, with scarcely a glance at her.

'Here it is!' announced Jake triumphantly, and tossed a key across to Mr Paget, who caught it and began unlocking the cuffs.

Miss Doomsday reached across and grasped one of Tom's arms. 'He's not going anywhere.'

Mr Paget stood up indignantly, his head slightly bowed within the confines of the vehicle. 'Look. What is your problem? My son is clearly hurt.'

Just then a policeman appeared from nowhere and stood behind Molly and Jake by the van's doors. He removed his helmet and asked: 'Is everyone okay?'

'Ah, officer,' said Miss Doomsday in a business-like fashion. 'Arrest this man. He's trying to free his son who's in custody.'

'Have you gone mad?' demanded Mr Paget.

The young policeman looked bemused, undecided.

'Your son,' persisted Miss Doomsday, 'is a criminal, like his father, and will go to prison.'

'Oh, that's what this is all about, isn't it?' said Mr Paget. 'You're using my son to get to *me*...'

'We've been on to you for some time now, Mr Paget,' sneered Miss Doomsday. 'We know all about your little activities, and your little group. Soon you'll be able to join your son behind bars.' She then turned to the policeman and said: 'Officer, this is Mr Paget. I'm sure you know all about him already. You can arrest him now for–'

But before she could say another word, Tom, who by now had regained his wits, reached across with the handcuffs, clasped one end around Miss Doomsday's outstretched wrist and the other to the frame of the bench to which he had previously been attached. 'We don't have time for this,' he said impatiently.

With her free hand, the teacher lashed out wildly and tried to grab hold of Tom, but, like a frightened mouse, he had already darted out of reach and was heading for the door.

'Stop him!' screamed the teacher at the policeman.

The policeman tried to grab Tom as he leapt from the back of the van, but Jake pushed the man in the back so he lost his balance and staggered forwards, allowing Tom to escape into the pouring rain.

'Now, let's not do anything foolish,' shouted the policeman, as he righted himself.

'Let me out of here,' yelled Miss Doomsday, her voice echoing inside the van.

Molly saw a faint smile creep onto Tom's lips as she, Tom and Jake stood in the rain at a distance from the policeman whose indecision froze him to the spot.

'I'll handle this,' said Mr Paget, climbing out of the van. Once he had positioned himself between the policeman and the three teenagers, he then promptly pushed the man in the chest, causing him to stumble backwards over his prostrate colleague. With arms and legs waving about, he fell into the interior of the van. Mr Paget then lifted up the gaping rear door and closed it before shouting: 'Run!'

No one needed to think twice. All four of them set off back

towards the car, soaked through to the skin, hearts pounding. Behind her, Molly heard the van door clatter open once more and when she looked over her shoulder, she saw another policeman, nursing a sore head, staggering to the back of the vehicle. There was a quick, frantic conversation between the two colleagues before they set off in pursuit.

Tom and his father climbed into the front of the car while Molly and Jake took up position in the back. In front of them, they could see the two policemen sprinting through the rain, black boots splashing through the water on the road. Mr Paget fumbled with his key, started the electric motor, slammed the car into reverse. One of the policemen jumped onto the bonnet, glaring through the windscreen, his angry face distorted grotesquely by the rain streaming down the glass. Silently the car's motor pulled it backwards, gathering speed as it went. The second policeman grabbed a wing mirror, then the door handle next to Tom. But the central locking held firm. With one hand on the wheel and his head turned, craning over his shoulder to look out of the rear window, Mr Paget continued to accelerate the vehicle, until without warning, he swung the car through one hundred and eighty degrees, and the two policemen released their grip and tumbled with a splash into the road.

'Are you okay, Michael?' asked Mr Paget, as they sped off down the road.

'Dad,' replied Tom softly. 'My name's Tom.'

Michael was wet and cold and alone. He was sitting on a bench under a large tree, staring out at the torrential rain that swept past in slanting waves, watching the road flow like a river, glancing up at the impenetrable blackness above. He had no idea what was going on, but it was all beginning to scare him witless. Every few minutes, lightning was exploding around him, the like of which he had never seen before. He had even seen a tornado snaking through the town. And all of it seemed to be gravitating towards him. Perhaps Tom was right: perhaps the two of them were causing all this. If that was the case, he had to find somewhere safe to hide while he waited out the storm. He could always try to go back to Tom's world, but then again it seemed impossible to get back to his house and the mirror, at least for the moment.

But, yes, of course. It occurred to him that there was one place he could go and wait in safety. So he stood up and headed out into the rain once more.

'Oh, Michael,' said Mr Paget wearily. 'Not you as well. Your friends have already told me this ridiculous story.' Then, raising his voice he demanded: 'Just what is this all about?'

Tom looked over his shoulder and threw Molly a glance, and just from the look she gave him in return, he could tell that she had told his father everything. 'It's true,' he said. 'Every word of it.'

'Listen to me, Michael,' said Mr Paget. 'Do I have to spell it out to you? In case you hadn't noticed what just happened back there, we're now on the run from the police – we have to go into hiding. Yet for some reason you're playing stupid, puerile games…'

'It's not a game,' persisted Tom. 'I'm not Michael. I'm nothing like him. For heaven's sake, Dad, surely you can tell I'm different. I've been asking you questions, acting differently these past few days. Please tell me you've even noticed.'

But before his father could respond they rounded a bend

and caught a view of the town in the valley below. By now, the rain was easing, the view of the town was therefore clearer.

'Oh, my goodness!' said Mr Paget slowly. With his mouth wide open, he brought the car to an abrupt halt.

All eyes had turned to look at the view, spellbound, horrified. Tom's father stepped out of the car as if in a trance, mesmerised by what he was seeing, drawn towards it like a moth to a flame. Tom followed him out. Against a backdrop of an oil-black sky, he could see a pair of tornadoes swaying massively through the valley – giant funnels of wind passing through buildings as if they were made of nothing more than paper, devouring all before them and leaving trails of terrible destruction in their wake. As the whirlwinds moved, small flashes of lightning were constantly erupting from inside them. And, slowly, inexorably, they were heading up the side of the valley towards them.

Molly and Jake joined the two of them in paralysed awe, the latter uttering a gasp and a curse.

Tom dragged his eyes from the scene, swallowed hard, grabbed his father by the arm, shook him gently to arrest his attention. 'Dad, listen to me. This is the Great Storm all over again. Remember? Fourteen years ago, when I was a baby, the same thing happened. Your old house was destroyed. Mum went missing for several days. Everything Molly told you is true. Grandpa was right. Only this time, it's me that's causing this. Me and Michael. We have to find Michael and stop all of this.'

'No, Tom,' said Molly, her voice straining with emotion at the destruction before her. '*You* have to go back. We don't have time to find Michael.'

Tom found himself glaring at Molly. 'No – I have to find

Michael and put an end to this for good, so it never happens again.'

'Tom,' urged Jake. 'We have no idea where to look for Michael. He could be anywhere.'

Tom stood brooding for a moment, before declaring: 'He's up there, near *Morladron House.*'

'How can you tell that?' asked Jake.

'Look at the tornadoes. They're heading up there. They'll go for either him or me.'

'We have to go back to our house,' said Mr Paget suddenly, his eyes still transfixed on the scene below. 'We have to go and get your mum and little Billy…'

Tom stopped him straightaway. 'No, Dad. They're safe where they are. As long as Michael and I stay well away from the house.'

His face full of shock and disbelief and terror, Mr Paget stared at Tom, seemingly unsure what to believe or what to do. 'How can you be so sure?'

'Trust me, Dad,' said Tom in a raised voice. 'Come on. We have to go – now, up to *Morladron House.*'

His father's shock worked in Tom's favour: without another word, all four of them leapt back into the car. And only a few minutes later, they were racing along the lane towards the old house. But even before the house came into view, they could see there was a problem. In the sky above where the house was located, a spiralling wisp of dark cloud seemed to break away from the low, heavy mass above and began to spin and spin, until in no time at all a giant whirlwind had formed and stood like a sentry before the house. It was as though the black clouds above were being sucked down to the earth and into a hole in the ground. Mr Paget brought the car to an abrupt halt, no more than two hundred metres from the twister.

Michael was nearby, Tom could feel it. Before anyone had the chance to say a word, he climbed out of the car for a better look. The spiralling giant stood in the road ahead, rotating at a terrifying velocity, yet scarcely moving, as if undecided which way to turn, as if considering whether to go after Tom or Michael. The danger was all too apparent, yet Tom was barely aware of the whirlwind before him. All he could think about was finding Michael and taking the second medallion from him.

When Jake stood at his side, Tom muttered: 'Michael's here.'

'He must be in the house,' replied Jake, fidgeting nervously with his hands.

'No,' said Tom, without taking his eyes from the twister. 'It would have destroyed the house if he was.'

A keen wind ruffled his hair, a wind that by now carried only a few drops of rain.

Molly hurried to join them. 'What are you doing?' she demanded.

'Looking for Michael,' came Tom's matter-of-fact reply.

Slowly the tornado moved sideways and tore into a hedgerow, shredding a small tree and the surrounding bushes into thousands of tiny pieces. Tom's father got out of the car and joined them, still in a state of shock, his eyes glued to the writhing vortex.

'Tom, for goodness' sake, you have to go back,' urged Molly.

Still he failed to look at her. Where was Michael? Where could he have gone? What was he doing? 'Michael's nearby,' he replied. 'We have to get that medallion back.'

Molly pulled at his arm to grab his attention. 'Go back now. We can worry about Michael later.'

His trance was broken, and he stared deep into those fiery hazel eyes that had enchanted him for so long. 'Don't you see?' he said. 'If we get that medallion back, we can stop this from ever happening again.'

'Or you could just go back now and destroy the mirror before anyone else gets hurt ...'

'And what if the mirror can't be destroyed? No, Molly, we have to end this for good. We have to stop Michael.'

Molly leant forward and grabbed both his arms, drawing him close. 'Don't be a fool, Tom. You're risking your life. And for what?'

Tom leant forward and kissed her on the lips. He lingered only for a second or two, but it felt good, until a moment later he felt a small pang of regret that he had not done it sooner. For he knew, when this was all over, he would never see Molly again. Soon he would have to return to his own world and close the pathway between the two worlds for ever. But at least he had now kissed her, and so he would never look back with regret and wish he had.

'What was that for?' asked Molly, visibly stunned but unable to conceal a faint smile on her lips.

'It was the only way to shut you up,' grinned Tom.

'I hate to break this up,' said Jake anxiously, 'but you either need to go back right now or start looking for Michael.' He then pointed down the road at the tornado which had evidently reached its decision and was now moving towards them, demolishing another tree in its path, turning it into a shower of tiny particles. Larger and larger sparks of electricity were flashing inside it, as if it were preparing to unleash a mighty bolt of lightning.

Even though it was not the first time that Tom had been chased by such a monster, it was no less terrifying. To see such massive power swirling towards him, knowing it was there because of him and existed solely to devour him and him alone, made his blood run cold. 'We can't get to the house now,' he gasped. 'We'll have to find Michael – it's the only way.'

'So where could he be?' continued Jake urgently. 'Remember, he's you. Well, almost, I guess. He thinks like you. Where would you go? What would you–'

'Of course,' interrupted Tom. 'You're right. You're a genius, Jake. I know where he is. Quick, follow me.' And with that, he turned and climbed over a low fence by the side of the road and began running towards the cliffs close to *Morladron House,* looking back only briefly to make sure the others were following.

Now that the rain had almost stopped, he could see into the distance, perhaps as much as a mile out to sea, where the heavy bank of black cloud ended abruptly. Beyond it, the sky was clear and blue, and the setting sun was beginning to peak from under the veil. He recalled the accounts of the Great Storm he had read, and realised that, just as it had done fourteen years ago, the storm was only raging over the small town of Porthgarrick.

But then his attention was jolted back to the present, when he heard the whirlwind to his right change direction, break through the wooden fence they had just scaled, and plough a path towards them. As it moved, he sensed it was accelerating, getting louder and louder, closer and closer, gaining in power.

At last, he reached the cliff top, ran along it until he found the path he sought and down he climbed, skidding, sliding down the wet rocks. Quickly, he glanced behind him to make sure the others were still safe, instantly wishing he had simply told them to wait in the car while he alone drew the beast away from them. Too late now, but at least they were still there, scrambling down with him, just about keeping ahead of the tornado.

Above them, rose the giant twister, roaring like a lion, picking up stones and boulders and clumps of grass, devouring some of them in its belly, casting out others at high speed. As rocks cascaded down around him, Tom continued to zigzag down the cliff, constantly putting out one hand or the other to steady himself, until they were both grazed and bleeding. But the sooner they got to the cave, he thought, the sooner they would be safe.

'Hurry up!' he shouted up to the others, but the words were swallowed by the noise from above, and from the turbulent waves crashing on the rocks below. Again, he looked up to check on the others and as he did so, he felt a hailstone hit his face, then another and another. At first, they fell from the sky like frozen peas, but quickly they grew into marbles, then golf balls. And then a hailstone the size of a football exploded on the rocks to his right, showering him with icy sparks. Another crashed to his left, then another whistled past his nose and plunged into the sea below.

But at last, the gradient had levelled out. He was standing on a large boulder close to the water's edge. He looked up to his friends and his father scrabbling down the path, straining to keep their balance, as mighty blocks of ice rained down around them. At the top of the cliff, the tornado was teetering on the edge looking as though it might topple down into the sea at any time, yet hesitating to proceed, as if it feared it might disperse into nothingness the moment it poked a toe over the edge.

In the next instant, Tom felt as if he had just been thumped between the shoulder blades by a giant fist. Scarcely able to breathe, he fell onto the boulder with small shards of ice tumbling down around him. He thought he was about to lose consciousness, but a helping hand reached out and grabbed his arm, tugging him back to his feet. Jake's big round face looked at him, full of concern.

Helped along by his friend, and frantically waving his spare arm, Tom beckoned to the others to what he hoped would be the safety of the cave, which he was certain had to exist in Michael's world as it did in his.

Sure enough, he then saw its gaping black mouth close to the water's edge. Everyone hurried towards it as more blocks of ice crashed into the sea and onto the rocks. Once they ducked through the narrow opening and clambered inside, the noise abated appreciably. A volley of giant hailstones flew down across the entrance, but by now, they were all safely inside. Almost immediately, the cave opened out into a bigger chamber, and Jake lowered Tom slowly onto a rock before falling back exhausted against the wall of the cavern. The distant sunlight out to sea flooded into the cave and lit up Molly as she leant over, hands on knees, gasping for breath. Behind her, Mr Paget was standing with a hand outstretched for balance against the rock wall. Everyone's face was contorted from the exertion of having fled from the whirlwind.

Catching his own breath, Tom turned to his left to peer into the impenetrable blackness of the cave's interior.

And a pair of small, disembodied eyes stared back at him,

no more than a stone's throw from where he was sitting. In the next moment, they were gone.

Chapter Seventeen

The Cave

Tom jumped to his feet. 'Michael!' he shouted, and his voice reverberated down the cavern. He heard the faint crack of what sounded like a stone being dislodged somewhere in the dark, but he could not see a thing from the direction the noise had originated. The rays from the distant sun were entering the cave and casting a pool of bright light around his feet but no further. Beyond was only a seamless blackness.

'What is it, Tom?' asked Molly, as the others hurried round him.

'I thought I saw someone back there.' He took a step forward, straining his eyes, willing them to grow accustomed to the dark more quickly than they were. 'I don't suppose anyone has brought a torch?' he asked.

Silence followed, until Molly said with sudden excitement: 'No, but I've got my mobile with me.' Triumphantly, she produced the smart phone from a pocket in her trousers.

Whilst she played with the buttons, turning it on, Jake said: 'How does that help? Are you going to phone somebody to bring a torch down here? No one'll come in this weather. And anyway, you won't get a signal underground.'

When Molly had finished entering the pin number to unlock her phone, she looked up at Jake, and said quietly: 'No, Jake. I meant my phone has a torch - we can use that.' And she held it up to demonstrate.

'Oh, right. I see,' replied Jake. 'I knew that. Of course I did.'

257

Molly stepped further into the cave, holding the phone in front of her. The light it shed from its tiny screen was barely adequate to see beyond a few metres, but it was all they had, and it nevertheless cast an eerie silver glow onto the walls and the floor.

More movement was heard up ahead. Then a shadow broke away from one of the dark walls and darted across to the opposite wall where it vanished once more. Mr Paget burst through the trio and strode deeper into the cave.

'What is going on?' he muttered. 'What is this all about?'

Once again, an indistinct shape darted about ahead of them. But this time it stumbled with a noisy clatter of stones and let out a curse. Mr Paget leapt forward and grabbed hold of a silhouette. Molly ran forward and shone the phone onto a forlorn figure on its knees, head bowed at Mr Paget's feet. The latter then proceeded to drag the figure to its feet.

When Molly shone the light into its face, Mr Paget gasped with shock: 'Michael?'

'Dad, what are you doing here?' he demanded, trying to shake himself free. But Mr Paget held firm. 'What are you doing with this lot?' he added, glancing at the other three figures peering at him

'Let's go back into the light,' said Mr Paget. 'I need to see what's going on here.'

When the group of five moved back towards the pool of wan light in the cave's entrance, Mr Paget released his grip of Michael, who promptly stumbled forwards having maintained his futile resistance. However, he quickly recovered his balance, and made for the cave opening.

'By all means go out there, Michael,' said Tom. 'But you'll almost certainly die.'

And, as if to emphasise the point, a rumble of thunder erupted nearby, freezing Michael to the spot. Slowly, he turned around and stared defiantly back at the group.

Mr Paget moved forwards and stood between Michael and Tom, glancing back and forth between the two look-alikes. 'Oh, my ...' His mouth was gaping wide, his eyes popping out.

Tom wanted to say something but could not find the words.

'Which one of you is my son?' asked Mr Paget.

'I am,' replied Michael in a flash. 'This ... this ... boy is an impostor. I don't know what he's told you–'

'Oh, shut up, will you!' spat Molly, and then turned to Tom. 'Tell him, Tom.'

'There's no time for this,' returned Tom, and stepped around his father. 'Michael, give me the medallion.' He held out his hand.

'Why?' said Michael with a sneer. 'What use is it to you now?'

'Because I'm taking both medallions back with me. And when I have, you'll never see me again ...'

'Woah!' said Mr Paget, and stepped between the two boys once more. 'What the hell is going on here? And who exactly are you?' he demanded pointing at Tom.

Tom swallowed nervously and said quietly: 'I've told you - I'm your son.' A lump grew in his throat from nowhere.

Michael stepped forward. 'No, he isn't. I am. Ask me what you bought me last Christmas, or for my last birthday. Or where we went on holiday last year.' He leered at Tom and then indicated with his head. 'He won't know any of that.'

Mr Paget looked at Tom and raised his eyebrows as if to say 'Well?'

The emotion was almost choking him. 'I'm your son ... in a

parallel world.'

'Tom!' protested Molly. 'For goodness' sake! Tell your father everything. Tell him you were swapped as babies.'

But he knew that would just complicate things too much, would confuse his father unnecessarily. And, moreover, that would cause himself too much pain. No, it was better to skip round the details and just get back to his old life. 'This weather,' he continued, 'is being caused by my being in the same world as Michael. I have to get back to mine. But before I do, I want to make sure this can never happen again.'

'Yeah, that's right,' said Michael bitterly. 'Go back to your own world, where you belong.'

Tom ignored him and looked at his father. 'Help me, please. I just want to do the right thing. I want to put an end to all this.'

Another crash of thunder exploded outside, and a giant hailstone shattered on the rocks close to the entrance of the cave.

Mr Paget glanced outside, then blinked and stared deep into Tom's eyes. 'What do we have to do?' he said finally.

'I somehow have to get back to *Morladron House*,' replied Tom.

Jake was already peering out of the cave, studying the elements and frowning. 'There's no way you can go out there at the moment. At least we're safe in here, I suppose.'

But just as he spoke, the ground rumbled and began to shake. Tiny particles of rock were shaken from the roof of the cave and floated to the floor like wisps of smoke. Tom momentarily lost his balance and fell against Molly, who had to reach out a hand and steady herself against the rocky wall. A few seconds later and the tremor stopped.

'We're not safe anywhere,' said Tom, looking at Michael. 'I have to get back.'

'I say we just throw him outside,' said Molly, glaring at Michael, 'and let the weather deal with him.'

'No!' snapped Tom before anyone else could speak. 'He may have done some bad things, but we'll not be killing anyone.'

'Pity,' mumbled Jake.

'What about the Smugglers' Tunnel?' suggested Mr Paget suddenly. 'It seems that some of what Sam used to rant on about was true. And he was always talking about *Morladron House* and the Smugglers' Tunnel. So maybe there really was, or is, some sort of tunnel.'

Tom, Molly and Jake looked at one another aghast.

'W-what smugglers' tunnel?' asked Molly.

'He said that years ago smugglers used a cave to bring treasure from the sea into the house. I must admit I never looked, but we are in a cave.'

'It's got to be worth a look,' Tom cut in with excitement. 'Molly, I'll take the phone and go and have a look back there. The rest of you had better stay here. Michael and I should be as far apart as possible.'

'I'll come with you,' declared Mr Paget.

Tom was not about to argue and agreed.

'Great,' said Jake. 'So we're left with the psycho.' He gave a contemptuous glance at Michael, who sneered back at him with equal disdain.

'It's better this way, Jake,' insisted Tom. 'I'm sorry. We'll come back for you once we find something.'

Jake shrugged his shoulders, whilst Molly folded her arms across her chest, clearly not happy, but biting her tongue.

Shining the meagre light before them, Tom and his father picked their way through the rocks and sand on the cave floor. The further in they went, the more the walls seemed to close in on them and the light from the sun behind became fainter and fainter.

'I'm still not sure I believe all this,' said Mr Paget softly. 'But I'll tell you one thing: you and Michael may look the same, but you're certainly two very different people.'

Tom smiled broadly to himself, knowing that his father could not see his face in the dark.

'So, what's this world of yours like, then?' continued Mr Paget, his quiet voice reverberating gently in the cave.

'It's pretty much the same as this one, really. Everyone looks the same, but the main difference is that people have more or less the opposite personality to the one they have here.'

'So what am I like in your world?' asked Mr Paget, with a smile in his voice.

Tom immediately felt sad and did not know how to answer. 'What are you like in *this* world?' he countered.

'Well, I'm smart, funny, good-looking …' He paused before adopting a lower, more serious tone. 'Is your father the complete opposite to me?'

'He is,' replied Tom flatly.

Silence filled the cavern, broken only by their footsteps on the rocky floor.

'What did Miss Doomsday mean?' asked Tom, wanting to change the subject quickly, as they clambered awkwardly over more rocks. 'She said they were on to you, knew what you were up to.'

Mr Paget laughed. 'Miss Doomsday and I go back a long

way. She's a member of the local secret police, and I happen to run the local underground opposition group. She's known for a long time what I do but has been unable to prove it. After what just happened back there, I can't really show my face in these parts again, can I?'

Just then, they heard Molly's raised voice echoing down the cave behind them. 'Michael, you're an idiot,' she shouted. They could not make out Michael's mumbled response, but Molly's voice, with its bitter tone, was crystal clear. 'This isn't even your world. You don't belong here.'

'What do you mean?' came Michael's booming reply.

Their conversation carried clearly down the cave towards Tom and his father, even though they were now some distance away.

'We went to your grandfather today,' continued Molly. 'In fact, he's not even *your* grandfather – he's Tom's grandfather. He told us you were swapped over when you were babies …'

'Rubbish!' exclaimed Michael.

Mr Paget stopped and turned to Tom. 'Is that true?' he murmured.

'I don't know,' sighed Tom. 'That's what grandpa says. I guess we'll never know for sure.'

As his eyes began to fill with tears, the whole cavern shook once again, more violently than before. Larger pieces of rock detached themselves from the roof, tapped the two of them on the head and pattered onto the floor. When the tremor had passed, Tom shone the light around and saw nothing but a rock face a short distance in front of him.

'There's nothing here,' he said with disappointment. 'The cave just stops here.'

'Give me that,' said his father, and took the phone from

Tom's hand. He moved forward, head bowed in the narrowing cavern and shone the light onto the wall of jumbled black rocks. 'Look,' he said, putting his free hand onto the rock and then rubbing his fingers together. 'There's water coming from somewhere.'

Tom joined him and looked closer. In the dim light, he could see several small trickles of water seeping out of cracks.

'Come on,' said Mr Paget. 'It's worth a try.' And he began to pull small rocks away and cast them to one side.

After only a minute or two, they had made a small hole in the back wall, and when Mr Paget shone the light into the gap, they could see a small chamber beyond, at the back of which, carved roughly into the rock, rose a line of jagged steps. With renewed enthusiasm, they pulled at more and more of the rocks, until the hole became large enough to climb through.

After checking that he still had the medallion in his pocket, Tom was tempted to press on into *Morladron House*, if indeed that was where the tunnel led, and escape. But in the next moment, he knew that was not a real option. He had to get the other medallion off Michael first. He turned to his father and said: 'Come on. Let's go back and get the others.'

And only a few minutes later, they were all lining up in the near pitch-black, ready to crawl through the hole. Mr Paget insisted on keeping the phone and proceeding first. So through they climbed and up the narrow, wet steps, holding onto the shirt or a hand of the person in front, feeling their way virtually blind in the dark. Up and up they climbed. The stairs had been formed in a natural fissure in the rock, so that they twisted this way and that, sometimes short steps, sometimes steep, but always wet from the trickle of water that crept down the fissure. Every so often they would turn a corner, and those at the rear would almost lose their balance entirely when the tiny glimmer of light from the phone disappeared from view.

But eventually Mr Paget cried out that he had come up to a trapdoor. He and Tom heaved and heaved, but the wooden boards above their heads refused to budge.

'Wait!' said Tom, and fished out the medallion and handed it to his father. 'Use that to smash a hole.'

And so he did, punching upwards with the wooden-framed mirror. And when the planks of wood began to yield, there was not a mark on the medallion. Once a large enough hole had been smashed, they climbed into the darkest of caverns, so large that the weak light from the phone found no walls and no ceiling to rest upon. Instead, a forest of large stone pillars came into view like the columns of an ancient temple, and no doubt, thought Tom, the foundations of *Morladron House*. In the gaps between pillars were dark and sinister shapes. Mr Paget swept the light to the left and a pile of wooden crates came into view. He swept it to the right, and a great chest emerged from the gloom, a chest chock full of gold and silver objects: cups and plates and cutlery. Everywhere they looked, more and more boxes and crates and precious objects appeared out of the darkness. It soon became apparent that they were in a vast, underground chamber, a chamber that was crammed full of treasure. And if the hidden trove existed in this world, thought Tom, the same store had to be buried under his *Morladron House*.

'Wow!' said Jake. 'Look at this place. What is all this stuff?'

'It must be the smugglers' treasure,' replied Mr Paget.

'Hey, Tom,' said Molly quietly. 'I bet the mirrors were brought here by the same smugglers who brought all of this.'

Tom agreed and shook his head in wonder.

Slowly, the group meandered along the aisles between the piles of treasure, until they came to a wooden staircase set into a wall of solid rock. When they ascended the steps, they came face to face with a large and square wooden door with an iron ring for a handle. On the wall next to the door hung a key the size of Tom's foot, which, when it was tried in the lock, turned and made a satisfying clunk. When Mr Paget pulled on the giant ring, the door creaked open towards them and they found themselves crouching in the large fireplace in one of the downstairs rooms in *Morladron House*. As Tom stepped into the room, he heard the distant, constant roar of a tornado and the violent crack of thunder overhead, pulling him back into the present, focusing his mind.

'Where's the mirror, Tom?' asked Jake.

'Come on,' said Tom, and headed towards the doorway. 'My grandpa took it upstairs.'

As he walked through into the large hallway with the grand staircase before him, his eyes were instantly drawn upwards to a room whose door stood ajar. From behind the door, a warm glow of flickering light was spilling out onto the landing. Urging the others to follow him, Tom ran up the staircase and then cautiously pushed open the door. Both on the floor and on a table in the centre of the room were half a dozen candles burning brightly and casting eerie shadows on the walls. In the centre of the room was the hole in the floorboards where the empty safe was. There was also a length of rope and a small toolkit on the table. And in the corner of the room stood the cheval mirror.

Having sighed with relief at the sight of the mirror, Tom was about to step into the room when a figure leapt out of the shadows and burst through the doorway, emitting a fierce groan as he moved. Reacting purely on instinct, Tom stepped out of the way and lost his balance, falling to the floor as the figure brushed past him and bounded onto the landing. Molly let out a brief yelp, Jake a gasp. Tom rolled onto his back just in time to see his grandfather, Sam, who was brandishing a short plank of wood in both hands, collide with Mr Paget, who had his arms raised in defence. Mr Paget fell backwards under the force of the surprise attack, and hit the wooden balustrade behind him, some of which snapped like twigs under the weight and spiralled away over the edge of the landing before clattering on the hallway floor below. As he desperately struggled to remain on the landing, fighting the deadly pull of gravity, he collapsed awkwardly and struck his head forcefully against the wooden floor.

'Dad!' yelled Tom, and dived towards his father who teetered on the edge of the now unprotected landing. He grabbed a leg, desperate to drag the dazed and barely conscious man to safety. Sam had his weapon above his head, poised for another blow.

As Molly and Jake took an instinctive step forward, Sam heard the creak of floorboards beneath their feet and spun round with the agility of a much younger man. He swiped the piece of wood back and forth in front of them, daring them to move closer. 'Stay back,' he barked.

Tom was on his knees, scrabbling towards his father, tugging at his shirt, his limbs, pulling him away from the edge. As he rose to his feet, he heard the words: 'You! Not again.' But before he could turn around, Sam's powerful arms wrapped around his chest from behind. The piece of wood, still in one of Sam's hands, was pressing into him, squeezing the air from his lungs. He was tugged backwards, twisted around to face his friends, his arms pinned to his sides. Sam's voice bellowed menacingly in his ear. 'Stay back!'

Before him, Tom could see the concern and shock in the faces of Molly and Jake as they froze in mid-motion.

'Any closer and I'll throw him over the edge,' snarled Sam, breathing heavily over Tom's right ear. And, as if to emphasise the threat, he thrust Tom a short distance towards the edge.

Tom found his eyes drawn inexorably to his left and down, and watched as dust and dirt kicked up from the landing, disappeared over the edge into the blackness below.

Lightning appeared to erupt all around the house, sending thin shafts of dazzling light through every tiny crack in every window frame and every hole in the roof, as if the sun had been switched on and off again several times in quick succession. Once the thunder had receded, the sound of a crackling fire could be heard.

Sam dug the wood tighter into Tom's chest and shook him. 'You don't belong here,' he cried. 'You have to go back. You are causing this weather. I've seen it all before.'

Tom could barely breathe, let alone speak.

'Mr Tranter,' said Molly, her voice almost squeaking with emotion. 'Let him go. It's not his fault – it's Michael's ...' She turned to look behind her. But Michael had gone. Aghast, she looked at Jake, then at Tom, and the terrible realisation struck her dumb.

'Where's my medallion?' continued Sam, tugging once more at the piece of wood as if to emphasise that he had expected to find the object below the section of wood he now held as a weapon. 'You've stolen it. Now give it back.'

'Let's talk about this,' pleaded Jake. 'I'm sure we can clear this up if we just stop and have a chat about it. Just let him go

– please.'

But Sam simply growled in response. And Tom knew there was to be no reasoning with the man. If what he had earlier told them was true, the terrible events of nearly fourteen years ago had taken their toll on his mind. A mind locked away for most of that time and driven mad by the death of his daughter, and the appalling thought that he himself had contributed to her death.

'Where is it?' he demanded once more. 'You have no idea what it is you have. It is *not* a toy. It–'

'It–it's in my pocket,' croaked Tom, almost inaudibly. He could not afford to relinquish the small mirror, but perhaps he could buy himself some time and, more importantly, some air. 'The medallion is in my pocket.'

Sam loosened his hold a degree. 'Show me,' he ordered. 'And don't do anything stupid …'

'Sam!' said a voice from behind them. 'What the hell are you doing?' demanded Mr Paget.

Tom felt the air return to his lungs in a flash and before he knew what was happening, the ground was rising up towards him. He crumpled to the floor and heard Molly and Jake rushing towards him.

'Are you all right?' asked Molly, stooping down to check.

'I'm fine,' answered Tom. 'Where's Michael?'

'He's run off,' said Jake. 'We didn't see where.'

With the help of Molly and Jake, Tom rose back to his feet. When he turned around, he saw Sam standing in the doorway to the lit room, waving his piece of wood back and forth in front of Mr Paget, keeping him at a distance.

'Put it down, Sam,' ordered Mr Paget. He then turned briefly to Tom, adding: 'Go! Find Michael. I can handle this.'

Without answering, Tom turned and walked past his two friends. 'Come on. Let's go and find him. He can't have gone far.'

As they rushed along the landing, a thunderbolt exploded around the house once again, and when the noise had abated, the faint crackle of flames could be heard from the rear of the house.

'What are you trying to do, Sam?' asked Mr Paget, holding up his hands in defence, as he eased forwards into the candle-lit room.

'You wouldn't understand,' snarled Sam, and swished the piece of wood in front of him, as if he were waving a dagger. Mr Paget staggered backwards in haste to avoid being hit. 'Now bring that boy back here and tell him to give me my medallion.'

'What is this all about, Sam?'

'I have told you before – on several occasions. And every time you refused to believe me. You had me locked up, remember?' he added, his voice dripping with bitterness.

'You tried to kidnap my son.'

Sam glowered menacingly at his son in-law. 'He's not your son,' he said through bared teeth. And he took another swipe at Mr Paget who again swayed out of harm's way.

A strong, warm wind whistled through the house, ruffling Mr Paget's hair and his still wet shirt, and bringing with it the smell of smoke and the cries of teenagers arguing in a nearby room.

'Then who is he?' demanded Mr Paget, in a booming voice. And then he lunged forward, and with faster reactions than the older man could summon, seized the piece of wood in both hands. As both men wrestled for control of the makeshift weapon, they drew close to one another, the taller Mr Paget looking down on his father-in-law and snarling with effort. The younger man wrested the wood from Sam's hands and tossed it across the room with disdain. Sam fell backwards and slipped ignominiously into a seated position on the floor.

Mr Paget moved forwards and looked down at him. 'I don't pretend to know what's going on here,' he continued in an agitated, impatient voice, 'but what I do know is that there are two boys in this house who look just like my son. And there's a great big tornado out there that appears to be trying to kill them both.'

'They're both here?' said Sam, with a flicker of amazement on his face, which quickly changed back to anger. 'That's impossible.'

'Why is it impossible?' asked Mr Paget in a softer, more conciliatory tone. 'What happened fourteen years ago, Sam? Tell me again.'

Michael was cornered in what had once been a large bedroom in a rear corner of the house with boarded-up windows in two adjacent walls. His eyes seemed to flicker alternately between anger and indecision. Or was it fear? Tom felt he should have been able to read the expressions in what looked like his own face. Yet somehow, he could not. Perhaps it was simply the lack of light in the room.

The two boys were squared up to one another a few metres apart, each one hesitant to make the first move after the discharges of electricity, which had occurred the last time they had fought.

'It's over, Michael,' said Tom calmly. 'Hand over the

medallion and we can all go home.'

After a pause that betrayed his anxiety, Michael barked: 'Why should I?'

His features were becoming more and more distinct, and it was not just because Tom's eyes were growing accustomed to the dark. A bright orange glow was seeping through the cracks around the boarded window behind Michael. The smell of smoke was filling his nostrils. Tom realised that a tree close to the house was ablaze, and that the flames were beginning to lick the rear of the house.

He took a step forward and was about to speak again, when there was a loud thud above them, followed by the distinctive rattling of tiles sliding down the roof. Then another thud resounded above; more tiles clattered away before shattering on the stone terrace below. Anxiously, Tom looked upwards at the flaking plaster of the ceiling and heard another bang, followed by another, like the heavy footfalls of a giant beast creeping across the roof. Pieces of plaster began to fall onto the floor.

There was another bang, followed by a crash, and suddenly, a giant, football-sized hailstone burst through the ceiling and shattered on the wooden floor between Tom and Michael. More hailstones thudded into the roof, and a strong, gusting wind carried a whiff of smoke and a deep, rumbling sound through the gaping hole in the roof.

'Michael, this is madness,' yelled Tom. 'Hand it over, and we can end all of this.'

'I said no,' hissed Michael. 'I've got an idea: why don't *you* give me *your* medallion?'

The wind began howling louder and louder; the rumbling grew ever closer; the thud of hailstones rose in intensity. Jake ran to the side window and pulled away part of the wooden board from the rotten window frame. 'Tom, the tornado's back,' he yelled back into the room.

Molly grabbed Tom's arm. 'Come on, Tom,' she pleaded. 'Go back. Come back and sort this out another time – please!'

'I'm not leaving without the other medallion,' he replied, without letting Michael out of his sight.

'For goodness' sake, Tom,' cried Molly, shaking him till she arrested his attention. 'What are you doing? You've become obsessed with that stupid medallion. You're not thinking straight.'

'She's right, Tom,' added Jake, in an uncharacteristically forceful tone. 'Don't be stupid, mate.'

Tom looked into Molly's fiery eyes flashing behind her glasses, and for an instant a flicker of doubt sparked through his mind. But in that moment, Michael made a break for the door. Tom reached out and grabbed a handful of shirt as his double tried to dash past. Michael, in turn, let fly with a fist which narrowly missed Tom's nose, but landed instead painfully on his shoulder. But he refused to let go and reached out with his other hand, seizing Michael's right arm. The two boys fell awkwardly against the wall, struggling to stay on their feet.

A fresh salvo of hailstones pounded against the weakening roof, whilst the wind moaned through the hole above. And then the wooden board over the rear window burst into flames, flooding the room with an orange, flickering glow and a whiff of acrid smoke.

Jake rushed towards the two wrestling boys but stopped dead in his tracks when a brilliant white streak of jagged energy burst from the duelling boys' hands. With a crackle, it shot towards the ceiling, vaporising a chunk of plaster, singeing an exposed rafter. Then it darted towards the floor, close to Jake, scorching the floorboard it struck. Jake and Molly scrambled backwards, horror etched in their faces, as the snake of energy attacked a fresh spot on the floor.

Tom shoved Michael away, and in the same moment the beam vanished. Michael steadied himself against the wall and scowled at Tom. 'Time's running out, Tom,' he snarled. 'Listen to your friends and go home.' Behind him, the fire was crackling, spreading up towards the roof.

'Sorry, I can't. I don't trust you.'

Before Michael could say another word, Tom lunged forward at his doppelgänger, trying to twist him around to get at his trouser pockets. Michael tried to grab his arms, then tried to get him in a headlock.

And then another giant tentacle of energy shot across the room straight towards Jake, who had to fling himself to the floor, as it exploded into the wall just above him. Molly screamed out Tom's name. But he could not hear her. It felt like the energy was coursing through every fibre of his being, energising him, filling him with strength and confidence.

The tentacle made a rapid change of direction, crashed into the boarded-up side window, vaporised the remnants of glass, blew out the wooden boards. A rush of wind immediately poured into the room, drowning out Molly and Jake's frantic voices and the grunts of Tom and Michael. Against the faint ribbon of sunlight far out to sea, the massive silhouette of a tornado stood out like a giant gnarled tree, moving towards the house, gathering speed, growing in size every second. All around it, giant hailstones hurtled to the ground like meteorites. But Tom could see none of it, so intent was he on recovering the second medallion. The boy could not be trusted. He could not possibly leave Michael to move freely between the two worlds, it was too dangerous. He had to be stopped.

Michael managed to grab both of Tom's arms. He heaved with all his might and spun Tom onto the floor. Instantly, the wind was forced from his lungs as he smacked into the wooden floor. And his own medallion clattered across the room and came to rest in the far corner. Tom looked up and for a second froze with terror. The swirling black mass of the tornado had filled the window, obliterating everything else in sight. It was heading towards the corner of the house, the corner where the medallion was lying. Desperately, he scurried on all fours across the floor, reaching out with a hand for the thick metal chain that lay tantalisingly close to his grasp.

The tornado burst into the corner of the room, devouring some chunks of stone and wood, casting out others in all directions. The whole house trembled under the onslaught, as if it were nothing more than a wooden shack. Tom's fingers were almost touching the chain. Just a centimetre more and he would have it. But the mighty wind was tearing at his hair, at his clothes, at every muscle, every bone in his body. Whether it was pulling him or repelling him, he could not tell. Maybe it was both at the same time. But if he could just …

He felt himself being pulled backwards, away from the whirlwind. Two large hands were pulling at one leg, while two smaller hands tugged at the other. Working quickly, the hands moved along his body, seized his arms, his torso, hauled him to his feet. But still his eyes refused to release their grip on the medallion. Until it vanished before him, swallowed in the blink of an eye by the avaricious twister, consumed together with a mixture of wood and stone. Not wanting to believe his eyes, Tom stared dumbfounded into the fast-revolving mass of wind, as his two friends hauled him backwards further and further away.

A plank of wood was ripped from the floor and swirled briefly in the room before it flew over their heads and crashed into a wall behind them. A block of stone was torn from the building and followed its path, smashing into the wall by the door.

Molly and Jake were shouting at him, imploring, commanding him to move, but their exact words were inaudible above the roar of the wind. Slowly, Tom was pulled backwards through the doorway, still looking, in case the tornado spat out the medallion at any moment. But then the roar lessened, the house ceased to tremble and the tornado moved away from the house, leaving a gaping hole where once the corner of the room had been. And the medallion had gone. More importantly, so had Michael.

Once back on the landing, Tom blinked and came to his senses. He glanced at the windswept and dusty faces of his two friends in turn, but before he could offer any words of apology or gratitude, a large timber fell down from the roof, burning fiercely, and crashed into the floor. He looked up and large parts of the roof were now ablaze. Clouds of smoke were being sucked into the room out of which the trio had just fled.

More flaming wood fell down in front of them, forming a criss-cross of burning beams on the landing, blocking their route to the stairs and their way out of the house.

'So I had to take your son through to the other world to protect him,' said Sam, as he stared defiantly back at his son-in-law, daring him to contradict him. 'If I hadn't, he might have been killed just like ...' He paused and looked away, unable to maintain eye contact for a moment. '... like your wife, my daughter, was killed.' His eyes filled with tears. 'So, you see, I have to do what I should have done years ago and destroy this cursed mirror and the medallion. I will never get my daughter back, or my true grandson, but at least I can prevent this tragedy ever befalling anyone else.'

'But I told you, both boys are here,' said Mr Paget. 'I don't understand how, but they are.'

A flash of anger spread across Sam's face once more. 'That's impossible. They can't be.' He then paused for a moment, his mind absorbing, processing the information, perhaps a flash of sanity returning. 'Of course! That must be why the weather has changed.'

Strange noises were echoing throughout the house: creaking wood, thumps and clattering tiles on the roof, the roar of a wind outside. And the house was trembling. The candles on the table wobbled and fell over.

'Then how do we stop this?' asked Mr Paget.

'They must go through the mirror together, both of them, for a short while at least, but immediately. Otherwise we could all die.'

Motionless, terrified, Tom stood and stared at the fire in front of them. Molly was squeezing his arm tightly. Just as his eyes began flitting about for a way out, a series of hailstones burst through the fiery roof like falling comets and smashed into the beams of wood that were blocking their path. Shards of ice splintered in all directions, and for a moment, the flames were doused. Plumes of steam rose from the floor where the ice had landed. Wasting no time, the trio leapt over the charred wood and headed for the staircase.

When Tom arrived at the top of the stairs, he could hear his father and grandfather still arguing in the room further along the landing. He stopped for a moment but quickly realised his father was more than capable of looking after himself and decided to head down the stairs instead. Now that his medallion had gone, he really did need to find Michael, and this time he knew his friends would not object.

As he rushed down into the gloom of the ground floor, a pang of regret struck him like a blow to the stomach. All of this, he realised, could have been avoided if he had only done as Molly had pleaded and gone home. He had placed his friends in danger. If anything happened to them now, he would never be able to forgive himself.

By now, the whole house was creaking and groaning like a dying giant. Only the hailstorm was keeping the blazing roof in check. But he knew that soon enough the whole roof would collapse on top of them. Time was running out. Where was Michael? He would be trying to escape out of the back of the house, Tom knew it.

He sprinted along the corridor towards the back of the house, heard footsteps ahead, burst into the back room through which they normally entered the house. And immediately, Michael ran into him, pushed him to the floor and fled out of the room. Even before he saw the raging fire at the back of the room, Tom could feel the intense heat on his face and hands. The boarded window had disappeared behind a mass of leaping flames, flames that had spread to the back door and the ends of the rafters.

Tom heard a scuffle outside the room, recognised the raised

voices shouting, cursing at one another. He scrambled to his feet, raced out into the corridor and back into the large hallway. Molly and Jake were standing in Michael's way, with the latter hurling threats and insults at the former.

With the howling wind, the pounding assault on the roof, the crackle of flames overhead and the shouting, Tom was able to draw nearer and nearer before Michael heard his footfalls and spun round. Suspiciously, they eyed one another, reluctant to make the first move, wary of the power they possessed when they touched.

'Come on, Michael,' said Tom. 'See sense. This can't go on.' And he took another step forward.

Michael flinched.

'Tom!' said Jake urgently. 'Stay back.' He threw a glance at Molly. 'We'll handle this.' And he glowered at Michael.

Michael turned round and smiled coldly at Jake, before turning back to the motionless Tom. 'Are you afraid to come and get it for yourself, Tom …?'

But then Jake lunged forward, his bear-like hands grappling with Michael's arms. Molly moved swiftly to his aid. But Michael was too quick, too strong to be held for long. And so, after the briefest of struggles, and before Tom could decide whether to risk helping or not, Michael had wriggled his way free and pushed Tom's friends away.

'Getting your friends to do your dirty work for you,' scoffed Michael, his fists clenched, his eyes darting between all three of his opponents. 'Shame on you …'

Suddenly, he turned and took a pace towards one of the downstairs rooms. But scarcely had he moved, when a huge flaming timber came plunging down from the roof above and crashed onto the floor just a few metres in front of him, breaking into several pieces on impact. Tiles and smaller pieces of charred or burning wood clattered down around it. After a brief, silent pause, giant hailstones began to fall through the newly created hole in the roof and exploded all around the smouldering timber.

'Michael,' snapped Tom firmly. 'Either go through the mirror now or give me the medallion. But either way, we don't have time for this.'

Michael's startled face flashed back round. When he caught Tom's eyes, the smirk returned in an instant, as if nothing had happened. 'You're sounding like a broken record. A very annoying, broken record.'

More hailstones continued to bombard the floor a short distance from where they stood. A brilliant flash of lightning burst overhead and filled the hallway with dazzling light for several, terrifying seconds.

'This storm will not stop,' continued Tom, his heart pounding out of control, 'until one of us is dead. And half of Porthgarrick could be destroyed before that happens. Is that what you really want?'

Michael snorted. 'You don't half talk a load of rubbish, you know.'

'Wake up, Michael,' he shouted and stepped to within millimetres of his look-alike's face. 'Look around you. You still don't realise just what's happening, do you? One of us is going to die.'

For once, Michael did not respond. Tom could see the doubt creeping across his face. Michael looked up at the smouldering roof, the gaping hole, the flames that were beginning to crackle upstairs, around doorframes, on the landing.

'We can stop it,' said Tom gently.

'Ah!' replied Michael suddenly, and the uncertainty was gone in a flash, the snarl back in its place. 'You nearly had me then. Do you think I was born yesterday? You'll do anything to get hold of this,' and he took out the medallion from a pocket and dangled it to one side just out of arm's reach.

Livid with rage, Tom grabbed Michael's scruff with one hand and reached for the medallion with the other. Instantly, Michael retaliated, tried to punch Tom in the stomach using the hand in which he held the medallion. But the blow glanced off Tom's flank as he swayed to one side. Briefly, there was contact: a short burst of energy erupted from the spot, as bright, as jagged as the lightning bolts outside. It sped across the hallway before plunging into a wall with an explosion of sparks and plaster and chipped stone.

Flames burst from an upstairs doorway, licking at the spindles around the landing. More burning rafters fell to the floor, in turn bringing more and more hailstones hurtling into the house. Immediately, the boys separated, eyes pulled upstairs.

Mr Paget and Sam came dashing out of an upstairs room, dragging the mirror awkwardly between them, as if it were a rigid and bulky corpse. A blazing piece of wood fell from above and somersaulted down the stairs, casting spirals of smoke into the air. A section of the landing burst into flames.

'Throw it down,' yelled Sam, as the two men stood at the top of the stairs, the mirror at their feet, and fire seemingly all around them. 'Don't worry – it won't break.'

Out of the corner of his eye, Tom could see Michael's attention was distracted by the scene above. His left hand sprang out like a striking snake and seized the chain that dangled from the medallion at Michael's side, and he heaved. But Michael was alive to the situation. Straightaway, his grip closed around the small mirror, whilst his other hand clenched into a fist. Fearing an imminent punch or a kick, Tom rammed his shoulder into Michael, and the two boys crashed to the floor.

Jagged tentacles of white-hot energy shot out in all directions like the legs of a terrible spider, as the two boys wrestled and writhed on the floor. Molly and Jake cowered further and further away as the tentacles flew around the hallway, striking the walls and the floor and the stairs, and with every strike came a shower of sparks and a gunshot crack.

Tom found himself on his back, pinned to the ground, staring up into Michael's face, a face of black smudges and seething rage. A hailstone exploded next to Tom's head, showering his hair with icy cold pieces. Tom could see the energy discharging from their hands and arms, flying around the room, adding to the chaos and destruction being wrought on the old house. And he felt afraid. Afraid of Michael's manic fury, of the crumbling house around him.

But then Michael rose up, as if he were taking off, and moved backwards, surprise written across his features. The moment he moved away, the tentacles vanished. Molly and Jake moved towards Tom in a flash, hauled him to his feet. Mr Paget had wound a piece of rope around Michael, pinning his arms to his waist. The boy wriggled violently, impatiently but ultimately with futility.

Another section of the landing creaked and groaned and then came crashing down into the hallway. As the upper steps on the staircase burst into flames, another hailstone pierced the roof and briefly dulled the blaze before the ice melted and the fire caught hold with renewed vigour.

Tom's grandfather rushed forward and seized him by the arm. Tom flinched, expecting a fight or an argument.

'You must go through the mirror, now,' said Sam. 'Both of you.'

Tom went to speak, but his grandfather was already pushing him towards the mirror, which he and Tom's father had erected close to the front door.

'If you both go through, this storm should stop quickly. If only one of you goes it may take longer. So go now!'

There was no time to think. Tom grabbed hold of Jake; a look was enough to express what they had to do. Mr Paget put an encouraging hand on Tom's shoulder and then gave him a sad smile. He handed over the medallion he had prised from Michael's hand, and then dragged the boy towards the mirror like a troublesome dog on a lead. Michael kicked and screamed, but Tom held onto the ropes while Jake seized the boy on the other side. Briefly, Tom turned to Molly who stood motionless, tears streaming down her face. He felt a horrible lump in his throat. There was no time for a farewell. Perhaps it was better that way.

'Go back down to the basement,' he said firmly. 'Wait out this storm down there.'

And with the deafening noise of destruction all around them, Tom touched the medallion's reflection in the large mirror, and the three boys vanished from the hallway.

Chapter Eighteen

Farewell

After what had gone before, the other *Morladron House* was quiet and serene, asleep on the hillside where it had been abandoned years before, and oblivious to what had befallen its namesake in another world. The room that housed the mirror was as gloomy and unwelcoming as the moment they had left it hours earlier. The low, setting sun was only allowed to peak through the cracks around the window frame, casting tiny beams of orange light into the room. Yet Tom felt an overwhelming sense of relief to be back.

Michael stumbled onto the floor when they released him. After wriggling for a moment, he soon realised he was not able to stand on his feet while his hands were tied and lay powerless on his back. 'Take me back,' he demanded.

Tom and Jake ignored him.

Tom turned to Jake. 'I should get back to make sure everyone's okay.'

'No, Tom,' replied his friend. 'Wait a while. They'll be fine.'

Tom knew his friend was right. But he just wanted to go back for one last time and say goodbye properly. But maybe it was simply too risky. And in any case, he was not sure he could face the pain of saying his farewells to Molly and his real father. Perhaps it was better to leave things as they were.

He heard footsteps outside on the landing, heading towards the room, and a beam of light appeared behind the half-closed door. When it opened, in strode a still perplexed-looking Mrs Meadow.

'Well, well,' she said. 'The travellers return.'

'Mrs Meadow,' said Tom excitedly. 'You're still here.'

'Well, I went home for a while. Then I came back because I wanted to make sure I wasn't going mad, after I watched you all disappear into that mirror.'

Tom was instantly reminded of Miss Doomsday, left seething and locked in the police van back in the other world. And a myriad of thoughts and doubts began to fill his head. 'And how is the town?' he asked.

'Well, I don't pretend to understand all this, but just like you said, as soon as you disappeared through that mirror the storm started to ease. Considering all that happened, the town isn't too bad. Apart from the school, of course. And what on earth have you boys been up to?' she added looking at their blackened clothing.

'It's a long story,' Tom chuckled.

'And what have we here?' continued the teacher, pointing her torch down at Michael, lying ignominiously in the dust.

'This is the idiot who tried to set fire to the school,' said Jake.

'I see. Well, in that case there's a nice young policeman who would like a chat with him.'

'Yes, but we can't really hand him over, can we, Tom?' said Jake looking at his friend.

But words failed to come out of Tom's mouth. His face betrayed him. Jake looked harder at his friend, and immediately saw a look that made him take a sharp intake of breath.

'You're not staying, are you?' continued Jake. 'You're going back.'

'I ... yes,' he found himself replying.

'What? What did you say?' boomed Michael, and wriggled anew on the floor but with the same result.

'Excuse me?' It was Mrs Meadow's turn to look puzzled. 'What's going on now?'

Tom swallowed hard and looked down at his feet. 'Michael and I - that's him - can't co-exist in the same world. Otherwise, you get violent storms like we just had. So, one of us has to go back through the mirror. And that someone will be me.'

'I don't think so,' hissed Michael in the background. But no one paid him much attention.

Jake looked crestfallen, but then smiled wryly. 'I should have guessed.'

'Sorry, Jake. But that's where I belong. That's where I was born.'

'You'll be going back to a police state where you're a wanted man … I mean … boy.'

'I know. But it turns out my dad is head of an opposition group. My place is with him. He needs me now …'

At last, Michael managed to wriggle himself into a sitting position. 'You can't do this,' he snarled through gritted teeth.

With no small amount of guilt, Tom turned to face Michael, whose face seemed to elicit a curious mix of pity and aversion in him. 'You're better off in this world, believe me,' he said. 'You won't be punished as badly here as back there,' he added, pointing to the mirror.

'I wouldn't count on that,' added Mrs Meadow with a mischievous grin.

'And,' resumed Tom, 'you'll be able to see Rachel …'

'Oh, I see. That's what this is all about,' said Michael with disdain. 'You want to stay with your girlfriend. See that, Jake? He likes the girl he's known for just two weeks more than he likes you. How small does that make you feel?'

But before Tom had time to worry how Jake would respond, his friend bent over Michael and glowered. 'Haven't you caused enough trouble already? Do us all a favour and just shut up.' The disdain in his voice sounded just like Sean.

Michael gave Jake a brief, cold stare, before turning his attention back to Tom. 'You have no right to decide where I live.'

'Sorry, Michael,' began Tom sternly, 'but you lost your right to anything the moment you forced your way into this world–'

'Oh, here we go with the little speech. I was just having a bit of fun, something you ought to try sometime. But no, you're too busy trying to be the hero, too busy being all high and mighty.'

It was as much as Tom could do to refrain from striking the boy. 'Thanks to your bit of fun, your so-called best friend Sean is now dead ...'

A look of instant shock spread across Michael's face.

'Come on, boys,' said Mrs Meadow. 'That's enough of this arguing.' After helping Michael to his feet, she turned to face Tom. 'I'm sure you'll find the time to come and visit us now and then, won't you?'

Tom looked sadly at her and then at Jake. 'I'm afraid I can't. This mirror is too dangerous. We can't let this sort of thing ever happen again.' He then moved forward and gave her a hug. 'Goodbye, Mrs Meadow. And thank you for everything you've ever done for me. I shan't forget you.'

'Oh, Tom, stop it,' she flustered. 'You'll make me cry.'

'And look after Jake for me,' he added.

'Of course I will. I'll need someone to help me keep an eye on this one here,' she said, tugging at the rope around Michael.

287

'I'm going to miss you, mate,' said Jake, his voice quavering.

'I would say come with me, but I guess you can't.'

'No, my family's here and they're great. Which must mean that Sean's are bloomin' awful.'

They both laughed nervously. Then Tom hugged Jake, who for a moment seemed unsure as to what to do.

'Steady on!' he said finally. 'That's not very manly.' But he then spread his bear-like arms around Tom and squeezed him warmly in return.

When they separated, Tom looked at his friend sadly. 'As soon as I go back through, I have to bury that God-forsaken mirror. So this is it.'

'I guess you're right.'

'And then you must bury this mirror, too. It can't fall into the wrong hands. Even with no medallion at this end, we don't know that there aren't any number of other ways to access the portal.'

'Okay,' agreed Jake reluctantly.

'Just one more thing,' said Michael in a surprisingly calm voice. But as Tom turned to look at him, his face suddenly creased into a picture of fury once more. 'I won't rest until I find a way back,' he hissed, with more malice than Tom had seen before. 'And when I do, I'll make you sorry for this, I promise you.'

Tom did his best to conceal the unease he felt looking at the evil in the boy's face, and said calmly: 'Michael, just get on with your life. You're not a bad person.'

In response, Michael simply swore vehemently in Tom's face, before Mrs Meadow tugged him away.

'Come on, you,' she said.

For one last time, Tom smiled at Jake and Mrs Meadow, and then turned to face the mirror.

'Good luck,' shouted Jake.

'Thanks, you too.'

And then he touched the mirror and disappeared.

Molly, Mr Paget and Sam were all standing around the mirror when he rematerialised into their world. To his surprise, he found himself outside on the overgrown gravel driveway leading up to *Morladron House*. Tom instantly felt a warm, gentle breeze on his face. Although there was still a mass of black cloud above, the setting sun in the east had appeared low on the horizon and was bathing the garden in an eerie light. A short distance away, the remnants of the roof crackled and smoked.

Molly was smiling with restrained relief; Mr Paget had a wry look on his face; and Sam seemed almost disinterested at his grandson's reappearance.

'Where's Michael?' asked Mr Paget.

'He's not coming,' replied Tom.

'You mean ...?' began Molly.

'I'm staying ...'

She ran forward and flung her arms around his neck.

'I rather hoped you would,' continued his father, and patted him on the shoulder, whilst Molly threatened to squeeze the life from him.

'It's the way it should be,' added Sam flatly.

When Molly released her grip, she looked at Tom with some doubt. 'But why, Tom? Have you really thought this through? I mean, I'm glad you're here. But you'll be leaving everything behind, including Jake.'

Tom thought for a moment. 'It was Michael, really. He showed no remorse whatsoever for what he'd done. And he never once mentioned his family or said how he would miss them. I realised I owed him nothing and that my place is here. Of course, I'll miss Jake terribly, and Mrs Meadow but not much else, really.'

There was a creak followed by a crash behind them. Holding Molly's hand, Tom turned round in time to see a section of roof collapse into the interior of *Morladron House*. The fire had died down and been replaced by a pall of thin smoke. With a corner of the house sliced off by the tornado, the roof largely missing and the windows burnt out by the fire, it somehow looked even more lifeless than it had ever done before.

'I guess that's the end of the old house,' he said.

'I'll rebuild it,' declared Sam, as quick as a flash.

'You're an escaped criminal now, Sam,' laughed Mr Paget.

'We're all escaped criminals,' returned Sam.

'Excuse me,' said Molly indignantly. 'I'm not.'

Tom laughed and, without thinking, felt the medallion around his neck. Immediately, he tugged if off as though it were somehow contaminating him. 'We have to get rid of this. And the mirror.' He then turned to face Sam. 'I presume we can't destroy them, Grandpa?'

'No, lad. It appears they are virtually indestructible.'

'Then we must hide them somewhere where they'll never be found again.'

'We'll weigh them down and throw them to the bottom of the sea,' said Sam, with a stern face and a tone that defied contradiction.

'You'll have no objection from me,' said Tom's father. He

then turned to his son. 'So, what are we going to call you now: Tom or Michael?'

Without hesitation, Tom replied: 'Tom. That's what I've been used to all my life. It would be too weird to change now.'

'Well, Tom,' said Mr Paget with a satisfied grin. 'We can't hang around here. We need to go into hiding, and then I need you to help me bring down Prime Minister Sheeran.'

Tom laughed. 'Now, that's not something I ever thought I'd hear someone say.'

He smiled to himself. It was strange how this bizarre world already felt like home. And, for the first time he could remember, he felt that he had at last found a place where he truly belonged.

The End

The story continues in

Book 2

The Book of Mysteries

John D. Fennell

If you would like more information on any of my books as well as news on new releases, please visit **www.johndfennell.com**

I really hope you enjoyed reading this book. If you did, I would be very grateful if you could add a rating and a short review on **Amazon** to let others know what you thought.

Many thanks,

John D. Fennell

Printed in Great Britain
by Amazon

78765991R00171